Final Ride

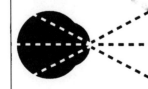

This Large Print Book carries the
Seal of Approval of N.A.V.H.

Final Ride

Rodeo Riders #3

Mike Flanagan

WHEELER
PUBLISHING

Published in 2002 by arrangement with
NAL Signet, a member of Penguin Putnam Inc.

Wheeler Large Print Book Series.

The text of this Large Print edition is unabridged.
Other aspects of the book may vary from the original edition.

Set in 16 pt. Plantin by Al Chase.

Printed in the United States on permanent paper.

Library of Congress Control Number: 2002105933
ISBN 1-58724-270-2 (lg. print : sc : alk. paper)

Final Ride

Chapter One

Jack Lomas brought the pickup to a stop beside the windmill and looked up at Clay Tory, who was sitting on top of the platform, by the turning vanes. Terry James was on the ground, pulling the rope that ran through the block and tackle and attached to the sucker rod in the well. Wedging a rod block against the sucker rod, he eased off the rope and let the twenty-foot length of rod settle against the block, then pulled off his hat and wiped the sweat from his brow. After making sure the rod was secure, Clay climbed down from the platform.

"How's it going?" Jack asked, looking at the number of rods lying on the ground.

"We've got about half of them out," Terry replied. "We should have the rest out in about two hours and ready for the new leathers."

"I brought them with me," Jack said, reaching into the back of the pickup and pulling out a box. As he looked around the pasture, he mentally cringed at the condition of his range. His eyes narrowed with concern at the sun-baked grassland that had once been green and lush. "We sure need another rain like the ones we got in May." It was the end of July, and there had been no rain for more than a month.

"Uh-huh," Terry agreed. "I thought we were

going to have a wet summer, but it sure didn't turn out that way."

"It sure didn't," Jack answered dispiritedly.

"Maybe we'll get lucky soon and have a gully washer," Terry quickly interjected, trying to improve Jack's rapidly souring mood.

Jack looked at the cloudless sky. "Yeah, maybe we'll get lucky."

Terry looked helplessly at Clay, who shrugged and shook his head, not knowing what to say. He thought it might be a good idea to change the subject, and so he said, "We'd better finish getting these rods pulled or we'll be here 'til after dark."

By the time they finished with the windmill and arrived back at the ranch house, Julie James had lunch prepared. Jack had hired both Terry and Julie two years earlier when Clay had turned pro and he and Jack had started traveling the rodeo circuit together. Terry's official title was ranch manager, but if truth be known, Julie was the true manager, even when Jack was home. She ran an efficient household and kept all three men in line. She cooked, cleaned, played nurse, and constantly admonished both Jack and Clay about their eating habits while on the road.

"We'll be leaving Thursday for Oklahoma," Jack said as they ate their lunch. "We should be back late Sunday night or early Monday." Looking at Clay, he sighed wearily, "If we don't get some relief from this drought pretty soon, you're going to have to travel without me." With his elbows on the table, Jack ran his hands through his gray, thinning hair in exasperation. "I can't afford to be away from the ranch for extended periods of time anymore. You'll be making three or four rodeos a week, which means you won't be here that often, and Terry can't do everything that needs to be done by himself."

Clay reflected on what Jack was saying. For the past two years he and Jack had traveled together. It was hard to think of going alone, but he knew Jack was right — Terry just couldn't manage the entire ranch alone. A wave of guilt flooded through him. He should be staying at the ranch and helping out, rather than traveling all over the country while Jack and Terry stayed home and did all the work.

"I think I should cut my traveling down some so I can be here to help until this drought's over."

Shaking his head, Jack replied in a voice that left little room for argument, "No, you won't. You've got a good chance of making it to the finals, and you need a good summer to clinch it. Terry and I can handle things here for another month, and by then you should have a good lead. You can cut back then, if need be."

Clay knew that when Jack used that certain tone, there was no use in arguing with him. He sat there in silent acceptance until Julie broke in.

"Don't you worry, hon. I'll be here, and I can help out with some of the work. I can drive the

9

hay truck to help feed, I can pull the stock trailer out to the pastures, and I sure can ride."

Clay smiled at her. "And she sure can cook, too! I swear, Terry, if you hadn't already got her for yourself, I'd snatch her up and marry her right now."

"I don't believe Tamara would think too highly of that," Julie said, referring to Clay's fiancée. She and Julie had become good friends over the past few months, often teaming up against Clay in the ongoing battle between the sexes. Tamara lived in San Angelo, Texas, and competed on the professional barrel racers circuit at the same rodeos as Clay, which was about the only time they had to be together, as Clay spent the rest of his time working on the ranch. Jack had encouraged him to take off and spend time alone with Tamara, but Clay felt obligated to the ranch.

"I'll take some time off after this drought is over. Tamara understands what it's like right now," Clay had said.

Jack and Julie had tried to convince him otherwise, but he ignored their comments, feeling he should be on the ranch helping out as long as conditions remained as they were.

After lunch, Terry left to check on some calves they'd put in the lower trap the day before and Julie returned to the nearby house that she and Terry lived in, leaving Jack and Clay to themselves. Jack sat at the table staring out the kitchen window, and Clay could see the worry etched on his furrowed brow.

"Are things really that bad?" Clay asked, concerned about this man who had become like a father to him over these past several years.

Jack looked at the young man sitting across the table, and a smile slowly replaced the worried expression. "No, things aren't that bad. I guess I've grown so used to worrying when things don't go as planned that I do it more out of habit than anything else. If things get too bad, we can always sell the older cows and try to keep the young stock until conditions improve. I'd hate to have to do it. I've spent a lot of years building up the herd I've got now. But I've done it before, and I reckon if push comes to shove, I can do it again."

Clay knew how proud Jack was of his herd — and with good reason. He raised some of the best beef in New Mexico, consistently bringing in top prices. He also knew it took time and careful planning to build a herd as good as Jack's, and to lose any of them would be a setback. "How long do you think we got before we have to start selling?"

His face falling, Jack sighed. "A month, month and a half. We've got enough hay to last longer, but I don't think the wells will hold out. We've lost three wells in the last month, and there's two more that will probably play out shortly."

"Can we haul water in?" Clay asked.

"I've thought about that, but I don't know where we'd haul it in from and I don't see how we could get enough to make a difference. I'm afraid if we don't get some rain in the next two to three weeks I'm going to have to ship at least two hundred head to market."

Two hundred head was only a small portion of Jack's herd. Clay was surprised by that figure. "Will that be enough to save the rest?"

Jack shrugged. "It depends on what happens. That should give us about three weeks' breathing room. If we don't get some rain by then, we'll have to ship some more."

"Aren't market prices down right now, because of the drought?"

"I thought I'd ship them to Colorado — the drought hasn't hit there. Cattle prices seem to be holding up there, but if the drought continues here I'm sure it won't be long until the Colorado market's flooded. It'll cost a little more for shipping, but we should still come out better than selling them anywhere around here."

They sat in silence, each considering the costs they faced if the drought didn't end soon.

Rising before the sun each day, they hauled hay to feed the cattle, alternating pastures so that all the stock got fed every other day. By ten o'clock the temperature rose to ninety, and by noon it topped one hundred. The heat scorched the already dry earth until the once hearty prairie grass became brittle, breaking off at ground level and leaving little to sustain the cattle.

Clay and Terry rode out every day to bring the weaker cattle — those that were pushed away from the hay or couldn't make the long treks to reach water — to the large trap near the house, where they could be cared for and watched more closely.

At four o'clock Thursday morning, Clay pulled out of the driveway with a reluctant Jack sitting beside him. It had taken Clay, Terry, and Julie all day and part of the night to convince Jack to go along. He had argued vehemently that there was too much to be done for him to be gone for four days. He had finally relented, but vowed that this would be the last time until the drought was over. If it hadn't been for the fact that his old friends Will and Dottie Hightower were furnishing the stock at the rodeo in Ada, he probably would not have gone at all.

Driving east on Highway 380 in the predawn hours, Clay talked about the rodeo in McAlester to take Jack's mind off the ranch and its problems. "I think Tumbleweed has become a top horse in the last few months. If he bucks like he did at Tucson, I should place in the barebacks."

"If you manage to ride him!" Jack chuckled.

Clay had to smile at the remark. Jack was already beginning to sound like his old, ornery self. "I plan on riding him in spite of the sorry training I've had."

A mock look of pain showed on Jack's face, causing Clay to grin widely.

"I'll have you know, big shot, that you received the best training available. Why, I know men who would have paid thousands of dollars

13

for instructions from me."

"Name one," Clay challenged with a smile.

"Thomas Holland!" Jack shot back quickly.

"Who in the world is Thomas Holland?"

"A man who didn't get the training you did," Jack replied innocently. "And see what happened? He didn't make it."

Clay laughed heartily. "I reckon I ought to count myself lucky, then. All it cost me was a lot of aggravation, having to put up with a hardhead like you. Not to mention all the free labor you got out of me in the name of training."

"Hmmph," Jack snorted. "I don't know where you get the idea *I'm* hardheaded. You're so stubborn you make a mule look like a whipped puppy. I was just standing my ground in an attempt to keep you straight. And all that work you claim to have done is just a small price to pay for the generosity I extended, takin' you in and givin' you the benefit of my vast knowledge and experience and all."

Once again, Clay burst out laughing. When he finally regained his composure, he said, "It'd be scary if you really believed all that bull you spread around."

Jack gave him a sly grin and pulled his hat down over his eyes. Leaning his head back against the seat, he said, "Just keep it between the ditches, Junior. I want to make it there in one piece."

Clay grinned and gripped the steering wheel firmly. It was great to be back on the road.

★ ★ ★

It was a little after seven in the morning when they entered the city limits of Abilene, Texas. Clay drove to a house on the east side of town where Tamara Allen was waiting. The house belonged to Kerry Tyler, a friend of Tamara's and fellow barrel racer. As they pulled into the driveway, Tamara came bounding down the porch steps and was opening Clay's door before he could bring the pickup to a complete stop. Her lithe blond figure flew into his arms as he stepped down from the cab.

"Boy, I missed you!" she said, squeezing him tight.

"I missed you, too," he replied, picking her up and swinging her around.

Breathless, she stepped back as he set her down. She kissed him quickly before saying, "I'll get Charger and Cash ready while you hook up the trailer. Kerry's gone to Dallas with Rob Tanner. She'll meet us in McAlester tonight."

Jack smiled with glee. "Good. Now I can have the entire backseat to myself so I can stretch out and sleep."

Tamara grinned back at him. "I'll have to tell Kerry how much her absence means to you."

"Now don't start spreadin' rumors," Jack said, causing Tamara's smile to widen even more. He groaned with stiffness as he got out to help Clay hook up the two-horse aluminum trailer.

After loading the horses, they were soon headed down Interstate 20 toward Fort Worth and Dallas. Tamara and Clay, ecstatic to be together again, talked nonstop all the way to Fort Worth and were still gabbing away as Clay negotiated the heavy traffic in Dallas. Turning north on Highway 75 and heading for the Texas-Oklahoma border, Clay was glad to see the large city fade into the distance.

Other than stopping for gas and a quick bite to eat, they drove straight through to McAlester, arriving at the rodeo grounds at six o'clock, an hour before the show was to begin. Clay parked the pickup and trailer in the contestant parking area, as close to the arena entrance as possible. While Tamara saddled Charger to limber him up from the trailer ride, Clay took his gear bag with his bareback rigging, glove, spurs, and chaps from the camper.

"I'll see you after the bareback riding," he said to Tamara, stealing a kiss.

"You better make a good ride and win some money so you can take me out to eat after the rodeo."

Clay chuckled. "Is that the only reason you stay with me, so I can feed you?"

Smiling coyly, she stepped into the saddle. "It's not the only reason, but it is one of the best." Reining the big horse around, she was gone before he could think of an appropriate answer.

Jack and Clay walked to the chutes together, stopping to look at the stock in the holding pens. Clay had indeed drawn Tumbleweed for the bareback event — he was a stocky blue roan that was slowly building a reputation as a solid bucking horse in the Three T's Rodeo Company. Watching the horse through the fence, Clay felt satisfied with his draw. Not so with Gruesome, his draw in saddle broncs.

"I doubt I'll place on that bag of bones," he lamented to Jack.

"Probably not, but you got two good draws with Tumbleweed and Wrangler." Wrangler, a large brindle bull with a wide horn span and lightning-quick moves, was Clay's draw in the bull riding event.

"I'm looking forward to trying Wrangler again. I almost had him ridden last time, but he pulled that quick move to the left, then swung right. I never saw it coming. I don't plan to let him trick me again."

Jack gave him a dubious look. "Just remember, he never bucks the same way two times in a row."

Clay sighed. "Yeah, I know, but I don't plan on letting him throw me with that move again."

Clay and Jack were studying the stock when a voice from behind brought them around. "There ain't no Shetland ponies for you in that bunch, youngster."

Clay held back his smile as he looked at Billy Ettinger. "Nope, and there ain't no old wore-out plow horses for you, either, old man."

Billy threw back his head and laughed at Clay's ribbing — he was only twenty-four, after all. "Jack, how do you put up with this young up-start?"

"It ain't easy, but we all have our crosses to bear."

"I can only imagine," Billy said, grinning at Clay. Billy was one of the top saddle bronc riders on the circuit and was presently ahead of Clay in the overall standings, though by only a slim margin.

Glenn Timmons was standing beside Billy, smiling at the friendly sparring between the two. "Hey, Clay, how's Tamara doing after her little episode last month?" He was referring to her being kidnapped and held hostage in a Dallas hotel in order to keep Clay from riding in the Denton rodeo. Though hers had been the most drastic attack, there had been other instances of harassment too — cowboys' tires slashed, batteries stolen, and even some cowboys knocked out and left in the boondocks in order to keep them from competing. It had all been caused by a gambling syndicate that had decided to bet on the outcome of the rodeo season.

"She's fine," Clay responded. "She really doesn't remember any of it, which is fortunate. I'm the one that still wakes up in a cold sweat just thinking about what could have happened."

"Too bad it wasn't you that got kidnapped," Billy said, breaking the somber mood. "I doubt if anyone would have noticed. Tamara could have found herself a real cowboy, and things would have worked out better for everyone."

"Thanks a lot," Clay said sarcastically. "It's good to know I've got friends."

"You don't have any friends," Billy chuckled. "We just put up with you 'cause we feel sorry for you."

It was Clay's turn to laugh. "And all this time I thought you hung around me 'cause you were too old to be by yourself and I was the only one that would put up with you."

"He's got a point," Glenn chortled.

Billy gave him a sour look. "Jack, I think you and I need to get some refreshments where the air's got a better flavor. These wet-behind-the-ears youngsters are starting to give off a bad odor."

"It gets that way quite often," Jack agreed, turning up his nose. "Come on, Billy, I'll buy you a Coke." Clay and Glenn followed a short distance behind.

The rodeo began with the introduction of the local dignitaries, followed by the grand entry, in which the mounted contestants rode in single file around the arena. After the invocation and the singing of the national anthem, it was time to ride. Bareback riding was the first event, and Clay was the seventh rider out. He stood behind the chutes with Jack, Billy, and Glenn to watch the other contestants.

The horses were in great form for the evening's performance, bucking hard and showing off their moves for the audience. The first rider,

Fielding Baker, had drawn Lively Liz, a strawberry roan mare. Coming out of the chute at a dead run, Liz ducked her head and cut hard to the left, then went airborne. Fielding tried valiantly to remain in the middle of Liz's back, but his right foot went over the mare's neck, and he found himself with his feet in the air and his head pointing toward the ground. One more quick jump to the left loosened him from his bareback rigging and sent him flying through the air. The second rider, Ross Calahan, made a qualifying ride on Thunderhead, a buckskin horse that had once been a top bucking horse but was now starting to show his age. Ross scored an even seventy, which probably wouldn't be high enough to place. The third rider, Daryl Melton, rode Galloway to a score of seventy-five. Cole Dwyer missed Millie out by not having his spurs over the point of the horse's shoulders on the first jump out of the chute. Reuben Sanchez scored a seventy-one on a good horse called TWA. Jack, Clay, Glenn, and Billy all knew Reuben could have had the winning score if he had just used his spurs more.

Tumbleweed was already in the chute with Clay's bareback rigging cinched on. As soon as the sixth rider nodded and turned into the arena, Clay stepped over the chute and stood astride the horse, placing his feet on the boards.

In the arena, George Beckel was bucked off a horse named Dewey four seconds into his ride, and while the pick-up men herded the stallion out of the arena, Clay worked his hand into the rigid suitcase-like handle of his bareback rigging and sat down gently on the horse's back.

With the arena clear, the action turned to chute number four. Clay was in position when the arena director called his name. Pulling his hat down tighter on his head, Clay leaned back, moved his spurs into Tumbleweed's shoulders and nodded.

The blue roan charged out of the chute, running two lengths before sticking his head between his legs and kicking high with his back feet.

Clay leaned back and jerked his knees upward, bringing his spurs all the way up the horse's shoulders as it lunged forward.

Tumbleweed bucked the length of the arena, twisting his body and kicking high with his back feet. The horse's bucking style was perfect for a cowboy to get in time with and spur hard — and that's exactly what Clay did, scoring a seventy-seven to move into first place. He wouldn't know until the end of the week whether it would hold through the second performance.

Clay retrieved his equipment from the derigging chute and watched the remaining three riders, breathing a sigh of relief when the last rider bucked out and he retained his first-place standing.

Chapter Two

Tamara tied Charger to the trailer when she saw Clay walking toward the pickup.

"Hey, cowboy, you really looked like a bronc rider out there," she said as he threw his gear bag into the camper.

"Thanks," he said, taking her by the hand and leading her back toward the arena. "I'm thirsty. How about something to drink?"

"All right, but it won't get you out of buying me supper after the rodeo."

"How about if I throw in a hot dog and some potato chips?" Clay asked, grinning.

"Not even," Tamara replied sweetly.

"Well, it was a good try," he said as he ordered two soft drinks at the concession stand.

As they walked around the arena, Clay and Tamara stopped to talk to several of the other contestants. Kerry Tyler caught up with them halfway back to the pickup. "Hey, guys, I've been looking all over for you two."

"Where have you been?" Tamara asked, concerned about her friend's tardiness.

"We got out of Dallas later than we thought. I swear Rob drove ninety miles an hour all the way to get here. I'm not sure I'm going to be able to run the barrels if I'm not traveling faster than eighty."

"I hate to leave in the middle of this story, but I've got to get my gear ready for the saddle bronc riding," Clay said.

"C'mon, Kerry, we need to get our horses saddled and warmed up before the barrel racing," Tamara said, and they all parted ways to prepare for the events ahead.

Clay stepped up on the platform behind the chutes as the last calf roper made his run. Billy Ettinger and Jack were there to give him a hand up. Jack took Clay's saddle and moved it to chute three, where Gruesome, a long-legged black with large, flaring nostrils, stood waiting. The platform was filled with cowboys preparing to ride and those that were there to help. Clay knew most of them by name and reputation, having competed against them numerous times. As he was setting his saddle on Gruesome, someone slapped him on the back. He turned around and smiled as he saw Tony Malloy standing behind him. Tony was a fellow saddle bronc rider on the circuit and was presently sitting ninth in the standings.

"How's it goin', Clay?" Tony asked, peering over his shoulder to get a look at the horse in the chute.

Shaking hands with his friend, Clay replied, "So far, so good. How about you?"

"I think I'm doin' better than you. I drew Pack Man."

Clay nodded his head. "If I had a horse to

draw, I'd pick that one anytime."

"Looks like you drew the bottom of the barrel. I don't know why Bronson keeps him in the string."

"Maybe he keeps hoping he'll get better," Clay said sarcastically.

"I wouldn't hang my hat on that happening. You and Tamara doin' all right since your problems in Denton?"

Jack finished pulling the cinch tight on Clay's saddle and looped the latigo back through the D ring, tightening it also. Clay nodded when everything was set to his liking, then turned back to answer Tony's question.

"We're fine. How about you? You had any more flat tires or stolen batteries?"

Tony grinned. "Nope, but at least I got a nice check from that investigation firm for my troubles."

"Tamara and I got some pretty good checks as well. It wasn't enough to make up for the worry I went through, but it did help. I'm just glad they got that kidnapper locked away in prison."

The arena director called for the first rider, bringing Tony and Clay's attention to the action in the arena.

The first rider out was Donny Landers on Dark Landing. Donny was presently twelfth in the standings in saddle broncs. Dark Landing was a good draw, so Clay expected a good ride. He wasn't disappointed. Donny showed perfect riding form, spurring from Dark Landing's shoulders to the saddle cantle in time with the horse's violent bucks while keeping his seat planted firmly in the saddle. Donny finished his eight-second ride and scored eighty-one.

The next rider was Collin Jordan on Starburst. Collin made it five seconds into the ride before blowing a stirrup and plowing up the dirt in the arena.

Clay was in the saddle and ready when Starburst was run out. Nodding to the gateman, he squeezed the swells of the saddle tightly with his thighs and placed his spurs over the points of Gruesome's shoulders as the horse turned into the arena.

It wasn't that Gruesome didn't give it all he had — he just wasn't as big and powerful as most saddle bronc horses. His bucking style was simple; he merely pushed off with all four feet, cleared the ground by three feet, landed stiff-legged, then repeated the same move over again.

Clay kept his spurs working from the horse's shoulders to the cantle. Keeping his rein held tight, he had to be careful not to pull too hard or he would pull the horse's head up. But if he held the rein too loose, he wouldn't be able to stay in the saddle.

It was an easy eight seconds, which didn't please Clay at all. When he slid off the pick-up man's horse, he knew he hadn't scored high enough to place. He grimaced as the announcer called out his score — sixty-nine. Climbing over the chutes, he was welcomed by Billy Ettinger's caustic remark.

"Hey, Junior, I see you finally drew a horse you could ride."

Clay couldn't help but grin, despite his disappointment. "Maybe one of these days I'll be able to ride grown-up horses like you old-timers," he shot back.

Billy's saddle was on a bay named Caution. Clay had drawn the horse before and knew he was one of the best in the string. If Billy rode him to the whistle — and Clay felt certain he would — he would stand a good chance of winning.

As Billy stepped into the chute, Clay held Caution's head and talked soothingly to him until the gate swung open.

Billy wasn't sitting third in the standings for nothing. His athletic ability, combined with Caution's bucking style, impressed not only the audience but the judges as well. Once out of the chute, Caution propelled himself skyward and kicked out with his back feet. The red horse looked as if he was stretching in midair. He came down with a hard landing that would have shaken many a rider loose, but Billy was prepared and put his weight in the stirrups to let his legs absorb most of the shock. From that point on, Caution kept his head between his front legs and bucked hard. Billy made it look easy as he spurred in time with each jump, keeping his backside glued to the saddle. Billy's ride was impressive enough to earn him a score of eighty-five.

Billy smiled at Clay as he climbed back up on the platform. "See what it's like to ride big horses?"

"You call that a big horse?" Clay asked. "The only reason you got a high score is because you're related to all the judges. That bag of bones you were on can't buck as hard as the saddle horses we got at the ranch. I'd love to stay and give you pointers on what you did wrong, but I've got to go watch a good-looking woman run barrels."

Billy chortled as Clay beat a hasty retreat. "Come back anytime you need advice on how to ride broncs."

Clay pretended not to hear. Hurrying to the arena entrance, he saw Tamara exercising Charger off to the side. He stood back and watched, waiting for her to notice him.

Slowing the big horse, Tamara walked him to where Clay stood.

"Gruesome lives up to his name, doesn't he?" she asked, stopping beside Clay.

"Not in his bucking, he doesn't," Clay responded.

"No, but it's a gruesome draw if you get him," Tamara smiled.

Clay chuckled dryly. "I hope I don't draw him again. If I do, I might just draw out of the saddle bronc riding." Some cowboys did this on a regular basis. Entering several rodeos on a weekend, they would wait to find out what stock they had drawn and then go to the rodeos where they'd drawn the best stock. They had to pay a draw-out fee, but it was less than the entry fees. Clay had done the same thing himself.

"You ought to tell that to Bronson. Maybe he'll pull him from the string," Tamara noted.

"I'm going to, the next time I see him," Clay responded.

The barrels were set in the arena, and Tamara had Charger warmed up.

"I'm third runner," she said, moving around Clay.

"You better win so you can take me out tomorrow night," Clay said with a mischievous smile.

"Is that the only reason you stay with me?" she chided him.

"Nope, but it's one of them," he responded.

Tamara laughed and moved to the arena entrance while Clay climbed up on the fence to get a better view.

"Our next barrel racer hails from San Angelo, Texas," the announcer called out. "Let's give Tamara Allen a big Oklahoma welcome as she enters the arena for her run."

Amid the applause from the crowd, Charger came through the gate running at full speed toward the first barrel, slowing only slightly before reaching it. Tamara cued him with a light tug on the reins as he turned the first barrel and lunged toward the second. In two lengths, the big horse was at full speed, slowing again as he came to the barrel. Circling the red-and-white drum and clearing it with only inches to spare, horse and rider sped toward the third and final barrel as the crowd cheered wildly.

Tamara's face showed intense concentration as she negotiated the last turn and spurred Charger toward the electronic timer located near the entrance.

Clay yelled loudly as Tamara crossed the timer line and reined Charger back to a walk. He knew her time would be good enough to place, and he wasn't surprised when her run was announced as the fastest of the evening by three-tenths of a second.

After walking Charger out, Tamara came to stand beside Clay to watch the remaining barrel racers. As the last run was made, Clay climbed down from his perch. "Looks like I got supper coming tomorrow night."

"Would you settle for a hot dog and a bag of potato chips?" Tamara asked innocently.

"Nope!" Clay shot back.

"Not even if I feed it to you under the stars with just the two of us alone at a romantic spot I have in mind?"

Clay looked at her suspiciously. "Just where is this romantic spot?"

"Ooh, that's my secret," she replied with a coy smile. "Is it a deal?"

Clay put his arms around her neck and leaned close to whisper in her ear, "I'd settle for a can of

Vienna sausages and some soda crackers if I could be alone with you."

Feeling hot and flushed, Tamara twisted her head and kissed him gently on the lips. "You got a date, cowboy. Tomorrow night after the rodeo!"

Clay squeezed her tightly against him, adoring the way she felt in his arms, loving the way he felt when he was with her. He kissed her once more, then released her and stepped away "I could do this all night, but I've got a bull to ride. I'd better get over there while I've still got the presence of mind to ride him."

"You take care of yourself out there and don't get hurt. I'd hate for you to miss our date tomorrow night," Tamara replied.

Clay gulped and tried to catch his breath. Just looking at her made his palms sweat and his heart race. "It would take more than a bull to make me miss it," he said as he turned and walked away.

Tamara took a deep breath and looked up in time to see Kerry grinning at her knowingly. She blushed and stuck out her tongue, then smiled back.

Chapter Three

Clay's bull rope was on the big brindle named Wrangler. His reputation of being a rank bull had been earned because of the large number of cowboys he'd managed to unload before the eight-second whistle. The animal had been to the national finals three times and would undoubtedly go again. Clay had drawn him once before and had managed to ride him for four seconds before being thrown.

Looking down at the large bovine in the chute, Clay vowed to even the score on this ride.

"Don't anticipate his moves," Jack advised, knowing what was going through Clay's mind. "Just stay in the middle, keep your spurs dug in, and don't let him pull you down into the well when he dips that shoulder."

"Shoot, is that all I got to do? Piece of cake," Clay chuckled.

"That, and stay on for eight seconds," Jack reminded him.

The battle between man and beast was being won by the beasts so far, as the first five riders failed to make a qualified ride. The bullfighters were earning their money today — two of the riders got hung up, and one of them was seriously injured when the bull stepped on him several times before shaking him clear.

With only one rider before him, Clay stood astride Wrangler and began warming up the resin on his rope by running his gloved hand up and down its length. The ride going on in the arena ended the same way as the earlier ones, with the cowboy being thrown before the whistle. Easing himself gently down onto the bull's back, Clay slipped his gloved hand into the braided leather handle of the bull rope and nodded for Jack to begin pulling the tail. The rope tightened on Clay's hand, and he nodded when it was snug enough. Jack laid the tail of the bull rope across Clay's open palm and waited for him to close his fist and wrap the rope behind his hand before bringing it back through his palm again, running the tail between his ring finger and little finger. Clenching the rope tightly, Clay moved forward as far as he could and dug his spurs into the bull's side, then nodded for the gate.

Wrangler bellowed as he swung into the arena, bucking into a left-hand spin close to the chutes. He made three quick rounds, shifted his weight, and spun right, the same move that had lost Clay on the previous ride and almost lost him again as he felt himself being pulled forward and down. Using all the strength he had, Clay strained to pull himself upright as Wrangler turned his massive body into a right spin and began tossing his head in an attempt to intimidate the rider on his back.

Five seconds into the ride, Clay was still sitting

tight with his spurs dug firmly into the bull's sides.

At the six-second mark, Wrangler stopped suddenly and twisted his body in an arch that placed his head near the ground and his hindquarters high in the air.

At seven seconds, the big brindle leaped forward in a powerful surge of energy and the rider slipped slightly backward.

Twisting to the right, with hind legs sweeping high, Wrangler had Clay sliding to the left just as the whistle blew.

Clay's feet hit the ground a mere second after the whistle, and he jerked hard with his right hand, relieved to feel it come free. Looking back over his shoulder as he ran, he spotted the bullfighters moving in to distract Wrangler long enough for him to gain the safety of the chutes.

"Ladies and gentlemen, not only did Clay Tory make the first qualified ride of the evening," the announcer began, excitement ringing in his voice. "He managed to score an eighty-nine on that ride. How about a round of applause in appreciation of that great performance?"

The crowd clapped and hollered while Clay waved his hat in the air, the exhilaration of the ride still coursing through him as the other cowboys behind the chutes congratulated him and gave him high fives.

"That was a great ride!" Billy Ettinger said as they slapped hands.

"I'm glad you approve, sir," Clay responded.

"Where ya buyin' supper?" Billy queried.

Clay gave him a surprised look. "Me? I figured since you beat me in the saddle bronc riding, you'd do the buyin'."

Billy grinned and glanced sideways. "How about we get Jack to buy?"

Jack was sitting on the top rail of an empty chute looking proud and pleased. "I'll buy, since Clay's winning the bull riding and you're winning the saddle broncs. Call it an added benefit for both of you riding so well."

"Sounds good to me," Billy grinned. "I know a great restaurant right off Highway 279. Since we're all heading to Ada, we can stop there on our way out of town. How long before ya'll are ready to go?"

"Tamara and Kerry are loading their horses now. All I got to do is get Jack loaded," Clay said, motioning to the pickup and trailer.

Jack looked at the girls and with a smirk turned back to Billy. "Your wife's not with you, is she?"

"Nope, she had to stay home. Her mother's not feelin' well."

"Good," Jack smiled. "Rob's not going to Ada, which means Kerry needs a ride. If she could ride with you I would have the backseat to myself."

Clay chuckled. "I can't get him to ride in the camper where he can stretch out on the bed and sleep. He says if I stop too fast or take a turn too quick it'll throw him out of bed."

Sniggering, Billy replied, "I'll be glad to take her with me. She can keep me awake — but it's an awful high price to pay for a meal."

After a full meal at the Roadhouse Cafe, they headed west toward Ada. Tamara had already made arrangements to board the horses at a friend's place. They drove there first and unloaded, fed and watered the animals, then headed to the Best Western, where Will and Dottie Hightower had made reservations for them.

"Where are you staying tonight?" Jack asked Billy after they checked in.

"I'm going to sleep in my camper," Billy answered, nodding toward his pickup.

"It's going to get awfully warm in that hotbox. Come on, you can bunk with Clay and me — but you'll have to share a bed with Clay!"

Billy grimaced and glanced sideways at Jack. "You know there's only so much a fella can endure in one day."

Jack roared with laughter. "I know what you mean," he said, looking at Clay and Tamara kissing each other good night, "but at least the air conditioner works."

Three groans sounded in unison the next morning as loud knocking on the door resounded through the small hotel room. Jack rolled over and looked at the digital clock on the nightstand. It was nine o'clock. He moaned once more and threw back the covers.

"If I had a gun I'd shoot that stinkin' Will

Hightower right now!"

When Jack opened the door, a grinning Will Hightower stood on the other side. "Nothing makes my day more than to rouse you from a peaceful slumber."

"Nothing would make my day more than to shoot you and save the world from your bad sense of humor," Jack replied dryly.

"Well, since you ain't got a gun, and you couldn't hit the broad side of a barn if you did, get dressed. Dottie and I ate a long time ago, but I'll let you buy me a cup of coffee."

"Now, that's right generous of you," Jack said, walking back into the room. "I'll meet you in thirty minutes."

"Don't forget to wash behind your ears." Will guffawed, closing the door and muttering to himself, "The world shouldn't have to see Jack Lomas in his underwear."

Tamara and Kerry woke Clay and Billy at noon so they could get something to eat and care for the horses. There wasn't much to do in Ada other than lie around the hotel pool and soak up some sun, so that's what they did for the better part of the afternoon. All four of them were a medium red by the time they decided to get dressed and head off to the rodeo grounds. Clay and Tamara drove out and got the horses while Kerry and Billy went on ahead.

Soon after they arrived at the rodeo grounds, Tamara and Kerry exercised their horses, while

Clay and Billy talked to the other cowboys. They then sought out Terry and Carl Hightower, Will and Dottie's sons and the main operators of Running H Stock Contractors.

The Hightowers, with Jack in tow, arrived shortly afterward. Dottie was the bookkeeper and the rodeo secretary and ensured that everything was ready for the evening performance.

Will and Jack had traveled the rodeo circuit together in their youth and had remained friends through the years. Though they had both vied for Dottie's hand at one point, Will had won out and Jack had gone on and eventually married the love of his life, Marie Gladstone. The four had stayed in touch until Marie's death, at which point Jack had become a recluse, staying at his ranch and avoiding company. Only when Clay had gone to stay with him and the two began traveling to rodeos was the old friendship rekindled.

Clay hurried over to shake hands with Will, and then gave Dottie a hug. Stepping back, Dottie looked him up and down.

"You've filled out even more since the last time I saw you! You're turning into quite a hunk. Tamara better keep her eye on you."

Clay blushed, but was secretly pleased with the compliment.

"You're just saying that because it's true," he said with a mischievous grin.

Dottie laughed and punched him playfully on the arm. "You've been living with Jack Lomas too long. You're starting to sound just like him."

"I talked to Terry and Carl a while ago," Clay said with an amused look on his face. "Sounds like you may have a new daughter-in-law pretty soon."

Carl, the younger of their two sons, was still living at home. Dottie had been wishing for some time that he would find a nice girl and settle down.

Dottie's face registered surprise. "Now, who told you such a thing? Surely not Carl?"

Clay's eyes sparkled with merriment. "No, it wasn't Carl — though I did question him about it."

With a stern look, she asked, "Well, if it wasn't Carl, who was it?"

Clay was savoring the moment and delayed telling her, pretending to struggle with remembering who it was that might have told him. "I can't recall exactly, but whoever it was, they were pretty sure that something serious was going on between Carl and Susan Blackwell."

Dottie gave him a scathing look. "Clay Tory, if you don't tell me right now who it was that gave you that information, I'm going to make sure you draw the worst stock we have at any rodeos you attend in the future."

Laughing outright, Clay took her by the shoulders and smiled. "Your elder son was the one that let the cat out of the bag. Carl told Terry a couple of days ago that he's thinking of asking Susan to marry him."

"Well, for heaven's sake, why didn't he tell me?" Dottie asked.

"Because you'd have booked the church, called the caterer, and sent out invitations within an hour of him telling you he was thinking about it," Will Hightower interjected.

"I kinda got the impression it wasn't quite absolute," Clay hurried to add, "so I wouldn't say anything to Carl just yet. It might mess things up."

Jack and Billy were standing off to one side watching and listening. Both wore roguish grins, knowing Dottie would be bursting to say something to Carl but would have to restrain herself.

Dottie was beside herself with excitement. "I promise you I won't say a thing to him. Did Terry say when Carl was going to ask her?"

Fighting back another grin, Clay answered innocently, "No, he didn't, but I gathered it was going to be pretty soon."

"Oh, my goodness," Dottie exclaimed, pressing her hands to her face, "my baby is getting married!"

Will Hightower rolled his eyes in disbelief. "Dottie, all he said was that Carl was *thinking* about asking her. Susan hasn't even had the opportunity to answer, and even if she says yes they haven't set a date. So calm down and leave them alone." He scowled at Clay, who quickly thought of something he needed to be doing.

"I'll see ya'll later. I've got to go help Tamara."

Billy and Jack could barely contain their laughter as Will followed Dottie to the trailer that served as their office.

"I'd hate to be in Clay's boots when Dottie finds out Carl isn't planning on asking Susan to marry him anywhere in the near future," Billy said.

Jack rolled his eyes in exasperation. "I don't think I want to be around when she finds out he's been pulling her leg, either."

When the rodeo began at seven, Tamara and Kerry were in the trailer visiting Dottie.

As the grand entry began, Dottie asked, "Aren't you girls going to ride?"

Tamara shook her head. "We'd rather stay with you. We've ridden in enough grand entries. We can stand missing one."

Dottie glanced around her as if checking to see who else might be in the trailer with them. Noticing her strange behavior, Tamara and Kerry exchanged puzzled looks.

"Have you two talked to Terry and Carl today?" Dottie asked in a hushed tone.

Looking surprised, Tamara nodded. "Yes, ma'am, we talked to both of them earlier this afternoon. Why, is something wrong?"

Dottie bit her lower lip, obviously nervous. "Did either of them tell you any, uh, good news?"

The girls looked at each other again, confusion plain on their faces. "Like what?" Kerry asked.

40

"Ohhh . . ." Dottie sighed in frustration. "If I tell you, you have to promise me not to say a word to anyone, especially Carl."

Neither of the girls knew what to expect. This was so unlike Dottie that it caught them both off guard. She was usually so matter-of-fact and straightforward. It was quite a change for Tamara to see her flustered and nervous.

"We won't say a word," Tamara promised. "What is it?"

"Well, I heard that Carl may ask Susan to marry him, but I'm not absolutely sure. I can't ask him for fear of meddling in his affairs. You know how men are about these things. If I ask him, he'll deny it and get angry with me for asking."

Tamara gave a sympathetic nod. "Neither Terry nor Carl said anything to me about it. I talked with Susan a little while ago, and she didn't say anything, either. Who told you Carl was going to ask her to marry him?" Tamara questioned, suddenly suspicious.

Once more, Dottie glanced around nervously, as if there might be someone eavesdropping on their conversation. "If I tell you, you have to promise not to say a word to anyone."

"Who told you?" Tamara asked again.

"Well, Clay told me that Terry said Carl was thinking about asking Susan to marry him," Dottie said, taking a deep breath and looking anxiously at Tamara.

"Clay told you?" Tamara asked in surprise.

Kerry was trying hard not to giggle.

"Yes. Just a little while ago," Dottie replied.

Tamara took Dottie's hand and held it gently. "Dottie, I suggest you find a tactful way to ask Carl. I wouldn't trust information that came through Terry and Clay. I wouldn't be surprised if Clay wasn't pulling your leg."

Tamara watched Dottie's face change from confusion to exasperation, and finally determination. "If that scoundrel was pulling my leg, I'll bend him over my knee and paddle his backside!" she declared.

"I suspect that's exactly what he's doing. You've mentioned on more than one occasion how much you'd like to see Carl married and settled down. Saying he heard it from Terry would make it almost impossible for you to verify. If you asked Terry and he said it wasn't true, you wouldn't know if he was being honest or just keeping Carl's secret."

"Oh, that rascal! He's turned out to be another Jack Lomas," Dottie said angrily.

Tamara said nothing, and Dottie could see she was mulling something over in her mind.

"I wish I knew some way to get even with him!" Dottie exclaimed.

"I think I know how we can turn this around and teach Clay a lesson," Tamara said with a sly smile. Kerry and Dottie looked at her expectantly. "I'm going to talk to Terry," Tamara said, walking to the door. "I'll be back later. Come on,

Kerry, let's go find him."

Usually Tamara would have been watching Clay ride in the barebacks, but this time she missed seeing him score a seventy-nine on Phantom as she worked her way through the holding pens behind the bucking chutes in search of Terry Hightower. It took her only a moment to get the information she was after. She briefly outlined her plan to Terry, then returned to Kerry. "We're going to give Clay a taste of his own medicine."

Searching for Tamara after his bareback ride, Clay spotted her coming from Dottie's trailer on the way to the pickup. "Did you see my ride?" he asked as he caught up to her.

"No, I'm sorry — I was talking to Dottie and forgot the time. She's so excited about Carl getting married that she kept us in her trailer talking until it was too late to watch."

Clay smiled sheepishly. "She told you about that?"

"Yes, she did! It's not every day a woman finds out her son is getting married. She's waited for this for a long time. It would sure be a shame if Carl changed his mind." Tamara gave Kerry a conspiratorial wink.

Clay nodded in agreement, the smile vanishing from his face. "It sure would, but I'm sure Dottie could handle it."

"I don't know," Tamara said with a shake of her head. "I think if he didn't go through with it, it would break Dottie's heart."

Clay's forehead wrinkled with worry. Tamara almost felt sorry for him, then she remembered the devious trick he was trying to play on Dottie, and it helped to strengthen her resolve.

As they walked around the parking lot visiting with the other contestants, Tamara and Kerry couldn't help but notice how quiet Clay had become.

It was almost time for the saddle bronc riding when he left them. Tamara took advantage of his absence to seek out Carl and Susan. She told them what Clay had done and briefly explained what she had planned. Both eagerly agreed to help her.

"Are you sure you're not being too hard on him?" Kerry asked as they walked back to the arena.

Tamara thought for a moment before answering. "I don't think so. Besides, it'll do him good to be on the receiving end for a change. All I have to do now is talk to Jack and Billy, and everything should be in place."

Dottie joined them in the bleachers to watch the saddle bronc riding, and the three of them whispered in hushed tones in between riders.

Billy rode before Clay and scored a seventy-eight on a horse called Ton-O-Trouble, a big rawboned bay that kept his head higher than most saddle bronc horses but bucked hard, jumping high and kicking out with all four feet. He would barely touch the ground before leaping forward again. Billy kept the bronc on a short rein, his spurs raking to earn every point the judges gave him.

Clay had drawn the best saddle bronc horse Running H owned, a dark gray named Gravestone. As horse and rider came out of the chute, Tamara, Kerry, and Dottie forgot about being upset with Clay and yelled encouragement to him.

Gravestone reared high as the chute gate opened; then he spun out into the arena. Clay dug his spurs into the horse's shoulders to keep himself centered in the saddle. Pushing off hard with his back feet, Gravestone arched high in the air, his front hooves coming down first. Clay struggled to get his spurs back at the horse's shoulders. The gray horse flexed his legs and pushed off again to complete another high arch, this time twisting his body to the right in an attempt to throw Clay off balance. Clay felt the move coming and leaned slightly to the left to compensate. The next leap was straight forward, followed by a quick jump to the left. Clay kept his thighs pressed into the swells of the saddle, his spurs raking Gravestone's sides. It was no surprise to anyone when his score of eighty-two was announced, which ended up helping him win the saddle bronc riding.

"That boy might be a pain sometimes, but he can sure ride," Dottie said as she watched him walk back to the chutes.

"That he can," Tamara agreed. "Now, you two keep him occupied while I talk to Jack and

Billy. And Dottie — don't forget to tell Will our plans."

"I won't!" Dottie grinned. "This is sure going to upset Clay's applecart."

Tamara giggled and hurried away to find Jack and Billy.

Clay retrieved his saddle and was taking it to the pickup when Kerry and Dottie walked up beside him.

"That was a great ride, Clay," Kerry congratulated him.

"Sure was," Dottie chimed in. "I haven't seen Gravestone ridden like that in quite a spell. Come by the trailer after you stow your gear and I'll get your check."

"Where's Tamara?" Clay asked, looking around the arena for her.

"She's talking to Gail Chambers. She asked me to get Charger for her," Kerry answered, trying hard to keep a straight face.

Clay nodded and headed to the pickup while Dottie went to her trailer and Kerry went to get the horses for the barrel racing event.

Tamara found Jack and Billy standing by the arena talking to several other cowboys. Excusing herself as she walked up, she asked the two if she could have a word with them. Once they were out of hearing distance, she explained her plan — and she wasn't disappointed with their reaction.

When Tamara left them to meet Kerry, both Billy and Jack were grinning in eager anticipation of the events to come.

Chapter Four

Tamara was pumped as she entered the arena on Charger. She set the pace in the barrel racing with a score of sixteen point five, and none of the other competitors topped her time. Kerry finished fourth with a sixteen point eight.

Clay watched from the gate and was the first to congratulate Tamara as the final runner exited the arena. "Looks like we both got in the money this time. But you get to buy supper."

Tamara smiled and kissed him. "It'll be my pleasure. But we'll have to postpone our romantic evening. Dottie wants us to go eat with them after the rodeo."

Clay was clearly disappointed, but he agreed they couldn't turn Dottie down. He left Tamara to go prepare his rig for his next event.

Clay's draw in the bull riding was a large black bull simply named Rank, a name that spoke of his bucking ability, and his surly attitude.

Tom Lowry was in first place in bull riding, with a score of eighty-four from the night before.

Tamara was biting her nails as she watched the big bull go into a spin just outside the chute. Clay used his outside spur to rake the bull's tough hide and improve the judges' score. Rank tested every bit of Clay's skill and strength as he remained in the tight, dizzying spin the entire eight seconds. The bullfighters had to rush in and attract the bull's attention before Clay could dismount with any degree of safety.

Clay finally separated himself from Rank's back and ran safely to the chutes. His ride earned him a score of eighty and put him in third place. The paycheck wouldn't be as large as the one he received for the saddle bronc event, but it was still a paycheck, and added points to his overall standing. He was sitting in fifth place for the year so far.

As the rodeo came to a close, everyone gathered at Jack's pickup to make final plans for the evening. They agreed on a place to eat and when to meet there. Clay and Tamara hauled the horses back to the stables, and fed and watered each one before driving to the restaurant. By the time they arrived, everyone else was already there.

Tables had been pulled together to accommodate the large group. Will was sitting at one end with Dottie on his left. Jack, Kerry, and Billy were beside Dottie. Carl and Susan were seated across the table, and Terry and his wife, Darlene, were next to them. The only two places left were at the head of the table. Tamara and Clay slid into them.

While food orders were taken, Tamara and Dottie exchanged knowing glances, and Carl winked at both of them.

Conversations were being carried on at both ends of the table when Tamara looked at Carl and nodded. Picking up a butter knife, he tapped lightly on the water glass in front of him, causing everyone's attention to focus on him.

"I know this may come as a shock to some of you and a joy to others," he began, looking at his mother, "but I have decided to do something that I swore I would never do." Turning to look down at Susan, who was seated on his right, he took a deep breath, then began, "There are rumors being spread that I was going to ask you to marry me. I think you know how I feel about you, and I want you to know the time we've spent together has meant a lot to me."

Tamara cast a cautious glance toward Clay. He was totally absorbed in what Carl was saying, and she had to cover her mouth to hide a smile that she just couldn't prevent. Turning back to Carl, she waited for him to say the words she knew were coming.

Carl took another deep breath before continuing. "And I want you to know that you are very special to me, but I want to tell you that I have no intention of marrying you. As a matter of fact, I don't think I'll ever marry, and I think it only fair to let you know now so you won't hold out any false hopes."

Susan's face registered first shock, then disbelief, and finally humiliation. If Tamara had not known it was an act, she could easily have believed that Susan was about to storm out of the restaurant. But the look on Dottie's face was priceless: her hands flew to her face in sheer horror and embarrassment.

Tamara glanced in Clay's direction and was gratified to see pure panic on his face.

Now it was Will's turn to perform. Standing upright in anger, he looked at his younger son and spoke, "Carl Hightower, in all your life I've never been ashamed of you. But what you have just done to this poor girl shames me to the bone. I will not tolerate such behavior. Since you have made your declaration in front of our friends, I too will make a declaration. I want you out of my house. Pack your belongings and get out. You no longer work for Running H Stock Contractors. You are on your own."

People at other tables were glancing in their direction, then turning away, embarrassed to be witnessing what was apparently a nasty family quarrel.

Dottie was hiding her face in her napkin and Tamara knew that though she was pretending to cry, she was actually smothering her laughter.

Carl sat down and stared at his father in stunned silence while Susan kept her head bowed in sorrow.

As silence spread over the room like a thick cloud, Tamara cast another glance at Clay. His face was ghostly pale and he looked ill. The others at the table managed looks of shock or embarrassment.

Dottie's shoulders sagged with grief as she got to her feet and walked slowly around the table to stand behind her son.

"You have broken my heart, and though I will always love you, I will never forget what you have done tonight." She looked around the table to ensure that she had everyone's attention before continuing. "But I will especially remember this night because it was the night I taught Clay Tory not to mess with this old woman." With that, she looked directly at Clay and smiled sweetly.

It took a moment for her words to register in Clay's befuddled brain. He stared at her in total bewilderment, then slowly looked at each grinning face at the table.

An embarrassed smile crept over his face as he realized they were all in on it. "I've got to admit, you got me, Dottie, and it looks like you had some help," he said, looking at Tamara, who gave him a wide smile.

Dottie bent down and hugged his neck. "I almost feel bad about doing such a thing, but you deserved it after telling me Carl was going to ask Susan to marry him."

"But I am going to ask her to marry me," Carl said. "Just not today." Everyone broke into laughter, and the other patrons grinned as well. Clay had to endure the rest of the evening, listening to jibes and snide remarks aimed at him. Leaning over, he whispered to Tamara.

"I'll get even with you, my dear!"

Tamara smiled back at him. "I look forward to it . . . my dear."

It was bad enough that Clay had to listen to all

the ribbing at the restaurant that night. But he also had to listen to it on the ride back to the hotel, and once they were in the room, Billy and Jack ragged him unmercifully. He took it all in good humor and the next day on the ride to Abilene, he managed to maintain his sense of humor as Tamara, Kerry, and Jack made numerous comments in regard to Carl's impending marriage.

"I guess the next time I set someone up, I better do it so's no one else will know," he commented as yet another jab was flung at him.

Tamara, sitting beside him, linked her arm through his and said, "Oh, don't do that. It would ruin all our fun."

When they reached Abilene in the early afternoon, Clay helped Tamara unload the horses and care for them before unhooking the trailer. It took them several minutes and many kisses to say good-bye.

"I'll pick you up next Thursday," Clay said, brushing his lips against hers one more time.

"I'll be counting the hours," Tamara said, squeezing him tightly. "Call me when you get home, okay?"

"I will," he promised.

"Come on, you two," Jack yelled. "I swear, you keep taking longer and longer to say good-bye."

Clay kissed her one last time, climbed behind the wheel and waved good-bye, then drove off.

Clay noticed Jack was fairly talkative until they

crossed the Texas–New Mexico border. As they got closer to Roswell, though, worry lines began to crease Jack's face. The rodeos had been a good diversion from the problems facing him at the ranch, but now that they were almost back home, Clay noticed the troubled mood that came over the old rancher. Looking out at the sunbaked prairie, he couldn't help the feeling of depression that washed over him, either.

"It'll be good to get home," Clay said, trying to lighten the mood.

"Yeah, it will," Jack said with false enthusiasm. "I'll bet Julie has something special cooked up for us."

"I hope it's pot roast. She makes the best I've ever eaten."

"I was hoping for spaghetti," Jack remarked. "I love her homemade sauce."

The conversation died, and they covered the remaining distance to the ranch in silence.

It was a somber homecoming as Jack and Clay carried their belongings into the house. Neither Terry nor Julie was around. Jack found a note from Julie, telling them that there was leftover fried chicken in the refrigerator and that they had gone to town to visit her sick aunt.

"I guess we're on our own tonight," Jack said, handing the note to Clay.

"Fried chicken, huh? That was my second choice," Clay exclaimed, taking the large pan of chicken out of the refrigerator. "There's peas and salad in here, too."

Jack merely nodded and got down two plates. He had really wanted to talk to Terry tonight. It was time to make decisions, and he needed to know just how much longer they could hold out before he would have to ship away part of his herd.

Chapter Five

Jack, Clay, and Terry moved the weak cattle from all the pastures to the traps closer to the ranch house, coaxed more water from the windmills, and fed out hay daily, working from sunup to sundown. They were all weary and disheartened at the end of each day.

As Thursday, and Clay's departure, drew nearer, Clay tried harder and harder to persuade Jack to go with him. He grew increasingly concerned about the old rancher as each day passed. Clay enlisted Terry and Julie's help in trying to convince Jack that he should go, but no amount of pleading, threatening, or cajoling would change his mind.

"Will you make it back Sunday night?" Jack asked as he watched Clay load his gear into the pickup.

"I may be back Saturday night if I can convince Tamara to let me drop her off and come home after the Stephenville rodeo."

"No. You just spend the night and come home Sunday," Jack directed him.

"But I can be home early Sunday morning to help around here," Clay protested. "I shouldn't be going at all with the amount of work there is to do here!"

Jack let out a weary sigh. "We've been over all

this before, and you know how I feel. You've got a good chance to make it to the finals, maybe even win the all-around championship. You've got to go for it now while you can. Terry and I will handle things here while you're gone."

Though Clay knew there was no use arguing, he couldn't help but add, "I just don't feel right about going off and leaving you two with all the work while I'm out running around the country having fun."

Chuckling, Jack reached over and slapped him affectionately on the shoulder. "I know you don't, and I appreciate your concern, but I want you to have the opportunity to compete at the finals. You're almost there. Don't make the mistake of blowing it when you're this close."

Clay nodded, understanding that his success, in large part, was also Jack's success. Jack had been a world champion saddle bronc rider, and he knew what it meant to make it to the top and what it took to be the best. Now he wanted that for Clay, to share the glory with the young man whom he'd taught so much.

Clay picked Tamara up in San Angelo Thursday morning, and they headed for Shreveport, Louisiana. Time passed quickly, and the miles fell behind them as they talked about upcoming rodeos and discussed their hopes and dreams as well as their concerns. They both missed having Jack with them, but they also enjoyed their time alone, which rarely happened.

After the night's performance in Shreveport, they would drive to Austin, where they were entered for Friday night. They would spend Friday night in Austin and drive to Stephenville for the Saturday night performance. It was the middle of what cowboys called Cowboy Christmas, and every weekend for the next month or so would be just as busy as this one. Making that many rodeos would mean being gone for the better part of each week. At one time Clay had eagerly anticipated this time of year, but now he had mixed emotions because it would mean being away from the ranch for long stretches. He didn't feel comfortable sharing this concern with Tamara, though. He just hoped that by some miracle the drought would soon end.

Shreveport was thirty miles across the Texas–Louisiana border and hosted several riverboat casinos.

"We could swing by Harrah's after the rodeo and try our luck at the slot machines," Clay suggested as they passed one of the billboards advertising the casinos.

"No, thanks," Tara remarked, frowning at the large sign. "I've had enough of gambling and gamblers to last me for a while."

Clay chuckled at her remark. Given the past, he could understand why she would say that. "Well, we can at least get us something to eat at one of their restaurants. I hear they have great food."

"Now, that I could go for!" Tamara smiled.

★ ★ ★

They arrived at the Shreveport fairgrounds thirty minutes before the rodeo started, which gave Tamara enough time to acquaint Charger with the arena and Clay enough time to get his gear to the chutes and talk to the other cowboys.

By the time the rodeo was over, Clay was holding second in bareback riding, first in saddle bronc riding, having beaten Billy Ettinger by three points, and fourth in bull riding. Tamara was winning the barrel racing with a comfortable lead.

After the rodeo, Clay and Tamara invited Billy and his wife, Diane, to join them for something to eat at Harrah's. They took advantage of the dinner buffet to stuff themselves until they all felt like gluttons, laughing at the huge amount of food they had consumed. Billy and Diane were driving to a rodeo in Oklahoma, then heading on to Missouri. As the four parted company in Harrah's parking lot, they wished each other good luck and made plans to meet the next weekend in San Antonio.

Clay pulled onto Interstate 20 heading west, and tuned the radio to a country music station as Tamara yawned and leaned her head on his shoulder.

"You going to sleep all the way?" Clay teased.

"I thought I'd catch a little catnap," she answered, snuggling closer to him. A few moments later she was sound asleep. Clay listened to her even breathing, and a feeling of peace and contentment stole over him.

It was nearing four o'clock in the morning when Clay saw the lights of Austin come into view. Tamara was stretched out on the seat beside him with her head resting in his lap. He nudged her gently to rouse her from her sleep. Sitting up, she yawned and scratched her head.

"Where are we?"

"That's Austin just up ahead," Clay answered.

"Austin!" she exclaimed in astonishment. "Why didn't you wake me up? You must be exhausted."

"I'm a little tired, but I'm all right. You were sleeping so soundly I didn't want to wake you. Besides, you talk in your sleep and I was enjoying listening to the things you were saying."

"I don't talk in my sleep!" Tamara responded with indignation.

"Yes, you do, and you say some pretty interesting things, too."

"Like what?" Tamara asked skeptically.

"Oh, you kept repeating my name over and over — Clay, Clay. Then you'd say you loved me and start breathing real heavy. It was all very intriguing. Kept me awake the entire trip."

Punching him lightly on the arm, Tamara giggled. "You're so full of bull, Clay Tory. You're just doing some wishful thinking, and your brain's done addled on you."

Clay laughed. "I had you going for a minute, though."

Sliding close to him, she put her arm around

his shoulder and squeezed it. "Listen, buster, I don't need to talk in my sleep to tell you I love you, and when I call out your name, I'll be wide awake."

"I like the sound of that," Clay said, stealing a quick kiss. "Now I need directions to the Crawfords' place. I'm ready to get that nag of yours bedded down so I can do the same."

"Are you going to get a room?" Tamara asked.

"I thought I'd get you one. I'm going to sleep in the camper."

"How gallant," she responded, kissing him on the cheek.

"No, I'm just tired and ready for some sleep. How about giving me those directions so we can get Charger taken care of?"

With the horse stalled and Tamara in her room, Clay climbed into the camper. It felt good to lie between the fresh, clean sheets Julie had put on the bed before he had left. Soon after laying his head on the pillow, he was fast asleep, but dry grass and thirsty cattle haunted his dreams. Only when a slim blond figure with sparkling blue eyes slid into his mind's eye did peaceful slumber come. He was sleeping soundly when Tamara knocked on the door at twelve o'clock that afternoon.

"Wake up, Sleeping Beauty," she said, opening the door.

He groaned as the bright sunlight that had been blocked by the tinted windows and dark curtains came streaming in through the open door.

"What time is it?"

"It's noon, and Charger is probably pacing his stall waiting to be fed."

"You could have just driven the truck and let me sleep," he protested.

"I thought you might like to take a shower while I was gone," she answered. "It'll take me about forty-five minutes to get there, feed Charger, and get back. That should give you enough time to shower and shave, and then we can get something to eat. I'm starved."

With a chuckle, he motioned for her to close the door. "Let me get some pants on and I'll be right out. I swear, woman, you're always hungry."

There were several other contestants staying at the hotel. After a hearty lunch, Clay and Tamara joined the crowd gathered around the swimming pool. The men talked about horses, bulls, rides, and women, while the women talked barrel racing, men, and relationships. Occasionally Tamara or Clay would look up and catch the other watching and they'd both smile before turning away.

The afternoon passed quickly, and soon it was time for them to retrieve Charger and get to the rodeo. While Tamara exercised Charger in the arena, Clay looked over the stock. A score of seventy-three was winning the bareback riding, and he had drawn Iceman, a feisty buckskin that he had drawn twice before, placing on him both times.

In saddle bronc riding, Glenn Harwell was leading with a seventy-eight. Clay's draw in that event was a large black horse named Coal. It would be hard to beat Glenn's score, but Clay felt he'd drawn a horse that could do it.

Loren Bates was holding the lead in bull riding with an eighty-four. Clay felt the bull he'd drawn himself, Bold Lancer, a large Charolais with drooping horns, probably wouldn't be able to top that score, but Clay would still give it all he had and hope for the best.

Clay's luck didn't hold as well in Austin as it had in Shreveport. He missed Iceman out in the bareback riding. He was late bringing his right foot off the chute and into Iceman's shoulder. The horse's front feet were already on the ground in the arena before Clay's spur touched his shoulder. In the saddle bronc competition Coal performed to Clay's expectations, bucking hard and high, straight down the arena. The big black horse was stout, and it took all of Clay's strength to keep him from pulling the rein away. Clay had to grip the rein tightly to prevent Coal from jerking it away from him. His spurring was smooth and precise, in perfect time with each buck. The judges' score of seventy-nine put him in first place after the first two performances.

Tamara's luck turned bad when she overcued Charger and knocked over the second barrel. She received a five-second penalty, and that added to her time to put her out of the running.

There's an old adage that says there's not a cowboy that can't be thrown and there's not a horse that can't be rode. Clay found that the same holds true in bull riding. His ride on Bold Lancer started out just as he had predicted. The Charolais bucked straight out of the chute and slowly came around to the left. Clay remained in position, forward on his bull rope, his spurs raking the bull's side. It looked as if it was going to be an easy ride, albeit a low-scoring one. But Bold Lancer had different ideas. With only two seconds remaining on the stopwatch, the yellow bull dipped his right shoulder and ducked left. Gravity worked its power on Clay's body, pulling him hard forward and down at the same time. He was caught by surprise, and no amount of skill or strength could prevent his inevitable departure from Bold Lancer's back one second before the whistle blew. All he would take home from his ride was a mouthful of arena dirt that he worked to spit out as he walked dejectedly back to the chutes.

Neither Clay nor Tamara felt very jubilant as they gathered Clay's gear. Several of their friends invited them to join them at a local restaurant, and though neither felt like being with a crowd, they reluctantly accepted. The evening with friends was balm for their wounded pride, and they were soon talking and laughing and enjoying the outing.

"I guess you can't win them all," Clay said in

reference to their performance that evening as he walked Tamara to her door.

"I can handle not winning 'em all. I just hate losing so badly. It was stupid of me to try cutting that second barrel so close, but I was trying to shave a few tenths of a second off my time."

"Sometimes you gotta go for it," Clay responded, "or else you'll never know if you could do it or not. I shouldn't have let that bull buck me off, but I knew if I didn't take some risk, I wouldn't score high enough to place. I didn't have my spurs locked in when he pulled that move on me and I came off my rope, but at least I know I was trying as hard as I could."

"You're right," Tamara agreed, "but I'd rather be taking home a paycheck."

Unlocking her door, Tamara turned and wrapped her arms around Clay's neck. She gave him a deep kiss before pulling away to catch her breath. "We'll get 'em tomorrow night!" she said with a smile.

Clay kissed her once more, said good night, then walked to his pickup.

Stephenville was a short two-and-a-half-hour drive from Austin, so Tamara and Clay could sleep until ten the next morning. When they got up, they fed Charger, then ate a late breakfast. They took a quick swim in the hotel pool and talked to some of the contestants who had come in for Saturday night's performance. Rested and relaxed, they left Austin at three o'clock and headed north on Interstate 35.

Clay was right about their luck changing. He placed second in bareback riding on Gold Plated, a palomino that bucked in a wide circle in a hard-lunging, high-jumping pattern that impressed both the crowd and the judges.

Loch Ness, a light-colored bay, cranked up the heat with a series of twists and lunges that helped Clay score a seventy-three and come in fourth in saddle bronc riding.

A gray-and-black bull named Two Tubs came out of the chute and went into a right-hand spin that had Clay working hard to stay aboard. When a bull spins away from a cowboy's riding hand, it's easier to ride than when it spins in the same direction as a cowboy's riding hand. Clay dug in with his right spur and attempted to use his left one to rake the bull's hide, but Two Tubs didn't spin in a smooth circle. Rather, he made a series of lunges and jumps as he came around. Clay worked his full eight seconds before detaching himself from Two Tubs's back in a graceful dismount that left him on his feet and running to the safety of the chutes. His score of seventy-six was good enough for fifth place and a paycheck.

Tamara placed second in barrel racing with a sixteen-three, going a little wide on the second barrel. Clay knew she played it safe, but at least she got a paycheck.

They left Stephenville after the rodeo, drove straight to San Angelo, and spent the night at

Tamara's house. Clay awoke the next morning to the smell of bacon frying and realized he was famished. Looking at the clock on the nightstand, he saw that it was ten-thirty. He had planned to be well on his way back to the ranch by now, and he had asked Tamara to awaken him early. Climbing out of bed, he stepped into his jeans, pulled a T-shirt over his head, and walked barefoot down the stairs. He heard voices coming from the kitchen and headed in that direction. He could soon see Tamara sitting at the kitchen bar drinking a cup of coffee while her mother cooked bacon.

In the kitchen, he was greeted with a smile from Tamara. "Good morning, sleepyhead," she said jokingly.

"Good morning, Clay," Tamara's mother said, turning at the sound of her daughter's greeting.

"Good morning, Mrs. Allen. It's nice to see you."

"And we're glad you finally decided to drop in and see us again. It's been a spell since you were down this way."

"Yes, ma'am. We've been pretty busy, with the drought and all."

"Tamara's been telling me how bad things are over your way. So far we've been pretty lucky, but it looks like we may be in for a drought, too, if we don't get some rain soon."

Clay turned to Tamara. "I thought you were going to wake me early."

"I tried," she responded in self-defense, "but you wouldn't wake up! I called you three times, and even shook you. I figured if you were that tired, I better let you sleep now or you'd fall asleep on the way home."

Clay chuckled. "I guess I was more worn out than I thought."

"It's a wonder the both of you don't fall asleep and kill yourselves. I swear, the way you two run from one rodeo to the next with only a few hours of sleep, you'll be old and worn out before you're thirty," Trish Allen said.

"Now, Mom, it's not as bad as that. We get plenty of sleep, and we keep each other awake on the road." She smiled sheepishly at Clay, remembering the drive from Shreveport to Austin.

"She's right, Mrs. Allen. We get plenty of sleep during the day and travel at night."

Mrs. Allen wiped her hands on the apron she was wearing and shook her head. "I remember what it was like traveling the circuit with Cliff. We'd drive all night and all day just to make it to a rodeo, then leave as soon as your father finished riding to head to the next one. I never did get enough sleep — but looking back on it, I think it was the best time of our lives. We still talk about it today and remember all the fun we had."

Tamara smiled at her mother. "There weren't as many rodeos in those days as there are now. We don't have to travel as far as you did."

"No, you don't, but you're making more

rodeos in a week than we did back then, too! How would you like your eggs, Clay?"

"Over easy, please."

Shaking her head, Trish Allen turned back to the stove and broke an egg into the skillet.

Seeing the gesture, Clay shot Tamara a questioning look, but she merely shrugged. "Did I place the wrong order?" he asked.

Trish looked confused, then realized what she'd done. "No, no," she hurried to say. "It's just that I'm still amazed."

"By what?" Tamara asked.

"By the fact that your father lets you go traipsin' all over the country with Clay. I can't think of another soul that he'd let you do that with. He must think mighty highly of you, young man."

Clay was at a loss for words. He'd had a few occasions to talk with Tamara's father and had to admit he'd felt ill at ease most of the time. Cliff Allen always seemed very solemn and businesslike.

"The reason he lets me travel with Clay is because he knows he can trust him. Just like I know I can trust him," Tamara said, giving Clay a sweet smile.

"Oh, I don't doubt he's trustworthy. So were several of the other boys you used to go out with, but I doubt very seriously that your father would have let you run around the country with them unchaperoned."

"It's probably because we're engaged," Clay

68

interjected, trying to provide a suitable explanation that would bring an end to this conversation. It was making him feel uncomfortable.

Trish smiled at him. "That does make him happy, I admit, but it's more than that. I think the real reason he doesn't object is because he sees a lot of himself in you."

Clay blushed. He wasn't sure it was true, but he had to admit he was proud to know Cliff Allen thought well of him.

Chapter Six

The glare of the hot New Mexico sun radiated through the windshield as Clay drove the last few miles to Roswell. He felt guilty for having stayed longer at Tamara's than he had planned to. Thinking about all the work to be done at the ranch, with only Terry and Jack there to do it, made him regret his leisure time.

Turning onto the caliche road, he watched the dust boil out behind him and hang in the still air. It settled on the parched grass on either side as if it were a burial shroud. Clay didn't think it was possible, but the prairie looked even more arid than when he'd left a few days earlier.

Turning up the drive to the ranch, he slowed down, remembering the reprimands Julie had given each of them for stirring up the dust that covered everything in the house. Clay hadn't really expected to see activity as he pulled up, but the feeling of abandonment hung starkly over the house as he stepped out of the pickup and opened the yard gate. When he opened the front door, he could feel the emptiness and knew immediately that no one was there. He looked once again at the front yard. Jack's pickup was parked in its normal spot, but the ranch pickup was nowhere in sight. He saw no sign of life over at Terry and Julie's trailer house, either. The place was deserted. All of this was no cause for concern. Clay's common sense told him they were out in one of the pastures and would be returning soon, but he still couldn't shake the feeling that something wasn't quite right. He went back to the camper and began bringing in his clothes, tossing the dirty ones into the utility room and carrying the rest to his room, where he hung them neatly in his closet. He would never forget the first time Jack had walked in and seen clean clothes strewn all over the room. He had made Clay wash, dry, and iron all the clothes for a month. Clay had learned his lesson about keeping his clothes in order. Returning to the camper, he pulled the covers and sheets off the bed and carried them to the utility room before going into the kitchen to find a snack. He stopped abruptly at what he saw. Dirty dishes sat on the table, food was still in pans on the stove, and chairs were pushed away from the table, as if whoever had been sitting in them had left in a hurry. Clay knew Julie would never have left the kitchen in such a mess unless there had been an emergency. He glanced around quickly, hoping to find a note explaining where they'd gone, but he found no such message in the kitchen. Next he hurried to his bedroom, to look on the headboard and dresser, but found nothing. He was on his way back to the kitchen, through the living room, when he saw the blinking message light on the answering machine. Hurrying to the phone, he pushed the Play button. Anxiety gripped him as he waited for the tape to rewind. Finally Julie's familiar voice erupted from the phone.

"Clay, we're at the hospital. Jack's had a little spell and we brought him to the emergency room. We're probably going to be here for a while — you know how these hospitals are. So if you get this message before we get home, you might want to come up here. There's no reason to panic. The doctor said it was probably just a mild case of heatstroke."

The message ended with the time of the call, and when Clay looked at his watch, he realized it had been left almost three hours earlier. He didn't bother to close the front door behind him as he ran to his pickup and jumped inside. This time he took no notice of the amount of dust that plumed up as he pushed the pedal to the floor, spinning the rear tires and causing the truck to fishtail. Fortunately, he met no other vehicles as he sped down the caliche road toward town. With tires squealing, he turned onto the blacktop highway and raced toward Roswell. Fearful thoughts raced through his mind, guilty thoughts. If only he had stayed home, if only he'd left Tamara's earlier that morning. All the rodeos in the world didn't mean as much to him as the man who was now in the hospital. If anything dire happened to Jack, Clay knew he would never be able to forgive himself.

He reduced his speed as he entered the city. Though he had to fight the urge to barrel through the slow-moving traffic, common sense prevailed and he held his anxiety in check.

The pickup had barely quit rolling before Clay was out the door and running to the emergency entrance of the hospital. Once inside, he rushed to the nurses' station and waited impatiently to be noticed by one of the three nurses.

"May I help you?" the closest one asked, finally looking up from her charts.

"I'm looking for a patient that was brought in earlier — Jack Lomas."

He waited while she looked up the name on her computer.

"He's in ICU. Only immediate family are allowed in, and only for a few minutes. Are you a family member?"

"Yes," Clay lied without hesitation. "I'm the only family he has."

"If you'll take a seat in the waiting room, I'll let you know when you can see him. Go down this hall, through the double doors, and you'll see the waiting room on your right," she said, pointing the way.

Clay started down the hall, but was stopped when the nurse called out, "I need your name for the records."

He gave her his name and waited until she typed it into the computer.

"That'll do it!" she said, tapping a final keystroke. "I'll come get you as soon as the doctor clears this."

"Thanks," Clay responded. He started down the hall once again, but checked himself and turned back to the nurse. "Excuse me — do you know where the couple are who came in with him?"

"I'm not sure, since I wasn't on duty when he came in, but I would think they're either in the waiting room or in the cafeteria. It's further down the hall through the next set of double doors. If you don't find them, come see me and I'll page them for you."

"Thanks," Clay said, smiling gratefully.

"No problem," she answered, returning his smile with one of her own.

Clay pushed open the doors leading into the waiting room and searched for Julie and Terry. Out of the corner of his eye, he spotted Julie coming toward him. Beyond her, he could see Terry sitting in one of the waiting room chairs. Julie stopped a short distance away. From the worry and anxiety that he saw on her face, he knew things were worse than she had let on. In the next instant she was clinging to him, tears running down her cheeks.

Panic gripped Clay's heart like a vise. Pushing her gently away, he asked the question that he dreaded to voice: "How is he?"

Wiping the tears from her eyes with her shirtsleeve, Julie tried to smile. "He's hanging in there. The doctors say it was a bad stroke."

Clay gently led Julie to a seat by Terry and saw the same concern etched on his face.

"He was sitting at the table eating lunch," Terry began. "We'd been out since daylight, feeding and moving cattle. We came in to eat around one-thirty. Jack hardly touched his food. When Julie asked him if he was feeling all right, he said he was a little tired and thought he might lie down and take a nap. He started to get up and just fell out of his chair onto the floor. We called the ambulance and told them we'd meet them on the road. Julie threw some blankets in the back of the truck and we laid him down on those. She rode in the back with him and I drove. We met the ambulance just before we reached the highway. They rushed him here, and the doctors stayed with him for about an hour before they came out and told us what was wrong with him. We didn't know what had happened — that's why Julie left you the message on the phone. The doctor says they won't know for sure how bad it is until they run more tests."

"Have you seen him?" Clay asked.

Julie shook her head. "He's in ICU. They only let one person in to visit. We thought it best to wait for you."

Clay nodded his thanks. "What's the doctor's name?"

"Lansing," Terry answered. "We called Doctor Johnson. He's been here about an hour, but he hasn't come out and talked to us yet."

"I guess we have to wait until he comes out, then," Clay said.

The three of them sank into their own apprehensive thoughts about the man lying in ICU, each wrestling with remorseful feelings over whether he or she could have done anything to prevent it. Clay's guilt was increased by the fact that he hadn't been there when it had happened. If he'd insisted on staying home to help with the work, Jack probably wouldn't be in this condition now. He was still brooding when he saw Dr. Johnson come through the door and look around. Spotting Clay, he walked quickly toward him.

The three rose anxiously to their feet to hear what he had to say.

After shaking hands with Clay and Terry and greeting Julie, the old doctor sighed heavily. "He's stable and resting. We won't know the extent of the damage until after we get the test results. Hopefully we'll be able to start running more of them tomorrow or the day after. It depends on how he does between now and then."

Clay listened intently to what the doctor was saying. "When can I see him?"

"You can go in now if you like, though I doubt he'll know you're there."

Clay nodded and followed the doctor down the hall. There was one other patient in the ICU ward, and Clay barely glanced at him as he was led to Jack's bedside. He was stunned by the number of tubes and monitors that were attached to Jack, but what shocked him even more was how pale and sick he looked. Jack Lomas had always seemed invincible to Clay, but now, as he stared down at the prone figure on the bed, a feeling of despair washed over him.

Taking Jack's limp hand in his, he squeezed it firmly, hoping to get a response, but none came.

"I'd like to stay with him for a while if it's all right," Clay requested.

"Fine," Dr. Johnson replied. "But don't stay too long."

Clay nodded and pulled up a chair. Dr. Johnson turned to leave, looking back one more time to see Clay still holding Jack's hand and resting his chin on the bed rail while he watched the old rancher.

It was late when Clay and the Jameses drove back to the ranch house.

"I'd better come in and clean up the kitchen," Julie said as they started up the walk toward the house.

"You go on and get some sleep," Clay responded. "The kitchen can wait until tomorrow."

"But it's in such a terrible mess," Julie argued.

"It'll wait," Clay said, gently pushing her in the direction of their home. She reluctantly joined Terry for the short walk to their house.

"Thank you both for taking care of him," Clay called after them.

Terry turned to him with a weak smile. "He'll pull through. Jack Lomas is as tough as they come. He won't let this get him down."

"You bet he will. Before we know it, he'll be back here barking orders and making our lives miserable," Clay replied.

Terry and Julie both grinned. "Good night,

Clay. You go get some rest. We'll see you in the morning," Julie said.

As Clay wandered through the empty house, the feeling of loneliness was overwhelming. Everything reminded him of Jack. He walked into his own room and looked around, his eyes coming to rest on the pictures that had been mounted on the wall before Clay had come to live with Jack. He had added some of his own on the opposite wall, but the ones he looked at now were of Jack when he was younger. Some others showed Jack's late wife and his son. Clay knew the story behind his son's tragic death and how Jack had lost his will to live after his wife's passing a year later. All of these thoughts came to mind now as he stood looking at pieces from Jack's past. Without thinking, he walked out of his room and down the hall to Jack's room. When he pushed open the door, he half expected to see the old rancher sitting on the bed, but the emptiness of the room only added to his feeling of gloom. He backed out and pulled the door closed, then went back to the kitchen. He began clearing the dishes from the table and carrying them to the sink. An hour later the kitchen was clean and the dishes were washed, dried, and put away. Clay saw from the clock on the wall that it was after midnight, and finally he walked wearily to his room, undressed, and got into bed. He lay there staring into the darkness, trying to figure out what he was going to do, until finally he fell into an exhausted sleep. When Julie arrived the next morning he was still in bed. She smiled when she walked into the kitchen and saw it had been tidied up. She tapped lightly on Clay's door, and when she received no response, she opened the door slightly and looked in to see Clay sound asleep. Quietly closing the door, she went back to the kitchen to start breakfast.

Clay woke to the sound of pots and pans rattling. Looking at the clock, he saw it was almost nine o'clock. He slipped on his blue jeans and walked into the kitchen.

"Why didn't you wake me?" he asked as Julie gave him a bright smile.

"I figured you must be worn out after yesterday and having to stay at the hospital 'til late last night." She smiled again. "And cleaning up the kitchen after you got home."

"I couldn't sleep. I was just going to straighten it up a little and before I knew it, it was all cleaned up."

"Thank you just the same. I wasn't looking forward to facing the mess this morning."

"Where's Terry?" Clay asked.

"He's out feeding the stock in the trap. He'll be here in a little bit. Why don't you go take a shower and I'll get your breakfast ready."

Clay nodded and headed to the bathroom. By the time he'd finished showering, shaving, and brushing his teeth, Terry had come in from feeding the cattle and was eating his breakfast. Clay pulled out a chair and joined him at the table. "How many head are in the traps now?" he asked as Julie set a plate of scrambled eggs in front of him.

"We got eighty-four head in the lower trap and another sixty in the upper trap."

"How does the rest of the herd look?" Clay questioned.

"Dry," was Terry's single-word response. "Jack was trying to figure out which ones to ship to market first. He was tellin' me yesterday that we'll probably have to sell three hundred head to begin with."

Clay chewed his eggs in silence for a moment before responding. "How's the hay holding out?"

Terry swallowed a bite of biscuit and jelly. "We've got enough to last about three months, but hay's not the problem. It's the water. Right now we've lost four wells, and three more are about to go dry. There's hardly enough water now to take care of all the cattle. Without more water there's no way we can keep the number of cows we got."

Clay gave a weary sigh. He knew how much those cows meant to Jack. The old rancher had spent years building up the herd. Clay felt sure Jack's stroke had been brought on partly by the worry of having to sell part or all of them. Now Clay was faced with the same dilemma while Jack lay in the hospital, unable to make decisions.

After breakfast Terry and Clay talked about the work that needed to be done. "I'm going to the hospital to see Jack," Clay said, assuming a leadership role. "Why don't you haul your horse over to the north side and check on the cattle and windmills? If there's any that need to be brought in to the traps we'll get 'em in the morning. We'll meet back here for lunch. This afternoon I'll drive over and take a look at the windmills in the southeast pasture and check on as many of the cows as I can."

Terry nodded. "Make sure to call Julie if there's been a change in Jack's condition."

"You bet," Clay promised, remembering that they were as concerned about Jack as he was.

Chapter Seven

Clay arrived at the hospital shortly after ten o'clock. There was another nurse on duty at the nurses' station when he walked up and asked to see Jack.

"Are you a relative?" she asked in an unpleasant tone.

"No, ma'am," he said, being honest this time, "but I'm the closest thing he's got to a relative and Doctor Johnson told me I could see him."

"If you're not a relative, I can't let you see him."

Clay, frustrated and not in a mood to argue with her, answered in a low voice. "Doctor Johnson has already cleared me to see him. I saw him last night."

The nurse picked up a metal clipboard and thumbed through several pages before turning back to Clay. "There's no authorization on Mr. Lomas's chart for anyone to see him, other than the doctor."

Clay's patience was worn thin. His anger barely concealed, he spoke through clenched teeth. "If you'll call Doctor Johnson, I'm sure he'll tell you it's all right to let me see him."

Giving him a nasty look, the nurse snapped, "I don't have time to be calling doctors. If Doctor Johnson calls me and tells me it's okay to let you in, then and only then will I allow you to see Mr. Lomas."

Fighting the urge to reach across the counter and grab the woman by the throat, Clay held his breath and then asked, "Is there a pay phone I can use?"

"In the waiting room," she answered in a chilling voice, pointing to the double doors that Clay had gone through the night before.

Without another word Clay hurried through the doors. The pay phones were on the wall to the left as he entered, but there was no phone book to be found. He dialed information and got the doctor's phone number, then deposited a quarter and dialed the number. Dr. Johnson's receptionist, Karen, answered the phone. When Clay asked to speak with the doctor, he was told that he was with a patient and couldn't come to the phone at the moment.

Clay's voice rose in exasperation when he spoke. "Look, Karen, this is Clay Tory. I've been trying to get in to see Jack this morning, and this Nazi nurse stationed at the front desk won't let me see him. Now the only way I can get in is for Doctor Johnson to call her. I don't have the time or the patience to sit here and wait for the doctor to get through with his patient, so you go in and tell him to call this nurse now, before I do something we'll both regret!"

"I'm sorry, Clay. I'll have Doctor Johnson call immediately. And Clay, I'm sorry to hear about Mr. Lomas. I hope he gets better real soon."

Hearing the sincerity in her voice, Clay felt bad about his outburst. "Thanks, Karen. I appreciate your help," he said in a calmer tone. "Would you also ask Doctor Johnson to tell the nurse when he'll be coming in to see Jack?"

"He's scheduled to be there in an hour," Karen answered.

"Great! I'll be here waiting. Thanks for your help," he said sincerely.

Clay walked back through the double doors and took a seat across from the nurses' station. Looking across the counter at him, the difficult nurse asked in a none too friendly voice, "Can I help you?"

Clay shook his head. "You'll be helping me in just a moment."

The nurse gave him a scathing look and was about to say something when the phone on her desk rang. She picked up the receiver and listened for a moment, then said, "Yes, Doctor. I don't know why his name's not on the chart. Yes, sir. Right away." Hanging up the phone, she stood up. "If you'll follow me, Mr. Tory, I'll take you to see Mr. Lomas."

Clay followed her into the ICU ward, saying nothing as she held the door open to let him enter. When he walked to Jack's side, he was surprised to see him lying there with his eyes open.

"How you doin'?" Clay asked, expecting an answer, but Jack just stared up at him.

Clay took his friend's hand and sat down in

the chair next to his bed. Jack's eyes followed him as he moved, but other than that there was no response.

Clay talked to him about the rodeos he'd been to and the people he'd seen. Occasionally Jack would close his eyes and open them again as if responding to something Clay said.

Clay was still talking when Dr. Johnson entered the room. "How's our patient today?" he asked in a cheerful voice.

Clay didn't know how to answer. The doctor listened to Jack's heart with a stethoscope, then took his pulse, giving an occasional "uh-huh" and a thoughtful "hmmm." Finished with his physical examination, he took the clipboard from the foot of the bed and flipped through it before turning to Clay.

"He's suffered a stroke that has caused the right side of his body to be paralyzed. It also affected his speech, leaving him for the time being incapable of talking."

"Is it permanent?" Clay asked, looking down at Jack.

"I doubt it, but we won't know for some time. The MRI and CAT scans show some damage, but we don't know at this point how much. We'll move him into a private room this afternoon and schedule some more tests before we begin physical rehab."

Clay looked down at Jack and was shocked to see him staring back. "Does he understand what we're saying?"

"I'm sure he does, even though he can't respond."

Clay took Jack's hand in his. "Terry and I'll take care of things at the ranch. Don't you worry." As the doctor stepped out of the room, Clay leaned over and kissed the old rancher on the cheek. When he straightened up he looked into Jack's eyes and could have sworn he saw a gleam in them. Smiling, Clay promised to come back the next day. He caught up with Dr. Johnson in the hallway. "Who's the doctor in charge of Jack?" he asked.

"Doctor Miles will be in charge of his rehab. He's one of the best. Jack will be in good hands. Doctor Lansing is his neurologist — he's the man who will be overseeing everything, but since I'm Jack's physician, he'll consult with me on all of his diagnoses and recommendations."

Clay felt better knowing Dr. Johnson was in charge. He didn't know the other two doctors, but if Dr. Johnson trusted their abilities, then they must be all right. "Thanks for getting me in to see him. I'm sorry I had to call you away from your patient."

"No need to apologize," the doctor said. "I left orders last night to allow you in. Apparently someone dropped the ball and didn't put it on the chart. The nurse should have called me herself. I had a word with her when I came in. She won't be doing that again."

While Dr. Johnson stopped to talk to another doctor, Clay called the ranch to update Julie about Jack's condition.

Clay walked out with the doctor, leaving him in the parking lot after finding out what time he would be in to see Jack the next day. On the way back to the ranch, Clay was deep in thought about the things he needed to do in order to save Jack's spread, and, rounding a curve, he didn't see the tanker truck in the middle of the road in time. The narrow road allowed only enough room for two vehicles to pass, and the truck was halfway on Clay's side. Clay jerked the wheel hard to the right just in time, and the pickup flew into the bar ditch, tilting precariously to one side before coming safely to a stop. As the truck passed, Clay eased the pickup back onto the road, his heart beating rapidly. He had seen the painted sign on the truck's door — YUCCA TRUCKING; he would call the owner as soon as he got home. And boy would he give him a piece of his mind! By the time he got to the ranch his heart rate had slowed and he had calmed down some. He still intended to call the trucking company and complain about the driver, but it could wait until after he checked the pastures.

Julie was putting the finishing touches on lunch, so Clay changed into his work clothes and set the table. Terry came in while he was fixing his plate, and Clay told them everything the doctor had said. "He's going to be in the hospital for several weeks. Even after he comes home there's no tellin' how much he'll be able to do, so it's going to be up to us to keep things going."

He hesitated before continuing on. "I know Jack was talking about selling off the cattle, and we may have to do it, but I want to do everything possible to hold on to them."

Terry was quick to respond. "There's no way we can keep all the cattle unless we get an awful lot of rain in the next week or two. Even then it would be tough. The land's so dry I doubt there'd be enough runoff to put any water in the dirt tanks. And you know we're going to have to have several hard rains before the water table comes up enough to replenish the wells that have gone dry. Right now there's just not enough water to sustain all the cattle we have."

Clay held up his hands. "I know. I'm not saying we won't sell any of the cattle. I'm just saying I only want to sell them as a last resort. Jack's spent too many years building up this herd for us to sell them off without trying everything possible first."

Terry nodded, understanding Clay's desire. "I've racked my brain trying to think of some way to shift them around, but there's just no way the water we've got will hold all the cattle for more than two weeks at the most."

"I know," Clay agreed. "But we've just got to keep trying. We can't give up."

"I'd do a rain dance if I thought it would help," Julie said, "but I doubt it'd do any good."

Clay chuckled. "I'll beat on the tom-tom if you'll dance."

That afternoon Clay drove to the southeast pastures to check on the windmills. His spirits sagged as he looked at the small amount of water in the tanks and the trickling stream that barely flowed from the pipe. He knew it was just a matter of time before the water table dropped below the depth of the well, and without rain, there would be no more water. Checking on the condition of the cattle as he drove the pastures, he was pleased to see that they were still in good shape for the most part.

It was after dark when Clay arrived back at the ranch. Julie had his supper waiting for him, and he ate a quick meal before taking a shower and going to bed. Lying in the darkness, he searched for a way to solve the problem of watering the cattle. As his mind wandered, he remembered the truck that had run him off the road that morning, and it dawned on him that he hadn't called the trucking company to report the driver. Suddenly he sat upright in bed, excitement coursing through him. He literally jumped out of bed, hurried to the living room, and turned on the lamp by the phone. He thumbed quickly through the phone book until he found Yucca Trucking. Jotting down the phone number and address on a piece of paper, he turned off the light and went back to bed, a large smile on his face.

Clay was already out of bed and dressed the next morning when Julie walked into the kitchen. Sitting at the table, drinking coffee and reading the paper, he smiled at her startled expression.

"What's gotten into you?" she asked.

"Nothing," he replied innocently. "I've just got a lot to do today, and I wanted to get a head start."

"If Terry finds out you're getting up this early, it'll scare the daylights out of him." She smiled.

Clay gave her a questioning look. "Why's that?"

"Because he'll think you'll expect him to get up this early too."

Clay laughed. "Maybe I should call him and wake him up."

Julie giggled. "You'd give him a heart attack."

Clay ate a quick breakfast, then left, telling Julie he didn't know what time he'd be home. When she tried to question him about where he was going, he simply told her he had business in town.

It was just a little after seven when he drove into Roswell. Dr. Johnson had told him it would be around ten o'clock before he looked in on Jack, so Clay had three hours to do what he needed to. Looking at the address on the sheet of paper, he drove south of town and turned right on an oil-topped road. He spotted the company sign a short distance down the road and drove up to the building with an OFFICE sign hanging between two truck grilles cemented into the ground. There were two cars parked outside, and he could see lights on inside. He entered without knocking and instantly recognized the girl sitting behind the receptionist desk.

"Hey, Brenda. I didn't know you worked here."

"Hi, Clay," she responded with a smile. "Long time no see! How you been doing? I hear through the grapevine that you're doing pretty well on the rodeo circuit."

"I'm doing all right, I guess. How long you been working here?"

"About six months now."

"Is that so? How do you like it?"

"It's all right. I get hit on by the truck drivers all the time, but most of them are harmless. What brings you out this way?"

From where he stood he could see an office on his left. The door was slightly ajar, and a light was on inside. "I came to talk to the owner. Is he in?"

"You're in luck. Carl Grey is the owner, and for once he *is* in. I'll tell him you want to see him. Can I tell him the reason?"

"I want to talk to him about renting a truck," Clay said.

Brenda gave him a strange look, then walked into Mr. Grey's office. Clay could hear them talking in low voices, but he couldn't make out what they were saying. Brenda soon returned and held the door open for him. "He'll see you now," she said.

Clay entered the office, smiling his gratitude as he passed. Carl Grey was a tall heavy-built man in his mid- to late forties. Clay stepped forward, extending his hand to the man standing behind the desk. "Thank you for seeing me, Mr. Grey."

"Please call me Carl. What can I do for you, young man?" he asked, shaking Clay's hand and motioning him to a chair. When they were both seated, Clay jumped right in to his reason for being there.

"I'm here to see if you can help me out of a bad predicament. Do you know a rancher named Jack Lomas?"

Carl Grey's eyebrows arched in interest. "Yes, I know Jack Lomas. He owns a ranch northeast of town. Why do you ask?"

"Did you know he's in the hospital? He suffered a stroke last Sunday."

Carl Grey's eyes widened in surprise. "No, I didn't know. How's he doing?"

"Right now the doctors don't know the full extent of the damage. We're praying it's not too bad."

"What can I do to help?" Carl asked, sincere in his offer.

"The reason I came to see you is to get your help with a problem at the ranch. As you know, we've been in a drought since April, and we're running short on water. If we don't do something soon, we're going to have to sell at least part of Jack's herd and that's something I want to avoid if at all possible. Yesterday I was run off the road by one of your drivers —"

"Where did this happen?" Carl Grey asked in an angry voice, interrupting Clay.

Clay held up his hand. "It doesn't matter. Thanks to him, I came up with an idea that might possibly be the answer to our water shortage."

Carl gave him an inquisitive look and waited for him to continue.

"You haul water to several of the drilling rigs in the county, don't you?"

"Yes, and in the surrounding counties as well."

"Where does the water come from?" Clay asked.

"From wells that I drilled north of here," Carl replied.

"And how many gallons of water do your tankers haul?"

"They haul a hundred and thirty barrels. A barrel is forty-two gallons, which means they carry almost fifty-five hundred gallons. Why?"

"I was thinking that if I could hire one of your trucks and tank trailers, I could haul water to the cattle. If I could get two loads a day I think that would be enough to take care of them."

Carl Grey leaned back in his chair, thinking. Then he said, "What you're talking about could be quite expensive. As far as renting my transports, that is just not possible at this time. I've got more orders right now than I can fill, and I'm assuming you'd want to haul water to several different pastures." He paused while Clay nodded.

"I can't have a truck and driver tied up for that length of time. My trucks haul to a site, dump their load, and come back for another. My drivers are already putting in ten-hour days, six days a week."

Clay's face fell as he listened to Carl. It had seemed like a good idea, but now he was seeing his hopes spiral down the drain.

Carl saw the look of despair on Clay's face. "That doesn't mean your idea won't work. As a matter of fact, I think it has a lot of merit. Do you have enough capital to invest in a rig of your own?"

Clay looked startled. Buying his own truck hadn't occurred to him before now. "Yes, sir, I've got some money. How much would a rig cost me?"

Carl rubbed his chin as he thought. "I know a man that's got a couple of transports for sale. He was asking twelve thousand each for them, but I bet we could get them for less."

Clay was turning over the idea in his mind. "How much will the water cost me?"

Carl picked up the pen lying on his desk and scribbled some quick calculations on the pad in front of him. "I wouldn't make this deal with anyone else, and if you decide to do this, you have to promise me not to tell anyone else what you're paying."

"I promise," Clay answered quickly.

"I'll let you have the water for thirty cents a barrel."

Clay realized that even if he could buy the water at that price, his plan was still going to be expensive, but it would be cheaper than selling cattle for less than they were worth. "If I get the truck, I'll have to hire a driver. Do you know anyone looking for a job?"

"You'll have to hire a couple of drivers if you're going to haul every day. But I happen to know a couple of old hands that are looking for part-time work. This would be right up their alley."

Clay felt his spirits rise. "Where can I see these trucks that are for sale?"

Carl smiled at his eagerness. "Why don't you let me negotiate the price? I'll have my mechanics check them over for you to make sure they're reliable. You don't want to be spending all your time and money on repairs."

"Mr. Grey, I don't know how I can ever repay you. I'm really grateful for your help."

"I just hope this works. I'll call you when I have a price on the trucks. How soon do you want to start hauling water?"

Clay thought for a moment. "I'll have to figure out where I'm going to haul the water to. We'll have to move some of the cattle. I'm guessing it'll take me three or four days to have everything in place."

"I'll get on it today."

"Thanks again," Clay said. He gave Brenda a broad smile as he left, thanking her as well.

Chapter Eight

Clay whistled along with the radio as he drove back into town. His mind was working fast, making plans for moving the cattle to pastures where it would be easiest to haul the water. At first, he had planned to tell Jack about his project, but after considering it, he decided it would be better to wait until he knew it was going to work. It wouldn't be good to raise false hopes. By the time he got to the hospital, he had a good idea of which pastures to employ.

Jack had been moved to a private room, and Clay was pleased to see that most of the monitors and tubes had been removed. The old rancher was sleeping when Clay entered, but he awoke when he felt Clay take his hand. His eyes looked searchingly into Clay's, and he struggled to speak but couldn't form the words.

"It's all right, don't try to talk," Clay said, seeing the frustration in his eyes. He pulled up a chair, sat down by the bed, and held the old rancher's hand. Dr. Johnson soon arrived.

"Our patient is looking much better today without all those gadgets hooked up to him," the doctor said, smiling at both Clay and Jack. He once again took Jack's vital signs and listened to his heart before glancing at the chart. "We'll have the results of two of the tests this afternoon.

The other one won't be back until tomorrow morning."

"And what will the tests tell you?"

"The two we'll get back this afternoon will tell us how much damage there is to his motor skills. The last one will tell us how much nerve damage there is."

"If I come back tonight, can I find out the results?" Clay asked.

The doctor smiled at him, then pulled a prescription pad from the pocket of his smock and scribbled something on it. Tearing off the page, he handed it to Clay. "Call me before you leave the ranch and I'll meet you here to explain the results."

Clay glanced at the paper in his hand and saw that it was the doctor's home phone number. "Thanks, Doc. I'm going to stay with him for a little while."

The doctor nodded. "I'm sure he'll enjoy the company."

Clay stayed with Jack for another hour before the old rancher dozed off. Stopping in the waiting room, Clay called Julie to let her know he'd be home for lunch.

"Oh, I'm glad you called. I just tried your cell phone and was about to call the hospital."

"What's up?" he questioned, expecting bad news.

"Jim Collins called and wants you to come by his office as soon as possible." Jim Collins, Clay knew, was Jack's attorney.

"Did he say what he wanted?"

"No, only that he needed to see you as soon as possible."

Clay looked at his watch and saw that it was eleven o'clock. "I'll go by and see him now," he said. "I should still be home in time for lunch. If Terry comes in, tell him to wait for me. I've got something I want to talk to him about."

Clay left the hospital and drove downtown to Jim Collins's office. He had to wait fifteen minutes before the attorney was free to see him. He borrowed a pad from the receptionist and took advantage of the time to make a list of the things that needed to be done. He was still writing when Jim Collins emerged from his office. Collins was a thin, slightly balding man in his early fifties, who wore horn-rimmed glasses. Clay had met the man only once before, when Jack had brought some papers over to be looked over.

Collins handed a folder to his receptionist, then turned to Clay. "Come in, Clay," he said, holding open the office door. Clay tore off the sheet of paper he'd been writing on and handed the pad back to the receptionist.

Jim Collins shook hands with Clay and motioned him to a chair, then settled into his own high-backed chair. "I'm sure you're wondering why I asked you here. About a year ago Jack came to see me. He wanted to make sure the ranch would be taken care of in case anything happened to him."

Clay remained silent, wondering where this was going.

"He had me draw up the papers giving you power of attorney if anything did happen," Collins continued, opening a folder in front of him and pulling out several sheets that had been stapled together. He slid them across the desk and pointed to the top paragraph with his pen. "This document gives you full control of all Jack Lomas's assets."

Clay was dumbfounded as he tried to comprehend what Collins had told him. "I don't understand," he barely whispered.

"I'm sure this comes as a total surprise to you, but Jack wanted you to have full control in the event that he was somehow incapacitated. I might as well tell you," he paused, looking for the right words, "in the event of Jack's death, his will states that everything goes to you, with the exception of a small cash allotment that goes to Terry and Julie James and another amount that goes to the church."

Clay sat in stunned silence. He had never thought about life without Jack Lomas. He couldn't imagine what it would be like without him, and he didn't want to dwell on it now. "Mr. Collins, right now I don't care if Jack left everything to me. All I want is for him to get well. As far as I'm concerned, his will is just a piece of paper that doesn't mean anything at this point."

Jim Collins's face turned red. "I'm sorry. I just thought you needed to know. I'm sure Jack is going to recover in due time, but in the meantime you still have to run the ranch, and thanks to Jack's foresight, you have the means to do that until he's well enough to do it himself."

Clay realized that the lawyer was just looking out for Jack's interests. "I'm sorry," he responded. "It's just that Jack's stroke has really been hard on me. He's been more of a father to me than my own father was."

Collins nodded. He had known Clay's father and the kind of man he was. "I know how you feel, and I know Jack feels the same about you. He's very proud of you."

Clay smiled and tried to swallow the lump in his throat, embarrassed by the attorney's praise. "Thank you. What exactly does this power of attorney mean?"

Collins went on to explain that Clay now had access to Jack's checking accounts, savings accounts, and all other assets. "As soon as you sign these papers, I'll send a copy to the bank. You can stop by there anytime after today and they'll help you with all of Jack's accounts."

Clay nodded. "Anything else?"

"I'm sure Jack's got bills to pay. You might want to go through his mail and make sure you have all of them. If you have a question about anything you find, bring it to me. I'll make sure they're all legitimate."

"Where do I sign?"

Collins showed him where to put his signature, then put the papers back in the folder. "I'll mail a copy of these to you. If you need help with anything don't hesitate to call me. And Clay — I hope Jack has a real quick recovery."

"Thanks," Clay responded.

When Clay got back to the ranch, Terry was seated at the kitchen table drinking a glass of iced tea, his face sweat-streaked from hauling hay to the cows. Clay filled both of them in on Jack's condition and what the doctor had said about the tests. "I'm going back to the hospital this evening to see how everything came out." He didn't tell them about his meeting with the lawyer. That news could wait. "I think I may have found a solution to our water problem," he said softly, not surprised by the doubtful looks on their faces.

Terry took a long sip of his iced tea before asking, "And what would that solution be?"

"Tanker trucks!" Clay exclaimed.

"Tanker trucks?" Terry asked in a questioning tone. "Whose tanker trucks are you going to use?"

"I'm buying my own. At first I thought I would need two of them, but after thinking about it, I realized I could buy one tractor and two trailers. We can rig the stock tanks with automatic waterers, and while one tanker is emptying the other can be pulled back to town and filled. Two loads a day ought to be enough, but if it takes more we'll be able to handle it."

"And just who's going to be doing the driving?" Julie asked. "You and Terry don't know anything about driving those rigs!"

Clay laughed. "You're absolutely right, and I don't have any intention of learning. I thought you could do it, Julie."

Wide-eyed, she turned from her cooking to stare at him as if he'd lost his mind.

Laughing at the look on her face, Clay said, "Carl Grey, the owner of Yucca Trucking, knows a couple of drivers that might be interested in the job."

"Sounds like this is going to cost a bundle," Terry said.

"Not as much as selling the cattle at a loss in this depressed market. And when the drought is over I can sell the truck and trailers."

"Sounds like you might have found the answer," Terry amended enthusiastically.

"I hope so," Clay answered. "It's going to depend on how much the tractor-trailers cost. If we can afford them, we have a lot of work to do. We'll have to move the cattle into two of the larger pastures. But first we have to move some of the larger water tanks in." He went on to tell them all of the plans he'd made. Terry and Julie agreed with each step and offered helpful suggestions.

Clay and Terry saddled up their horses after lunch and rode to the southernmost pasture. Terry had found four head of weak cattle that needed to be moved to one of the traps. By the time they had them roped and inside the trailer, it was late afternoon. When they finally got the cattle unloaded in the trap and the horses unsaddled, it was almost dark. Clay left Terry to finish the chores while he went into the house to take a shower and change clothes. Later, after eating a quick supper, he called the number Dr. Johnson had given him and told the doctor he was leaving for the hospital. He arrived a little after nine o'clock. The same nurse that had been on duty the night of Jack's stroke was sitting behind the desk when Clay walked in. Giving him a bright smile, she asked, "How's he doing?"

"He's better," Clay answered.

Jack was asleep when he entered the room. Clay read the ranching magazine he had brought to Jack for fifteen minutes before Dr. Johnson showed.

"Sorry I'm late," he exclaimed, hurrying into the room. "I had to look at one of my patients in the emergency room."

Jack woke at the sound of the doctor's voice and looked at Clay, a spark of recognition shining in his eyes.

The doctor motioned for Clay to follow him out into the hallway. Once the door closed behind them, he turned to Clay and said, "I talked to Doctor Lansing earlier this evening. His prognosis after reviewing the test results is very optimistic. He feels certain that, with the proper rehab, Jack should fully recover. How long that takes depends on how fast Jack regains his strength. A stroke like this weakens the patient. It's usually a slow recovery."

Clay gave the doctor a questioning look. "What do you mean by a slow recovery?"

Shrugging his shoulders, the doctor answered, "It could be six months to a year before he's fully recovered. But we also have to guard against its happening again."

"What do you mean?"

"Jack's stroke was brought on by an ischemia, which is a narrowing or blockage in the arteries. It's common in older people with a high cholesterol intake. We'll use drugs to help open the arteries, but reducing the stress in his life will be just as important. I know this drought is causing problems for the ranchers, and if I were to wager a guess, I'd say it's been causing Jack a good bit of worry."

"That's an understatement," Clay said. "He's worked for years to build up the herd and for a while it looked like he might have to sell almost half of it. But I've got a plan that may save it. I don't want to tell him about it until I know for sure it will work, though."

"That may be a good idea," the doctor said. "I want you to meet all the people that will be taking care of Jack. You'll have to schedule time to come in."

"How many will there be?"

"Let's see . . . there'll be an internist, Doctor Taylor; then there's the physical therapist and the speech therapist — I don't know who they'll be as yet. And there's usually a head nurse that specializes in stroke victims — that will probably be Gail Roberts, she's one of the best. And of course you've met Doctor Lansing, the neurologist."

"Thanks for all your help, Doc. I appreciate you coming up here tonight."

"Jack and I've been friends for a long time. I'm glad he's got you to worry about him. I've done it long enough."

Clay laughed as the doctor turned and walked back down the hall. When Clay reentered Jack's room, he thought Jack had fallen asleep, but as he walked across the room, Jack's eyes fluttered open and followed Clay all the way to the chair. Clay took his hand once again and began telling him about the ranch, and what he and Terry had done that day. He stayed for another two hours, talking and reading articles from the magazine he'd brought. As he finished an article on a new feed supplement, Clay looked over and saw that Jack was asleep. He tucked the covers up under Jack's chin and felt tears well up in his eyes. Fighting to control his emotions, Clay hurried out of the room.

Chapter Nine

Clay was up at five-thirty the next morning despite getting home at a late hour. He was sitting at the kitchen table drinking coffee and reviewing his list of things that needed to be done when Julie came in. She walked around behind him and held her hand to his forehead.

"What are you doing?" he asked, turning in his chair to look at her.

"I was checking to see if you had a temperature," she responded with a mischievous grin. "This is the second morning in a row that you've gotten up before me. Normally, we have to drag you out of bed."

He chuckled. "I just have a lot of things to get done and I can't afford to lie in bed. When Jack gets home and starts running things again, I'll go back to sleeping late."

Julie snickered as she put on her apron. "Oh, I almost forgot to tell you," she exclaimed in an excited voice. "Tamara called last night. She was real upset because you hadn't called her. I told her about Jack and she understood, but she wants you to call her as soon as you can. Are you entering the rodeo this weekend?"

Clay gave her a blank look. He had been so preoccupied with Jack and the ranch that he'd forgotten all about Tamara and the rodeos. He'd already missed the call-in dates to enter. But there was no way he could leave the ranch at a time like this.

"I won't be going to rodeos while things are this bad at the ranch," he answered.

Julie didn't say anything. She merely set a frying pan on the stove and opened the refrigerator door. Clay noticed her lack of response, but didn't realize how disappointed she was in his answer.

After Clay and Terry had finished breakfast and were about to head to the barn to saddle their horses, the phone rang. It was Carl Grey.

"I can get you both rigs for nine thousand each," he told Clay.

"I've been meaning to call you," Clay said. "I've decided I only need one truck. What would it cost for one truck and two trailers?"

After a moment's hesitation, Carl said, "I could probably get them for twelve thousand."

"If you can arrange it, I'll hire both of the drivers you mentioned. They can alternate days."

"Sounds like a good plan. I'll make a call this morning. If I can get them, I'll have them delivered tomorrow. When do you want the drivers to start?"

"I'll try to have everything in place in two days. I'd like to have them start then — that would make it Friday morning. I'm going to have a bunch of thirsty cattle in pastures with no water. Tell them the first few days will probably be real hectic, 'til we get things organized."

"I'll take care of it and call you tomorrow morning."

Clay smiled to himself, then spoke. "Carl, I can't thank you enough for all you've done."

"No need to," Carl replied. "I'm glad to be able to help. Tell Jack I said hello."

"I will," Clay said. Hanging up the phone, he let out a whoop that brought Julie running from the kitchen. As she came through the door with a look of alarm on her face, Clay grabbed her, lifted her feet off the floor, and twirled her around twice before setting her back down.

"We're going to save Jack's cattle!" he shouted with glee.

Still shaken, Julie brushed her hair back in place and stared at him with astonishment. "I gather you got the truck."

"Sure did," he said, excitement gleaming in his eyes.

Terry walked through the door as Clay made his announcement. "Sure did what?" he asked.

"The truck!" Clay yelled. "I got the truck and some tanker trailers! We can start hauling water to the cattle as soon as we get the water tanks in place. We'll fill them first, then move the cattle."

"That's quite a task," Terry remarked.

"But one that we can handle. I want to start moving tanks today. We can use the tractor and flatbed trailer to move them. I've already figured out which ones to move. We'll move half the cattle to the north pasture — it's right off the county road. If we put the water tanks close to the gate, we'll have easy access to them. We'll move the other half of the cattle to the west pasture. We'll have to haul a little further off the main road, but it'll still be closer to town, making it a shorter run overall. Both of those pastures are big enough to hold all the cattle."

Terry nodded, considering what Clay had said, then added, "There's only one problem with your plan."

"What's that?" Clay asked.

"Feeding that many cattle in one location is going to be hard to do. There's no way we can haul enough hay to feed all of them at one time. We'll have to make at least three trips, and by the time we feed one load and get back with another, they'll have finished the first load. Some of the cows will get fed two or three times while others won't get any."

Clay pondered the situation. "You're right, that does pose a problem. We'll have to figure out either how to haul all the hay at one time or how to separate the cattle while we feed. I think we can work that out. Right now we have to start moving tanks."

Terry grinned at Clay. "I'm with you. Two days ago I was ready to sell the entire herd, so who am I to doubt?"

Clay slapped him on the back. "That's the spirit! Let's get to work."

They worked until after dark moving two of the water tanks to the north pasture. Julie had their supper warmed when they came in. Clay ate quickly, then showered and drove to the hospital. He spent two hours with Jack, reading to him from the local newspaper. Jack was sleeping soundly when he left.

Up early the next day, Clay and Terry got the other water tank moved to the north pasture, then moved two more to the east pasture. While Clay and Terry were moving water tanks, Julie went to visit Jack and pick up a few groceries.

Once again, it was well after dark when they got back to the house. Clay ate while listening to Julie tell him about the physical therapy program Jack would be following. Then he washed off the dust and rushed to the hospital once again.

When he arrived, he saw that Jack's bed had been raised to a sitting position, and he was propped up on his right side with pillows supporting his back. He held a soft drink in his left hand and was attempting to sip it through a straw. Clay could have sworn he almost saw the old rancher smile as he entered the room.

"How ya doin'?" Clay asked cheerfully, pulling the chair up to the bed.

Jack's eyes followed his every move with an almost pleading look that didn't go unnoticed.

Clay spent the better part of two hours telling Jack about the ranch, the cattle, Terry, and Julie. He refrained from telling him about the truck and trailers, not wanting to say anything until he had everything in place and was sure it was going to work. He then read the newspaper to him until the nurse came in and lowered the bed.

"I guess I'd better be getting back to the ranch," he said, straightening the covers. He was about to turn away when he noticed a slight nod of Jack's head. At first he thought he'd imagined it, but stepping back to the bed, he was sure that Jack's eyes followed him. Clay asked, "Did you just nod at me?"

This time he knew he wasn't imagining it — Jack's head moved slowly up and down. He smiled and squeezed the old man's hand. "I'll see you tomorrow. You keep getting better. We miss you at the ranch."

Carl Grey called the next morning to tell Clay he had bought the truck and trailers and would have them and the drivers ready to go by Friday morning.

Clay and Terry finished moving the water tanks that morning and fed hay to the cattle in the afternoon. That evening Clay, Terry, and Julie all went to visit Jack. The visit seemed to lift Jack's spirits. Clay noticed he even attempted a lopsided grin, which made him look more like he had a bad case of indigestion.

It was late when they got back to the ranch that night, but Clay was up before sunrise the next day, as usual these days. He had to be at Carl Grey's early to meet the drivers and give them directions to the pastures where the tanks were located. After breakfast, he told Terry which pastures were to lose a significant number of cattle. They would leave a few head in each of these pastures and move some of the weak ones in with them. There would be enough water for twenty-five to thirty head to stay in each of the pastures, but the main herd would be moved to the two large pastures that could be reached by the water trucks. Clay figured it would take at least a week to move all the cattle, maybe longer. It would be an arduous task for the three of them to accomplish, but he knew they could do it.

Carl Grey took Clay out to his lot to look at the truck and tankers he'd purchased for him. "They're in pretty good shape. The rig's had an engine overhaul and has been driven about thirty thousand miles since. The tankers have good brakes and don't show any signs of rust."

Clay realized how little he himself knew about trucks and trailers, and he was thankful once again for Carl's help. As they were walking back to the office, a pickup arrived and two men stepped out.

"There's your drivers now!" Carl said, motioning to the two. "Come on, I'll introduce you and you can get started."

Larry Colmbs was tall and skinny, with a thick handlebar mustache. He wore an old straw hat that looked as if it had seen better days, and he spoke with a slow Southern drawl and moved almost as slow. Jerry Paris was several inches shorter than Larry and almost as broad as he was tall. He wore a baseball cap with the brim bent down on each side. His voice boomed when he talked, and when he shook

Clay's hand, his grip was like a vise.

Clay had drawn a map to the two locations to which they would be hauling the water. Both men would make the trip today to learn the route, then they would alternate days. "I want to go ahead and fill all the water tanks before the cattle get moved in," Clay said. "You'll probably have to make two or three trips today. Is that all right with you?"

Both Larry and Jerry nodded. "Sure, no problem," Larry said.

Since both men had driven for Carl, they knew where his wells were located. Clay watched as the transport pulled out of the yard with Larry at the wheel and Jerry riding shotgun. Returning to the office, Clay wrote a check to reimburse Carl for the purchase of the truck and trailers and thanked him once again for all his help.

After Carl left, Clay stopped by the feed store to put in an order before driving back to the ranch. He arrived at the north pasture half an hour before the truck showed up. He watched as Larry expertly backed the big rig next to the water tanks. As Larry and Jerry unhooked the trailer, Clay looked at the long, three-inch-diameter hose and valve that released the water from the tank. It was going to take some pipe and fittings and a bit of work to set up all the water tanks with automatic float valves, but it could be done. With the tanks on automatic, the crew wouldn't have to drive over several times a day to fill them.

Larry and Jerry were on their way to retrieve the other trailer, and Clay was still making sketches of piping configurations when he heard the bawling cattle being driven into the pasture. He could see dust roiling in the distance and knew it was Terry bringing in part of the cattle, so he began filling one of the tanks from the hose. The sound of the water running into the metal container was music to his ears.

After the second trailer was delivered, Clay went to the hardware store to buy the plumbing fixtures he would need. It took him the rest of the afternoon to attach the pipe and automatic floats, and it was after nine by the time he got to the hospital to visit Jack. After two hours of reading and talking to him, then driving back home, it was after midnight by the time Clay got to bed. Nevertheless, he was up before daylight the next day. He and Terry moved more cattle into the north pasture in the morning, then fed them hay in the afternoon. Exhausted, Clay drove back to the hospital that evening to visit Jack but spent less time than he had intended to because when he tried to read to Jack, he himself kept nodding off. He could tell Jack was improving, though. He had been to physical therapy that day, and the nurse bragged on his progress, saying that he could now move his head from side to side. Clay could hardly keep his eyes open as he drove home that evening. He fell into bed so exhausted that he didn't even bother to take off his clothes.

Julie arrived at her usual time the next morning, expecting to see Clay seated at the kitchen table. When she walked into the kitchen, the light was on and the coffee was made, but Clay wasn't there. Listening down the hallway, she could hear the sound of the shower running. She prepared breakfast and put it on the table before Clay made his appearance. His steps were slow, and his face wore a haggard look.

"Why don't you take a little time off and get some rest?" Julie asked, concerned about him.

"I can't," Clay answered. "Not until we have all the cattle moved."

"Well, at least let me go visit Jack today so you can go to bed early tonight."

"I wouldn't feel right, not going to see him."

"I'll explain it to him. I'm sure he'll understand."

Clay thought for a moment. It sure would be nice to get a good night's sleep, but he felt guilty at the thought. "No, I better go see him."

Julie decided to change tactics. "No, you're not! You're going to get to bed early tonight and get some sleep. You're so tired now that it's a wonder you haven't wrecked the truck on the way home. If you don't take care of yourself, pretty soon you won't be any good to anybody, especially Jack."

Surprised by the authoritative tone in her voice, he could only stare at her, dumbfounded. Several objections ran through his mind, but each time he thought about voicing them, he considered what her response would be and chickened out. Finally he nodded his head slowly in assent. "I guess you're right. I'll help Terry move the cattle from the two south pastures this morning and while he's putting out hay this afternoon, I'll move the stronger cattle out of the traps. There's about eighty head that have regained their strength and are ready to be put back with the others. The water in the traps is starting to run low. We can't afford to hold any more than necessary."

Julie started to remark about the amount of work he had planned, but decided she'd gotten enough with his commitment to turn in early. "I'll fix y'all some lunch and leave it on the stove. You can warm it up when you get in. I'll tell Jack you're moving cattle and won't be in to see him. That's a partial truth, anyway."

Clay gave her a weak smile, still harboring feelings of guilt. He had finished his breakfast by the time Terry came in, but he sat and drank two more cups of coffee while Terry ate. After that, he felt almost revived and ready for the day's work.

It took close to an hour of riding to reach the southernmost part of the pasture and another two hours to get the cattle rounded up and moving. They were pushing almost two hundred head of cattle through three pastures, and it was all the two of them could do to keep them bunched and moving. Looking at the windmills as they passed, it was evident that the water stored in most of them would be gone in a few days. Driving the cattle was hot, dusty work, made harder by the parched prairie. Dust coated both men and horses. Their sweat ran off them in muddy drops.

As noon approached and the sun grew hotter, the cattle became harder to drive, constantly trying to turn back to the last water source they'd known. Clay and Terry pushed their already weary horses to the limit, trying to keep the cattle headed in the right direction. As they passed through the last barbed wire gate, the cattle picked up the scent of the water tanks and headed directly for them.

Dead-tired and covered from head to toe with dust, Clay couldn't help but smile as he watched the thirsty animals surround the tanks and drink their fill. He and Terry waited until the cows had finished drinking before moving up to the tanker. Unhooking the hose from the pipe feeding the four water tanks, Clay opened the valve and let the three-inch stream of water pour over his head, then turned it on Terry and washed him down. After cooling themselves off, they used the hose to wash the dust off their horses.

"How much water is left in that tank?" Terry asked. Only one watering tank was below a quarter full.

Looking at the sight glass on the side of the big tanker trailer, Clay saw it was still three-quarters full. "There's still quite a bit, but we haven't moved all the cattle in yet. By my estimate, it'll take a load every other day to hold them."

"All we got to do is figure out a way to feed all of them," Terry interjected.

"I may have a solution to that as well," Clay added.

"Oh?" Terry questioned, cocking his eyebrow. "I can't wait. Are you going to use helicopters or something?"

"Who told?" Clay asked, with a sly grin. "No, I'm not using helicopters. I'll let you know when I've got all the details worked out."

The lunch Julie had prepared for them was devoured quickly when they got back to the house. Both really wanted a short nap, but they headed to the barn instead. Clay helped Terry load the flatbed trailer with hay before saddling another horse and riding out to the traps. Each trap consisted of about thirty acres, and they were connected together on the east side by a barbed wire gate. The trap farthest from the house bordered the county road that led to town, and the pasture where the cattle were being moved was on this same road. Clay planned to drive the cattle straight down the road. The fences on either side provided a natural lane that would keep them from straying, so all he had to do was stay behind the herd and keep it moving. Cutting the healthy cattle out proved to be easier than he had anticipated, and he soon had them on the road.

Later, Clay would swear he hadn't been dozing in the saddle. The cattle were moving along nicely, with little prodding, and the cow horse he rode had enough savvy to herd them without guidance. The lack of sleep, the hard day's work he'd already done, the hot sun draining his strength, and the gentle motion of the horse beneath him all played a part in the accident. Had he been alert, he would have seen the dust raised by the fast-moving vehicle long before it reached him. But he wasn't alert. As fate would have it, the herd had come to a large washout caused by the runoff from rain. The washout was too deep for the cattle to cross, so all but a few had moved to the middle of the road when the Ford Mustang topped the rise only yards away, traveling at a speed that would have made a professional race car driver nervous.

Clay was jerked back to reality by the blare of the car's horn, followed by the sound of metal scraping metal as the Mustang left the road and careened sideways through the five-strand barbed wire fence, coming to a stop in a cloud of dust. The cows, frightened by the commotion, turned as one and ran in the opposite direction, thundering past Clay before he could react. His horse, unnerved by the stampeding cattle as well as the wreck, danced frantically sideways, trying to turn in the direction of the fleeing cattle. It took Clay several seconds to bring him under control and take stock of the matter. Then he urged the big gelding onto the road, around the washout, and through the mangled fence.

The car's engine was still running, and he

could hear the radio blaring out rock music. Coaxing his horse around to the driver's side of the car, he peered down, trying to see through the tinted window. He could make out long, dark hair pressed against the window from the inside, but there was no movement. Stepping down from the saddle, he held tightly to the reins of his nervous horse and tapped gently on the glass. He was relieved to see a dazed face turn toward him, and he opened the door slowly. Sitting behind the steering wheel was a female, sobbing hysterically, her hands held to her face.

"Are you hurt?" Clay asked gently.

She gave a slight shake of her head, but the sobbing continued.

Clay chewed on his lower lip, not knowing what to do next. He stood there, holding the door open and feeling like an intruder, as the woman wept, her shoulders shaking. After what seemed an eternity, her crying subsided except for an occasional shuddering sob, and she slowly turned to face him.

In spite of her tearstained face and disheveled look, Clay was struck by her beauty. Underneath the long black hair were the largest brown eyes Clay had ever seen. She had fine features and high cheekbones that hinted at Indian heritage. She wore makeup, but only enough to accentuate her eyes and full lips.

"Are you all right, ma'am?" Clay asked.

"I . . . I . . . I think so," she stammered.

"Do you want to get out?"

She looked first at him, then at his horse, and nodded.

He took her arm gently by the elbow and waited for her to swing her legs out. Allowing him to assist her, she attempted to stand. She was nearly to her feet when her knees gave way and she fell against Clay, who let go of the reins he was holding and wrapped his arms around her for support.

"Are you sure you're not hurt?" he questioned again.

"I can't make my legs quit shaking," she responded with a weak smile.

Still supporting her, Clay led her to the back of the car and helped her lean against the trunk. When he had made sure she wasn't going to fall, he walked around the wreck to survey the damage. The left front tire had been flattened and was sitting at an odd angle. Dropping to his hands and knees for a better look, he could see many broken parts on the car's undercarriage. He didn't know what they were called, being unfamiliar with front-wheel-drive cars, but he knew it couldn't be driven, and that created a dilemma. Down the road he could see a few of the cows grazing on the dry roadside grass, but the rest weren't in sight. He knew if he didn't get them rounded up soon, he'd have a devil of a time catching up to them. The woman was still leaning against the trunk of the car, apparently in shock. How was he going to get her out of here and get the cattle rounded up at the same time?

The only way out was on his horse — but he wasn't sure if she could ride or if she was up to it. And if he did get her on the horse, the closest place to take her was back to the ranch. If he took the time to do that, though, the cows would be scattered from here to Roswell when he got back.

The driver pushed herself upright, wobbling slightly as she did so, and surveyed the damage. "Oh, my God!" she groaned, when she saw the long scratches running the length of the car where the barbed wire had sliced through the paint. Clay grimaced as she continued to walk around the car. He had seen the large gash where the fence post had struck the right front fender, but she hadn't seen it yet. Her mouth opened wide in dismay as she found more and more damage. When she came to the ripped fender, her hand flew to her mouth. "I can't believe this! This is a brand-new car. I just got it three weeks ago. Do you have any idea how long I've waited and saved to own this car?"

Clay didn't respond, feeling it was better to remain silent.

She gave a hysterical laugh, and Clay took a step away from her, not sure what her next move might be. "I saved for two years to get enough money for a down payment. I have dreamed of owning this car for years, and now it's wrecked! Just like that, it's ripped to shreds!"

"It can be repaired," Clay said tentatively.

"Ha!" she spat. "It'll never be the same." She

looked at the flat tire and spoke in a calm voice that scared Clay more than her hysterics did. "I've got a spare in the trunk — if it didn't get flattened as well."

Taking off his hat and wiping the sweat from his brow with his shirtsleeve, Clay shook his head and said, "I'm afraid it's going to take more than a spare tire. Something's broken underneath. See the way the tire leans away from the car?"

Bending over to inspect the damage more closely, she staggered and almost fell. Clay rushed forward to catch her, holding her close until she regained her balance.

"How am I going to get back to town?" she whimpered.

"Well, ma'am," Clay said, "we got a bit of a problem. The only way out of here is on that horse over there."

She cast a hesitant look at Clay's horse, which was ground-hitched a few yards away. "You mean we have to ride him?" she asked in a weak voice.

"I'm afraid that's the only option we got, unless someone comes along and gives you a lift. Do you know how to ride?"

"I've ridden a few times at the stables back home, but only in the ring."

"Well, ma'am, if you want to leave here, we're both going to have to ride my horse. But before I can take you to a phone, I've got to get these cattle moved to pasture."

"Cows?" she exclaimed, suddenly remembering why she had swerved off the road. "Those cows are the reason my car is wrecked! I could have been killed, and now you're telling me I have to go with you on that horse to take them to some pasture instead of finding some place where I can call a tow truck?"

Clay grimaced. "Yes, ma'am. I'm afraid that's exactly what I'm telling you. I can't let those animals roam up and down the road while I take you to a phone. I'd never be able to get them all rounded up again. Besides that, if they're left out on the road, they might cause someone else to have an accident."

Straightening to her full height of five feet three inches, she looked Clay in the eye. "Well, cowboy, I'm not too keen on the idea, but if that's the only alternative I have, then let's get to it. I have to meet someone in town this evening and I don't want to be late. And quit calling me ma'am. My name is Ginger — Ginger Loring."

Clay had been expecting her to throw a fit. He had even been prepared to ride off and leave her if she had demanded to be taken to a phone, but her sudden acceptance caught him totally off guard. "Yes, ma— I mean Ginger. Uh, my name is Clay Tory."

"Well, Clay Tory, let's go!"

Chapter Ten

It took Clay the better part of an hour to get all the cows rounded up. Normally it would have taken only a fraction of that time, but he ended up riding behind the saddle, with Ginger in front, holding on to the saddle horn with both hands. Clay's gelding, being a cow horse, fought the bit in an attempt to turn the cattle with his normal cutting skills, but Clay held him in check, since a quick turn or fast stop would likely topple the both of them off his back, and Clay certainly wasn't eager to experience that. He had first tried letting her ride behind him, with her arms wrapped around his waist, but after a bloodcurdling scream that almost pierced his eardrum when the gelding had jumped the small ditch beside the road, he realized that neither Ginger nor his ears would survive this ordeal. Changing places would slow things down considerably, but it was the only alternative he had.

When the cattle were finally headed in the right direction and moving along with little prodding, Clay and Ginger had an opportunity to get acquainted. Ginger told him she had moved to Roswell from Virginia just two weeks earlier, to take a job with an investment company, and today she had decided to take a drive in the country.

"It turned out to be some kind of drive, didn't it?" she remarked dryly. "So what's your story, cowboy?"

Clay told her about the ranch and living with Jack. She seemed sympathetic when she heard about Jack's stroke. He explained about the drought and what it meant to the ranchers and the community, but when he told her about traveling the rodeo circuit and the events he worked, her eyes widened in surprise.

"Isn't that dangerous?" she asked, turning in the saddle to look at him.

With a chuckle, he shrugged. "I guess it is, but I don't think about it. I just love riding broncs and bulls."

"I think you're crazy," she stated emphatically.

Clay smiled and was about to reply when he realized that they were almost to the gate that led into the pasture. He turned the horse to circle around the cattle. Kicking him into a trot, Clay had to fight back a smile as Ginger bounced in the saddle in front of him.

"What are you doing?" she asked angrily.

"I've got to get around these cows and open that gate up there. This is the pasture they belong in."

"If you'll let me off, I'll run around and open the gate," she offered.

Clay pulled the horse to a stop. "All right. That gate's a little hard to open, though. You have to wrap your arm around it and push with your shoulder to get the latch off. After you open the gate, stand in the road and turn 'em."

Throwing her leg over the horse's neck, she slid to the ground and would have landed hard had Clay not caught her arm and eased her down. She looked up at him and asked, "What if they don't want to turn?"

Clay chuckled. "Just wave your arms and shout. They'll go in."

Though she looked doubtful, she began to walk around the cows, keeping a wary eye on them as she passed.

With a fair amount of groaning and swearing, and with Clay yelling encouragement, she finally managed to open the gate. The cows, used to being herded, barely glanced her way as they passed through the gate and into the pasture.

"I've got to push them on to the water tanks," Clay said, riding through the gate.

Ginger groaned. "I thought we were done. You said you had to get them into the pasture. They're in."

"I know," Clay replied, "but I've got to show them where the water is. It's just a little ways over that rise."

"You mean these cows are so stupid they can't find water?"

"That pretty well sums it up."

"Well, you go on and show your stupid cows where the water is. I'm going to wait right here."

Clay nodded and touched the gelding with his spurs. "I'll be back before you can say scat."

Clay pushed the cattle to water in short order, then trotted back to the gate. Ginger sat there with her arms propped up on her knees, her head resting on her arms. Clay felt sorry for her, knowing how exhausting this whole ordeal must be for her. He called out to her as he rode up, "Ginger, I'm back."

She looked at him through tired eyes and struggled to a standing position. "I'm already sore. I know that tomorrow I won't be able to get out of bed!"

Clay grinned sheepishly. "A long soak in a tub of hot water will take care of a lot of it, and I've got some horse liniment that'll take care of the rest."

She gave him a scathing look as he dismounted to close the gate. "I'll take the long hot bath, but you can keep the liniment for your horse."

Once the gate was closed, he helped Ginger into the saddle. She groaned as she lifted her foot to the stirrup, and she didn't object when Clay held her waist as she mounted. Seated behind her, he headed home. Normally he would have put the horse in a ground-covering trot, but now he held him to a slow walk for Ginger's sake.

Ginger's head was nodding by the time they reached the drive that led to the house. Clay knew the trauma of the wreck, not to mention the ordeal of having to ride double for the last three hours, had sapped her strength. He kept one arm around her waist to prevent her falling, and her back was pressed close against his chest.

Feelings of excitement coursed through him, but he fought against them. He couldn't explain why this woman triggered such feelings in him. Only Tamara had ever made him feel this way. At the thought of Tamara, he was reminded that he hadn't called her since Jack's stroke. How could he have forgotten such a thing? Other than Jack and the ranch, Tamara meant more to him than anything in the world. By now she was in San Antonio, but he promised himself he would keep calling her on her cell phone tonight until he reached her.

Clay had to shake Ginger gently to awaken her. She climbed groggily off the horse's back, then leaned against Clay's leg for a moment before she could will her legs to carry her.

"You go on up to the house and rest. Julie's home, so she can get you something to eat if you're hungry."

Ginger nodded and walked unsteadily toward the house. Clay smiled as he watched. Terry walked into the barn while he was feeding his horse and rubbing him down.

"Where'd you pick up the hitchhiker?" he asked with a smirk.

Clay gave him the abridged version of what had happened. "She's a real spitfire," he said.

"She could be trouble if she decides to sue."

Clay mulled that over. It had never occurred to him. "It was as much her fault as it was mine!" he said.

"Uh-huh, but it's your word against hers."

"What do you think I should do?"

Terry thought for a moment, then replied, "I think you ought to call Ben Aguilar and have him come out and take a look at the accident site before the tow truck hauls her car away."

"You're right. I hate to drag Ben all the way out here, but it's probably best for both of us if he makes a report."

Ginger was drinking iced tea at the kitchen table when Terry and Clay came in. Her color seemed to have improved — or maybe she had just washed the dust off. Either way, Clay thought she was very attractive.

"Julie called a towing company for me. They said they would be here in an hour or so," Ginger said.

"Will that give you enough time to get to town for your meeting?" Clay asked.

"I called and postponed it until tomorrow. I don't think I could handle a business meeting to-night."

"Probably a good idea. The offer for the horse liniment still stands. Tomorrow you'll be wishing you'd accepted," Clay claimed, grin-ning at her.

"Thanks just the same, but I think I'll pass," she responded, as if the thought were absolutely distasteful.

Clay excused himself to wash up, but instead he passed the bathroom and went into Jack's bedroom to use the extension phone. He felt sadness wash over him as he looked around the room where Jack had slept most of his life. If only these walls could talk, Clay thought. Sitting on the edge of the bed, he dialed the number for the Chaves County sheriff's office. The phone was answered on the second ring by one of the female deputies. "Deputy Dupree speaking. How may I help you?"

"Hello, Linda, this is Clay Tory. Is Ben in?"

"Hi, Clay. How's Jack doing?"

"He's getting stronger every day. Won't be long 'til he's back here making my life miserable."

"That's good to hear! Ben's in his office. I'll put you through. Don't be a stranger."

Clay and Linda had been classmates and had known each other for years. It still surprised Clay that the shy, slightly plump girl with the freckled face had chosen a career in law enforcement. His train of thought was broken when Ben Aguilar's voice came on the line.

"What's up, Clay?"

"I'm fine, Ben, how are you?"

Ben chuckled into the phone. "Okay, sorry. It's been a long day and I was about to go home. I was on my way out when Linda put your call through. How's everything going, Clay?"

"Fine, thanks, but I'm afraid you're not going to be pleased with what I've got to tell you."

Clay could hear the weary sigh at the other end of the phone line. "What is it?" Ben asked.

"There's been a wreck on the county road about two miles east of the house."

"Anybody hurt?" Ben asked with concern.

"No, just shaken up a bit."

"Any property damage?"

"One barbed wire fence wiped out and one car damaged pretty badly," Clay responded.

"What happened?" Ben asked.

Clay briefly explained how the accident had occurred, leaving out none of the details. "I feel it would be best if we had a law officer look at the scene before the tow truck removes the car."

"Oh, you do, do you?" Ben asked, a touch of humor in his voice.

"Isn't it standard practice for the sheriff's department to investigate accidents that occur in the county?"

Ben laughed lightly. "I'll be there in thirty minutes."

Clay sighed with relief. "I'll be waiting for you."

"By the way," Ben said before Clay could hang up, "I went by to see Jack today. He seems to be improving."

"Thanks, Ben. I'm sure he enjoyed seeing you."

"I'll see you in a little while," Ben said.

Clay stopped by the bathroom to wash up. After cleaning the dust from his hands and face, he walked into the kitchen. Ginger had before her a plate filled with Julie's pot roast, potatoes, and green beans. He took the plate Julie handed him and began piling it high with food.

"Ben will be here in a little bit," he said to Terry.

Julie looked surprised. "What's he coming all the way out here for?"

Casting a glance at Ginger, Clay answered, "Whenever there's an accident on a county road, the sheriff's department has to be notified." He watched Ginger to see what her reaction would be, but her facial expression never changed. She merely cut another piece of roast with her fork.

While they ate, Clay and Terry made plans for moving the rest of the cattle into the two pastures. Ginger seemed to pay attention at first, but soon she was looking around the kitchen at the knickknacks on the wall. Julie tried to engage her in conversation, but after getting only monosyllabic answers and the feeling that Ginger wasn't interested in talking, she finished her meal and began clearing the dishes. Ginger made no offer to help.

Clay had just finished eating and was rinsing his plate in the sink when he heard the car coming down the drive. He turned to Ginger as he picked up his hat. "I think you should come with us so you can tell Ben what happened."

Nodding, she rose and followed him outside.

Ben was getting out of his car as Clay and Ginger walked out. "You want to come in for a cup of coffee?" Clay asked as they approached the sheriff's car.

Ben looked at the sky and shook his head. "I reckon we better get on over to the accident site while there's still some light left. Come on, you can ride with me."

Clay introduced Ginger to Ben, then opened the back door for her, but he missed the angry look she gave him as she slid into the backseat. When they reached the site, Ben pulled the car to the side of the road and killed the engine, surveying the situation. Ginger's car was still sitting in the pasture, headed in the opposite direction from the one in which she'd been traveling. The marks where her tires had torn into the earth were clearly visible.

Ben flipped open his metal clipboard and paged through several forms before finding the one he was looking for. Placing it under the clip, he turned to Clay. "Why don't you stay here while Miss Loring and I take a look at her car?" Clay watched the two walk into the pasture. He could hear their voices but couldn't make out the words. From Ginger's hand gestures, he surmised she was explaining how the accident had occurred. Ben took notes as he looked at the skid marks and walked around the car, tallying the damage. Ginger stood to one side as the sheriff stepped off the distance between the car and the fence, then the distance between the fence and the road, and finally the length of the skid marks on the road. After jotting down his measurements, Ben closed the cover on his clipboard and walked over to Ginger. "Would you mind waiting by the car while I talk to Mr. Tory?" Without answering, Ginger turned and walked to the car. Ben stood in the middle of the road watching her.

"It's your turn with the gestapo!" she said as she passed Clay's window and opened the back door.

Ben and Clay walked down the road away from the sheriff's car in the direction where Clay had been when the accident occurred. "Tell me your version of what happened," Ben said, not bothering to open his clipboard.

Clay gave his explanation, making mention of the fact that he might have been dozing when he heard Ginger's horn. Ben nodded and looked around at the scene once more before walking back to the car. Ginger was sitting in the backseat with the door open. She wore an unconcerned look as Ben and Clay approached.

"It looks like we have a case of both parties being at fault here," Ben told her. "It is true that Mr. Tory's cows were in the middle of the road and hidden by the rise so that you couldn't see them. By the length of tire marks, both on the road and in the pasture, however, it's safe to say you were traveling at an excessive rate of speed. It's an unspoken law in these parts that the ranchers can use these roads for moving cattle from one pasture to another, but since you're not from around here, I can't very well expect you to know that. I'm not issuing any citations in this case. My official report will state 'Accident caused by extenuating circumstances.' "

Ginger let out a gust of air. "I suspected you two would stick together on this. My car is ruined, the cowboy here got his cows moved, and all he has to do is repair a little fence. Sounds fair to me." She stood and started walking toward her car. "I'll just wait here for the wrecker. There's no use in me putting you out any more than I already have," she said in a voice that dripped sarcasm.

"Now, there's no sense in you waiting out here alone. Let's all go back to the house where it's cooler," Ben said.

"I'll be fine, thank you," she said, perching herself on the hood of the car.

Clay winced, knowing that the metal on the car hood had to be at least 150 degrees, but she didn't budge, and if it burned her backside, she gave no sign of it. Maybe Northerners have tougher backsides than those of us from the South, he thought. "Look, Ginger, it could be another hour or more before that tow truck shows up. Why don't you come on back to the house and have some more iced tea? It'll be a whole lot cooler than sitting out here," Clay suggested.

Her only response was to turn and look up the road as if expecting to see the tow truck coming.

Clay shrugged his shoulders at Ben's exasperated look. "We can't just go off and leave her here by herself!" Clay said.

With a disgusted sigh, Ben said, "No, I reckon we can't, but it sure is tempting." Calling to Ginger, he pleaded, "Why don't you come sit in the car? I'll turn on the air conditioner. We'll wait here with you until the tow truck arrives."

Ginger looked at him skeptically, then started toward them, but before she took three steps they all heard the sound of a large truck coming down the road. Squinting against the sun, Ben exclaimed, "Thank God. Maybe I'll get home at a decent hour after all."

Chapter Eleven

Clay awoke to the sound of the alarm clock at five o'clock. Though he'd gone to bed early the night before, he was still tired, and the thought of turning off the alarm and going back to sleep was almost too tempting. He hit the button a little harder than was necessary to turn the alarm off and swung his legs over the side of the bed. He had a lot to do today; he couldn't afford the luxury of sleeping in. He was meeting Jerry and Larry at the north pasture later this morning and had to get the tanks set up with automatic waterers. Terry was going to move part of the cattle into that pasture today, and he and Clay would move the rest of them in the next two days. Clay also had to be in town first thing this morning for a meeting he'd set up with Jake Montoya. Jake dealt in anything that would make a dollar, and after talking to him, Clay felt pretty sure he could provide what he needed. He just hoped Jake could do it for the price he had in mind.

Clay had the coffee made and was sitting at the kitchen table drinking a cup and making notes on his pad when Julie came in.

"Feel better?" she asked.

"A little," Clay answered truthfully.

"How much longer do you think you can keep

up this pace before you go into the hospital your-self?"

"Two more days of this, and we should have everything in place. If things work out the way I hope they will, we should be able to relax a little then. I know Terry's almost as wore out as I am, but we're almost there," Clay explained.

"I hope you both last two more days," Julie said, banging a pan down on the stove for emphasis. "Did you call Tamara last night?" she asked.

Clay groaned. "Oh, man! I forgot all about it. I was going to call her when I got in, but it completely slipped my mind. I guess with the wreck and getting Ginger's car out of the pasture, I just forgot."

"I didn't care too much for that Ginger," Julie said in an offhanded way.

Clay glanced up at her, but she had her back to him. "She's not that bad. She was just upset because her new car got wrecked."

Julie turned to face him. "She's cold. I tried to talk to her several times and she wouldn't say hardly two words to me."

"She had a traumatic experience," Clay said, defending Ginger's actions. "And to top it off, she had to ride with me while I took those cattle to the pasture. She's not used to being on a horse, and it probably took a lot out of her."

Julie gave him a skeptical look and turned back to the stove. "Maybe, but I didn't care for her."

Clay didn't pursue it any further. Instead, he

changed the subject to talk about Jack. "I'm going to go see him while I'm in town this afternoon."

"He's making good progress," Julie said. "He was sitting up in bed yesterday, and they're teaching him to write with his left hand. He has a hard time remembering the letters, but it won't be long before he'll have those down."

Julie set Clay's plate in front of him and said, "You know, he's not going to be happy with you when he finds out you missed the rodeos this weekend."

Clay picked up his fork and began eating, ignoring Julie's remark. She didn't understand that he was doing this for Jack. Or was he? Was it Jack that he was working so hard for, or was he trying to prove something to himself? Clay knew that if he managed to save Jack's cattle, he would have accomplished something that he could always look back on with pride.

Terry came in looking very weary.

"Think you can hold out for a couple more days?" Clay asked.

"That's about all I got left, but I'll make it. How about you? You going to last?"

"I think it's going to be a draw as to which of us drops first. I'm heading into town, then to the north pasture to meet Jerry and Larry while you start moving the cattle. Can you think of anything we need?"

"Vitamins," Terry said dryly.

"I need some laundry detergent and dish

soap," Julie piped up.

"I'll run by the store and pick some up," Clay said and hurried out the door.

Since it was Sunday, Clay did not spend very much time in town after visiting Jack. On the way, he passed by the church where he and Jack spent their Sunday mornings when they weren't out of town, and the sight of the crowded parking lot brought on a feeling of depression as he thought about Jack lying in the hospital. After picking up the few things from the store, he headed straight back to the ranch to finish hooking up the automatic waterers and help Terry move more cattle to the pastures.

On Monday morning Clay had a meeting in town, and he was eager to get there. He told Terry and Julie he would be back around noon, then hurried out.

Jake Montoya's business consisted of a three-acre lot on the west side of town that contained everything from worn-out washing machines to cement trucks. Jake was in his office, thumbing through an equipment sales brochure, when Clay walked in.

"Hey, Clay," he greeted, glancing at his watch. "You're a little early!"

"I hope you don't mind," Clay said in an apologetic tone of voice. "I got a lot to do today."

"Nah, I don't mind. So, you ready to look at those trailers?"

"Where are they?"

"I got 'em parked on the lot across the street.

They're behind the shop."

Clay followed Jake on a zigzag path through broken bicycles, lawn mowers, car engines, and piles that contained a wide assortment of what looked like discarded junk. What amazed Clay was that Jake knew exactly where everything was. If you needed an axle for a 1966 Ford pickup, Jake could take you right to it. If you needed a carburetor for a two-cylinder Briggs and Stratton, he could tell you which path to take and which pile of parts to look in.

When they crossed the street and walked around the end of the large metal building, Clay saw what he was looking for. Parked side by side were four enclosed freight trailers. Each one had a roll-up door on the back and a large door on the side that swung open. He circled the trailers and inspected the tires, springs, and framework. Jake stood off to the side, remaining silent until Clay had finished his inspection.

"How much are you asking for them?" Clay asked.

"You want all four?"

"No, I just need two of 'em."

"I'll make you a heck of a deal on all four," Jake said.

"I don't need all four, so why don't you make me a heck of a deal on two of them?" Clay replied.

"Which two do you want?" Jake asked innocently.

Clay started to point to the two that he'd already decided on, then caught himself. He knew that whichever two he picked Jake would claim they were the best ones and ask a higher price for them, so he decided to play the game to his advantage. He pointed to the two he didn't want.

"You got a good eye," Jake said. "Those are the best ones."

Clay had to struggle to keep from smiling. "How much?" he asked, knowing it was going to be high.

Jake seemed to be considering his asking price, but Clay had no doubt he already knew what he wanted for each of the trailers.

Rubbing his chin while appearing to reflect upon a price that would be equitable to both him and Clay, Jake seemed to be deep in thought. Finally he reached a decision. "I'll let you have both of them for eight thousand."

Clay winced. "I thought you said you'd give me a good price."

"That *is* a good price!" Jake exclaimed. "By the time I pay for having them brought here, I'm not making anything. I wouldn't let anybody else have them for that price."

Clay considered for a moment, then said, "I'll give you six."

Jake doubled over as if hit in the stomach. "Ow, you're trying to take advantage of me! And I thought we were friends."

Clay allowed himself to smile. "If you thought we were friends, you wouldn't have tried charging me twice what these wore-out trailers are worth."

"You wound me, Clay. These trailers are worth twice what I'm asking, but since you think I'm asking too much, I'll let you have them for seven thousand."

Clay seemed to think about his offer for a moment. "You know, now that I think about it, these trailers are only going to sit in the pasture with hay stored in them. I really don't need the two best ones. How much will you sell me those two sorry ones for?"

Jake looked at Clay suspiciously. "Those two are good trailers too. I couldn't take less than sixty-eight hundred for them."

Clay laughed. "That's only two hundred less than you were asking for the two trailers that you said were the best."

"Yes, but the best ones are only two hundred dollars better than these," Jake said with a straight face.

"I'll give you a check right now for fifty-five hundred," Clay offered.

"Make it six thousand and they're yours," Jack countered.

Clay had been willing to pay fifty-eight, but no more. He needed the trailers and he needed them soon, but he couldn't afford to waste money. He knew that if the drought didn't end soon, he'd have to buy more hay and feed. "I reckon we can't trade today, Jake. Maybe next time." He turned and started back to his pickup.

He was almost to the street when Jake called out.

"Hold up, Clay. I'm losing money on the deal, but if you'll give me a check, I'll let you have 'em for fifty-five."

Clay hadn't realized he'd been holding his breath, but now he allowed himself to smile as he stopped and turned slowly around. "I suppose you got the titles. I wouldn't want to buy stolen property."

Jake crowed with laughter. "I've got a bill of sale on each one of 'em. You won't have any trouble getting them titled."

Clay wrote out a check and handed it to Jake, who looked it over carefully before putting it in his wallet. "There'll be a truck here to pick 'em up later today." He turned to go, but Jake stopped him.

"Do you mind if I ask what you're going to do with two trailers?"

"I'm storing hay in them."

"Did Jack's barn burn down?"

Clay chuckled. "No, we had to move all the cattle into two pastures, and this is the only way I can feed all of them. These trailers will be left in the pasture. The only problem I got now is getting 'em loaded."

"If you need some help, my sister's got two teenage boys that could use some extra spending money."

"I could sure use 'em, and a couple more, too."

"When do you need them?" Jake asked.

"First thing in the morning."

"Call me this afternoon. I'll talk to my sister. I'm pretty sure you can count on at least two."

"Thanks, Jake. I'll call as soon as I get back to the ranch."

Clay drove straight from Jake's place to the hospital. When he walked into Jack's room, he was surprised to see the bed in the upright position and Jack sitting up, holding a carton of milk with a drinking straw in it. The tray in front of him held a half-eaten bowl of Jell-O and an almost full bowl of what looked like some kind of broth.

"Looks like you've been eating high on the hog," Clay remarked as he looked at the unappetizing food.

Jack emitted a sound like several grunts, and Clay realized he was attempting to chuckle. "I got some good news to tell you," Clay said, and was pleased to see Jack turn his head slightly and look at him. "We don't have to sell the cattle!"

At Jack's questioning look, Clay began to tell him what he and Terry had accomplished. When he finished, Jack merely looked at him. Clay didn't know what he'd expected from the old rancher, but it certainly wasn't the placid response he got. As Clay stood there, Jack reached over to the table on his left and fumbled with a pad of paper and a pencil, until he was holding them in his lap. Clay watched as Jack scrawled with his left hand in large letters across the page, R O D E O? Clay stared at the word and wondered

146

just what Jack meant. Did he know that Clay had missed last week's show or that he'd already missed the call-in date for the rodeos this week? Or did he want to know how Clay had done at the last shows he'd entered? Taking the only option he could, Clay pulled up a chair and began.

"I did real well at Shreveport, ended up third in barebacks, second in saddle broncs, and fifth in bull riding. Saddle broncs were the only thing I made any money in at Austin. I finished up third. I bucked off my bull and missed my bareback horse out. Tamara knocked over a barrel, but she won in Shreveport and in Stephenville. I placed second in barebacks, fourth in saddle broncs, and fifth in bull riding at Stephenville. It was a pretty good week overall," Clay said, watching closely to see what Jack's reaction would be.

For a few moments Jack just sat staring into space, then he took his pencil and began writing shakily on the pad in his lap.

Clay watched intently as Jack slowly wrote N E X T? and held the pad for Clay to see. At first he was perplexed as to Jack's meaning, but as he saw Jack's expectant look it dawned on him what he was asking.

Struggling to find the right words, Clay said, "I . . . I haven't entered any rodeos this week. I've been so busy trying to get the water to the cattle that I just haven't had time to think about making any shows. I'll start back as soon as everything's in order and I know we're out of danger."

The look of disappointment on Jack's face, however slight, didn't elude Clay, and it was all he could do to keep from stomping out of the room. He had worked himself and Terry past the point of exhaustion, and Jack didn't even appreciate it. The only thing he seemed interested in was how Clay was doing in the rodeos. Well, the dickens with him! I'm going to save those cattle whether he appreciates it or not, Clay thought to himself.

Jack squirmed in the bed. He was watching Clay and could see the anger that suddenly blazed in his eyes. Struggling to explain to the young man that Clay's happiness was the only thing that mattered to him, he searched for something or some way to convey his message. Without realizing it, he was trying to talk, but the only sounds that came out were more like grunts than words.

Clay didn't understand Jack's sudden movements and guttural sounds, and was about to press the call button to summon a nurse when Dr. Johnson entered the room. Noticing the agitated look on Jack's face and the look of fear on Clay's, he asked in a calm voice, "What's going on in here?"

"Thank God you're here," Clay said. "I don't know what's happening to him. We were just talking, and suddenly he started looking all around, making grunting noises and getting upset. I thought he was having some kind of spell."

Dr. Johnson went to Jack's side and leaned down so his face was even with Jack's. Jack had ceased his spastic movements, though his face still bore an agitated look. "Are you feeling all right, Jack?" the doctor asked. He received an affirmative nod. "Do you want something?" This time Jack looked at the doctor, and Clay could see the pleading in his eyes. "Are you hungry?" Jack shook his head. "Thirsty?" He got the same response. "Are you in pain?" Again Jack shook his head, this time more vigorously. The doctor turned his gaze on Clay. "Let's step out into the hall for a moment and let Jack have a moment to calm down."

Clay led the way, wondering why Dr. Johnson wanted him out of the room. As soon as the door closed behind them, the doctor began questioning him. "You said you were just talking before Jack became agitated — what were you talking about?"

Clay hesitated before answering. "I had just told him what I'd done at the ranch, then I told him about the rodeos in Shreveport, Austin, and Stephenville."

Dr. Johnson was listening intently. "Did he start becoming agitated when you told him about the ranch, or the rodeos?"

Clay couldn't look the doctor in the eye when he said, "No, sir."

"So when did he get upset?"

"He asked me which rodeo I was going to next. I told him I wouldn't be going to any until I'd taken care of everything at the ranch."

"So, that's when he started getting upset?" the doctor asked.

Clay started to answer, then stopped. "No, not right then. It was a few minutes later."

"Did you say anything that might have upset him?"

Clay took a moment to consider the question. "I don't think so. After I told him I wasn't going to rodeo for a while, he seemed disappointed, but not upset like he was when you saw him."

"Uh-huh," Dr. Johnson said as he thought about what Clay had told him. "You said he seemed disappointed when you told him you weren't going to any rodeos for a while. How did you know he was disappointed?"

"By the look on his face."

"And how did you react?"

There was a moment's hesitation when Clay remembered the anger he'd felt. "I guess I got mad. I've worked hard to save Jack's herd, and he didn't even care!"

Giving Clay a moment to calm down, Dr. Johnson opened the door to Jack's room and peered inside. Jack stared at him from the bed. The look on his face was a mixture of sadness and frustration. Stepping back and letting the door close, the doctor turned to face Clay. In a soft voice he asked, "Can you possibly imagine how frustrating it must be, not to be able to communicate your thoughts, your feelings, your ideas?"

Clay blinked in surprise at the doctor's question. When he didn't answer, Dr. Johnson continued, "I would imagine Jack's agitated state was caused by his inability to communicate with you. You're going to have to be patient with him."

Clay glanced through the small window in the center of the door. Jack looked as if he were talking to himself. His lips were moving and he was shaking his head from side to side. "I just wish he could tell me what's bothering him," Clay said.

Dr. Johnson looked over Clay's shoulder. "We'll just have to be patient. I'll talk to his doctors and see if there's any way to help him communicate better."

By the time Clay and the doctor reentered Jack's room, the old rancher had settled down considerably. "I want you to behave yourself and quit getting riled up," Dr. Johnson said with a smile, and was rewarded with Jack's lopsided grin. "I've got real patients to see, so I'll leave you alone. Can I trust you not to throw any more tantrums?" Jack nodded and watched the doctor leave.

"I've got to run too," Clay said. "I'll be back as soon as I can. If you need anything, tell the nurse to call Julie." He didn't miss the dejected look on Jack's face. He knew there were things that remained unresolved, but he had no idea how to go about resolving them right now. Taking

Jack's hand, he squeezed it tightly. "We'll talk later. You get some rest."

Clay's mind was in turmoil as he drove to the ranch to meet the truck.

Chapter Twelve

Ginger Loring paced nervously back and forth in her office. Jay Crawford was supposed to have been there thirty minutes ago. Glancing out her office window once more, she saw his Corvette pull into one of the parking spaces. She hurried to her desk, sat down, and opened a folder, pretending to be studying its contents when Jay walked in with a grin on his face that told Ginger he'd had a successful morning.

Standing two inches over six feet, with wavy brown hair and light green eyes, Jay could make Ginger's pulse race just by being in front of her. He was trim and fit, and he could always find a gym to work out in, no matter where they were. Today he was wearing a colorful Western shirt with pearl snaps, blue jeans that looked as if they'd been tailored to fit, and a pair of ostrich-skin boots that shone from recent polishing. It hadn't taken him long to adopt the local fashions. In Boston he had worn the clothes of a successful businessman, looking as if he'd been one all his life. Only Ginger knew that before Boston, he'd been a blackjack dealer in Atlantic City, and before that he'd been involved in a real estate scam in Florida.

Ginger had met Jay Crawford in Boston when he approached her in the lounge where she often went after work. He had asked her to dinner that night at a very classy restaurant. Plying her with expensive champagne and lobster, he had manipulated the conversation until he found out everything about her. Ginger had been enthralled by his total interest in her life. He was unlike the other men she'd dated since moving to Boston; they had only wanted to talk about themselves and their accomplishments. By the time he drove her home that evening, he knew how much she wanted the finer things in life. She had come from a poor family and had grown up in abject poverty with an alcoholic father, always longing for the things that other kids took for granted. Determined to rise above her station, she worked hard in school. Since the other kids shunned her — partly because of her threadbare clothes and partly because of her aloofness — she had plenty of time to study. She had always excelled at math, and therefore upon graduating from high school she enrolled at New York's City College and earned a degree in accounting. Her first job was with a small firm whose clientele consisted of small- to medium-size businesses that couldn't or didn't want to hire their own accountants. It didn't take Ginger long to become bored with the daily routine of entering accounts payable and accounts receivable into the computer. Her real interest was in banking, where the big-money deals were. She attended every seminar she could find where she would meet people in the industry. Finally her perseverance paid off, and she landed a job with an investment banking firm. She started out as an assistant to one of the vice presidents, helping him research and track investment opportunities for several of the firm's larger customers. Her hard work and a natural ability for recognizing good investments quickly earned her a promotion. She was given several small accounts to manage and even brought in new ones on her own. Her salary, while enough to cover her living expenses, wasn't large enough to allow her to invest, but her dream was to have her own investment portfolio someday. It had all been only a dream until Jay came into her life. It hadn't taken him long to discover her desire to make money and only a little longer to convince her she could make it faster than she'd planned. Setting him up as a customer, she used the ten thousand that he had to begin making investments. Each night they would sit in the small living room of her apartment, researching companies and tracking their stock performance. It took them three months to find the right opportunity. It was a chance to invest in a conglomerate of several different small Internet firms that were either expanding or merging with other businesses. The plan was for Ginger to place phony orders to buy stock for Jay through her firm, driving up the price of the stock. When it reached a peak, they sold off their phony shares and walked away with a bundle. Everything had gone smoothly, though Ginger had been a nervous wreck throughout the ordeal. Everything would have continued without a hitch if it hadn't been for a broker at one of the investors' companies, who noticed all the buy orders that Ginger was placing and began asking questions.

Ginger had covered her bases well, but at Jay's suggestion she left her job and moved to Wisconsin with him. They made a little over forty thousand between them, which Ginger had already invested back in the stock market, not trusting Jay to handle the money. They pulled a similar scheme in Wisconsin, netting another fifteen thousand. Ginger had stayed on for three months afterward to make sure there was no danger of discovery, then they left for New Mexico. In Albuquerque, Ginger landed a job with the largest investment firm in the state. Six months later, she was offered the position of managing the company's satellite office in Roswell. She wanted to decline the offer, but Jay talked her into taking it: "Just think, we'll have access to all the records and no one to look over our shoulder."

Ginger reluctantly agreed, but she made him buy her a new car before she would move. As in the past, they set Jay up as a client so that the two assistant brokers and the secretary would suspect nothing when he came and went.

Now, as Jay entered her office wearing his mischievous grin, Ginger wondered for the thousandth time what it was that drew her to him. She did not doubt that one day he would leave her, but she didn't dwell on that. She only knew that he stirred her as no other man ever had.

"I gather you had a successful morning," she said as he took a seat in the overstuffed chair and threw one leg over the arm.

"I sure did," he answered, inspecting the nails on his right hand. "There was a report filed by the sheriff's department about the wreck, but it's forgotten."

"That's good. I'm still not sure they haven't pressed charges against me in Boston."

"Will you stop your foolish worrying! If they'd filed charges, we would have heard about it. I've told you a thousand times, I've got contacts keeping an eye on things in Boston."

"I can't help it. I still worry. How many more of these schemes are we going to pull before we have enough money?"

With a Cheshire cat grin, he said, "We may have to pull off only one more, if what I learned is true."

Giving him a skeptical look, she asked, "What did you learn?"

"It seems your cowboy is in line to inherit one of the best pieces of property around these parts."

"What are you talking about?"

"That cowboy you met yesterday is the sole heir to the Lazy L, which is one big chunk of prime ranchland. I've got contacts that would grovel for the chance to invest in that property."

"What on earth are you talking about?"

Ginger demanded incredulously.

Standing up abruptly, Jay leaned across the desk and stared into her eyes. "What I'm talking about is getting our hands on that piece of property and selling it. All you have to do is butter up your cowboy and get him to sign over the ranch. I'll have it sold before the ink dries. And then we'll head to California."

Ginger could only stare at him as if he were a lunatic. "Are you out of your mind? How am I going to get him to sign over his ranch to me?"

"You're going to make him fall head over heels in love with you, then trick him into signing."

Ginger shook her head. "What makes you think he's going to fall for me?"

Looking her up and down, he said, "Because, baby, you got all the right equipment to make a hardworking cowpoke fall for you."

Ginger gave him a withering look but said nothing. She didn't like the idea at all. It sounded way too risky. But she had learned never to discount anything until you'd had time to analyze it from all points of view.

As soon as Larry and Jerry dropped off the tanker at the north pasture, Clay sent them to Jake's to get the two trailers while he began piping in the automatic waterers. When he got back to the ranch, well after lunchtime, he was surprised to see one of the trailers already backed up to the barn. He found Julie in the utility room washing clothes.

158

"I was beginning to wonder if you were going to come back before dark. There's a plate of meat loaf and potatoes in the oven."

"Thanks," Clay said, heading to the bathroom to wash up.

"Terry liked your idea of using the cargo vans to store the hay in the pastures," Julie said as she walked by with a load of clothes in her arms.

"He figured it out, huh?" Clay responded.

"Yep. He's real impressed, but he was wondering who was going to load the hay into the trailers."

Clay chuckled. "I'm sure he is! Jake's got some nephews that we might be able to use. I've got to call him in a little bit. If I don't get them, I'll find somebody else."

"I may know a couple of young boys that may be able to help."

Clay gave her a dubious look. "Does Terry know about these boys?"

Julie laughed and said, "They're his cousins — they live between here and Artesia. Do you want me to give them a call?"

"Let me talk to Jake first. If his nephews can't do it, you can call Terry's cousins. We may use them anyway. We're all going to need a rest pretty soon, and it would be nice to have someone to feed the cattle and keep an eye on things around here."

"How was Jack today?" she asked.

"He wasn't happy with me for missing rodeos, and when I told him about saving the cattle, he acted like it didn't matter."

"Oh, I'm sure it mattered," Julie said. "But remember, I told you earlier today that he wouldn't be happy with you for missing those rodeos. In case you haven't noticed, the thing that gives him the most pleasure is for you to do well. I think that through your achievements, he's able to relive his past and the times when he was the happiest."

"But what about the ranch? I mean, he worked and struggled and sacrificed to build it up, and if we don't save the cattle, we could lose a big part of what he worked for."

"I know," Julie said, "but I wonder if the ranch and cattle mean as much to Jack now as they once did."

"What do you mean?" Clay asked.

"It's just that I'm not sure he's as concerned about the ranch as he is about you making it to the finals."

Clay frowned at the suggestion. "If that's the case, why was he so worried about having to sell the cattle? That's what caused his stroke and put him in the hospital."

"I think most of it was just habit. He's been worrying about this ranch for so long, I don't think he knows how to not worry. But I do know the only thing that really makes him happy is watching you ride and helping you make it to the finals."

Clay reflected on her words and knew that in part she was right. He himself had seen the difference it made in Jack when he was at rodeos with him. "You may be right," Clay agreed, "but if I can save these cattle, I'm going to. As soon as we're out of the woods I'll go back on the road."

"Have you called Tamara and let her know what's happening?"

Clay smacked his head with the palm of his hand. "Oh, no, I forgot to call her!"

"Well, you get in there right now and do it."

Clay rushed to the telephone and dialed Tamara's cell phone number. When he got no answer, he dialed her home number. After three rings, her mother answered the phone and said Tamara was out helping her father move some cattle. She inquired about Jack's health and promised to tell Tamara that he called, then asked Clay if he would be entering the rodeos the next weekend.

"I don't know yet. It depends on how things go the next few days."

"Her father and I both feel a lot better when we know she's traveling with you."

Clay sighed inwardly. "I've really missed being with her these past two weeks. Hopefully we'll have things running smoothly here pretty soon so I can get back to riding."

"I certainly hope so," Mrs. Allen responded. "You can't afford to miss too many rodeos and keep your place in the standings, but I know what it's like when you have responsibilities. Tell Jack we said hello. If there's anything we can do, give us a call."

Clay thanked her and said good-bye. He hung up the phone and took a deep breath, remembering how simple things had been only a couple of weeks ago.

Clay had Julie haul him and his horse to the pasture where Terry was rounding up cattle. Before he left the house, he called Jake and arranged for two boys to start loading hay into the trailers. Julie was going to call Terry's cousins and see if they wanted to earn some extra money by helping out.

Terry had most of the cattle rounded up by the time Clay and Julie arrived. Clay had thrown three bags of feed in the truck, and now he broke one open and poured it out from the back of the pickup while Julie drove slowly toward the gate. Soon all the cattle were following the pickup. Terry and Clay pushed the cattle along and kept them from straying while Julie stayed just far enough ahead to open the gates and keep the cattle moving after her. This method proved to work much better. In short order, they had the cattle moved into the large pasture and drinking from the tanks. As soon as Clay was sure all the cattle had drunk their fill, he watered the horses, then loaded them in the trailer.

As he drove back to the ranch house, he asked Terry and Julie, "How would you two like to have supper in town tonight?"

"Sounds great to me!" Julie said quickly. "I was just sitting here dreading having to cook."

"As long as I get back early," Terry said, stifling a yawn.

"I thought we'd eat and then go visit Jack," Clay said. Secretly he didn't want to see Jack alone tonight. He wasn't sure he would know what to say to the recuperating rancher if the subject of rodeos came up.

Terry and Clay did the chores while Julie went in to clean the dust off of herself. It took the two men only a few minutes to wash up and change clothes, and then they were all on their way to town. Clay bought them steaks at the Cattlemen's Cafe and then drove to the hospital. As he pushed open the door to Jack's room, he was thankful for Julie and Terry's presence.

It was obvious that Jack was surprised to see the three of them, but the awkward grin on his face showed how delighted he was. Julie went immediately to his bedside and hugged his neck, kissing him on the cheek and smiling brightly.

"How are you feeling?" she asked.

He nodded his head, and the grin remained on his face. Terry and Clay sat back and let Julie carry the conversation. She told him about the things she'd been doing and the people she'd talked to, eventually getting around to telling him about Clay's accident and the fact that she didn't think too highly of Ginger Loring.

Jack sat and listened with rapt attention, nodding occasionally. His eyes widened in surprise at the mention of the accident, and his eyes turned quickly to Clay in a questioning gaze.

Clay grinned and explained what had happened, finishing his tale by saying he thought maybe Julie was a little jealous, since Ginger was such a looker. That brought something that resembled a chuckle from Jack and a sharp look from Julie.

With the ice broken and Clay's tension gone, he and Terry began telling Jack about the work they'd been doing, each trying to outdo the other by embellishing on the amount of work and how worn-out they were.

Jack's eyes twinkled with merriment as he listened to them spin their tales. Julie was rolling her eyes and giggling, but not once did she dispute anything they said, seeing how much it pleased Jack.

Clay and Terry were still telling stories when the nurse came in with Jack's supper. They started saying their good-byes, but Jack held up his hand in a gesture for them to wait. Reaching around to the nightstand, he retrieved his paper and pencil and began writing while the nurse was busy setting up his dinner tray on the rollaway stand. Clay, Julie, and Terry stood to one side while Jack wrote in his slow scrawl, then handed the pad to Julie. She read what he'd written, then with a puzzled frown handed the pad to Clay. Clay read the words and frowned as well.

"TOMORROW TYPE," Clay read. "What does that mean?"

The nurse stopped what she was doing and turned to Clay. "I think it means that tomorrow

164

he's going to start learning to type. Rehab has special keyboards with large keys and a monitor that help patients like Mr. Lomas communicate by typing."

"That's wonderful!" Julie exclaimed. "I can't wait to see how well you're going to do."

Clay nodded in agreement. "That's great, Jack." Then he chuckled. "Just think — you'll be back to giving orders and driving us crazy in no time."

Jack's smile remained until long after the three said good night and left.

Chapter Thirteen

It took all of Jay Crawford's charm to convince Ginger that his plan would work — if she were willing to do her part. Her part meant working her charms on Clay Tory and, by hook or crook, getting him to sign the ranch over to them.

"I'll have the deal made and the land sold before they know what hit them. We'll both be in California living the good life before the lid blows, and by then it'll be too late."

"But what happens when they find out their land has been sold out from under them? Won't they fight it in court?" Ginger asked, still skeptical.

"Of course they will. And with all the friends Jack Lomas and Clay Tory have in this town, I imagine they'll get an injunction to stop any development until they can sort things out. But by then we'll be long gone and out of reach."

In the end he had convinced her it could work. Playing on her greedy nature, he talked about the amount of money they could expect to make off this deal. In the end, it was Ginger who laid out the logistics and planned the timetable. Jay smiled inwardly when he noticed her growing excitement. According to her calculations, things would be set into motion in about a week. That would give Jay enough time to scout Clay's scheduled visits to Jack and give her enough time to do some shopping.

It took Clay and Terry another day and a half to get all the cattle moved into the pastures. Larry and Jerry had their routine down for hauling water, and so far it was working well. Jake's teenage nephews, Gilbert and Thomas, were loading hay out of the barn onto the two trailers. Two of Terry's cousins, Shawn and Timmy, were coming today to help with the feeding. Clay planned to use all the boys for at least two weeks so he and Terry could get some badly needed rest. He planned to start back rodeoing as soon as possible if things kept going as well as they had. Tamara had called and left a message the night before, saying that she was coming to the ranch today. Excitement had swept through him as he listened to the sound of her voice on the recording. He had tried to return her call, but there was no one home. Presently, he was pushing the last of the cattle to the north pasture, herding the cattle faster than he should have, eagerly anticipating Tamara's arrival in the afternoon.

"Hey, slow down!" Terry yelled from the other side of the herd. "You push these cows any harder and they're going to start dropping dead."

Clay gave him a sheepish grin. "Sorry. I reckon I'm just a little impatient for some reason."

"You better slow down while you can, or

you'll be rushing yourself right into a wedding."

Clay laughed. "You're a good one to be talking. You're not that much older than me, and you've been married for five years now. And that brings up a good point — when are you and Julie going to start having rugrats?"

Terry shrugged and shook his head. "Julie's ready right now, but I'm not sure I'm ready to have kids."

"Why not?" Clay asked, surprised by Terry's answer. "I think you'd make a great father."

"It's not that. It's just that I'm not sure I'm ready for the responsibility. I mean, what if they turn out to be like you? How in the world would I ever be able to deal with that?"

"You should be so lucky, Mr. James. But you and Julie would make fine parents, and raising a kid on the Lazy L would be great. I could teach him how to ride broncs and bulls."

"No son of mine is going to ride bulls!" Terry stated adamantly. "He's going to have more sense than that. If he wants to ride broncs, that's all right, but no bulls!"

"I don't see why not. I think bull riding is one of the greatest sports ever."

"It may be a great sport, but as far as I'm concerned, you got to be a few bricks shy of a load to climb on the back of one of those things."

Clay smiled. "I can't argue that point, but I can't think of anything that offers the thrill that bull riding does."

"I can!" Terry said.

"What's that?" Clay asked.

"Not getting on one of those things to begin with."

Laughing, Clay answered, "I guess it's all in the way you look at it."

They soon had the cattle moved into the pasture and headed toward the watering stations. Though Clay was anxious to be away, he waited until all the cows had finished drinking before he and Terry left. He could see Tamara's pickup parked at the house long before they rode in. With the horses already in a long trot, it was all Clay could do to hold himself in check and not let them run.

"You go on to the house," Terry said with a grin as they rode up to the barn. "I'll take care of the horses."

"Thanks," Clay said, tossing him the reins. Before he was halfway to the house, Tamara came bursting through the door, running toward him and almost bowling him over as she flew into his arms.

"I ought to be mad at you instead of being so happy to see you," she said, hugging him tightly.

"Why?" Clay asked innocently.

Stepping away from him, she said, "Because you didn't call me for almost two weeks! If it hadn't been for Julie, I wouldn't have had any idea what was happening. Why didn't you call me?"

Clay gave her a sheepish look. "I planned to call you a thousand times, but things were so

169

hectic I kept forgetting."

"That's no excuse! But I'll forgive you anyway. Julie's been telling me about all the work you've been doing. I'm surprised you and Terry aren't in the hospital with Jack."

"It ain't been that bad. We just finished moving the last of the cows into the pasture and everything's in place now. With Terry's cousins coming tomorrow to help with the feeding, he and I can take a couple of days off and rest."

"Good," Tamara said, "because I want you to show me around. Every time I come here you're too busy working to do anything. I've always wanted to go to Ruidoso. I hear it's beautiful there."

"It is!" Clay said. "And Ruidoso Downs is running horses now. How about we go see Jack this afternoon, then get a good night's sleep tonight and leave early in the morning?"

"Sounds fine to me. Julie says Jack is recovering nicely."

Clay nodded, a slight frown on his face. "He's improving, all right, but he's got a long way to go. Don't be too surprised when you see him."

"Do you think he'll fully recover?"

Clay shrugged. "No one knows. It's going to be up to Jack and how hard he works at it, and even then it will depend on how much damage was done. But with Jack's stubborn constitution, I think he'll recover as far as possible."

While Clay showered and changed clothes,

Tamara told Julie about their plans for the next day. "I'd love to go to the races again," Julie said.

"Why don't you and Terry come with us?" Tamara asked.

Julie considered the invitation for a moment, then shook her head. "No, you and Clay haven't seen each other in two weeks. You need this time to yourselves."

"Don't be silly. We'd love for you two to join us. Besides, we're not going to be alone at the races anyway."

"Are you sure we won't be intruding?"

"I'm sure! Why don't you go talk Terry into it, and we'll make a day of it?"

Julie gave her a sly smile. "I'll go tell him we're going! He hasn't taken me anywhere in so long, he won't dare say no."

Tamara giggled as she watched Julie hurry off. When Clay came out of the shower, Tamara bit her lip nervously as she told him what she'd done.

"That's great!" Clay responded, much to her relief. "It'll be a fun day."

Julie came back in the house smiling broadly. "He said he'd love to go. What time are we leaving?"

The three of them made plans to leave early in the morning so they could get to Ruidoso and show Tamara the town before the races started.

"You've done a good job of organizing things around here. I'll bet Jack's really proud of you," Tamara said as they drove into town.

"I'm not so sure," Clay responded dryly.

"Huh?"

"When I told him what I'd done, he didn't seem too enthused at all. But when I told him I hadn't been to any rodeos for two weeks, he had a conniption fit."

"I can understand that," Tamara said.

Surprised by her comment, Clay asked, "What do you mean?"

"Ever since Jack took you in, you two have been traveling to rodeos. He's been a big part of your success and wants nothing more than to see you become a world champion. I imagine he would give up the ranch and everything else he owns to see you make it."

Clay sat in stunned silence. Suddenly it all made sense. Sure, Jack was upset about the drought and having to sell off part or all of his herd. But while he was worrying about that, Clay was still making rodeos, at least up until the time of Jack's stroke. Thinking back to the day in Jack's hospital room, Clay remembered his own anger when Jack got so upset. Now he knew why Jack had become agitated!

"I think Julie tried to tell me the same thing, but I guess I was too busy thinking about what a good job I was doing, I wasn't considering how Jack felt."

"You did what you thought you had to. Considering what you accomplished in three weeks, I'd say Jack's going to be very proud of you. All you have to do now is get back on the circuit and

172

make it to the finals. You've already dropped two places in barebacks, one place in saddle broncs, and two in bulls."

Clay was stunned to realize he'd dropped that many places in such a short time, but he knew he still had plenty of time to get back in the game and regain his position.

"I've already called and entered the Del Rio and Brownwood rodeos," Clay said, pleased to see the smile that spread across Tamara's face.

At the hospital, Jack was obviously happy to see Tamara and his eyes lit up at the sight of her. She smiled and hugged his neck. If she was shocked by his weakened condition, she gave no sign of it. "I hear you're about ready to break out of this place and get back on the road," she said.

He gave her his lopsided grin and shook his head vigorously, causing both Clay and Tamara to laugh. "Well, you keep up the good work and I'm sure they'll let you go home soon," Tamara responded.

He held up two fingers, which prompted a confused look from Tamara. She looked at Clay, but he only shrugged and asked, "Does that mean you get to go home in two weeks?"

Jack smiled and nodded. "Two weeks," he mumbled in a slurred voice, causing Clay's eyes to widen in astonishment.

"You're talking!" Clay shouted, and Jack nodded slowly.

"That's great!" Tamara cried, kissing his cheek.

With obvious effort Jack spoke again. "Typed!" he managed to say.

Again Tamara looked confused and Clay grinned at her. "He means he's been using a special typewriter." Turning to Jack, he asked, "What did you type?"

"L . . . Letter f . . . f . . . for you."

"For me? Where is it?"

Jack held up his hand, indicating he wanted Clay to wait.

"I think he wants you to take it with you," Tamara said.

Jack nodded again, and Clay said, "All right, I'll wait. By the way, I've entered two rodeos this weekend. One in Del Rio and one in Brownwood. We got the cattle in two pastures now, and we have two moving vans full of hay that'll be taken in with them tomorrow so we can feed them all at one time. Jake Montoya's nephews and a couple of Terry's nephews are helping out for a few days, so Terry, Julie, Tamara, and I are going to Ruidoso in the morning."

Jack nodded, obviously pleased with the news. They talked to him for another hour before running out of things to say. As they started to leave, Jack motioned Clay over to him. Taking out an envelope that was tucked under the blanket in his lap, he handed it to Clay. Clay put it in his back pocket, then said, "We're all ready for you to come home. It's not the same without you."

Jack's eyes misted, and he held up two fingers again.

Clay smiled. "I'll be counting the days. If we get back in time tomorrow, we'll come by and see you."

Later that evening when he was undressing for bed, Clay pulled the envelope from his back pocket and opened it. Tears came to his eyes as he read what Jack had typed.

CLAY

I KNOW YOU HAVE WORKED HARD TO SAVE THE HERD. I AM PROUD OF YOU BUT I WOULD GIVE UP ALL THE COWS AND THE RANCH FOR YOU TO BE WORLD CHAMPION. YOUR DREAM IS MY DREAM. THANK YOU FOR ALL YOUR WORK. NOW GET BACK TO RODEO.

I LOVE YOU LIKE A SON
ALWAYS
JACK

Clay put the letter back in the envelope and laid it on his dresser. He wondered how he could feel so good and so bad at the same time. He fell asleep thinking about how one man had made such a difference in his life.

The trip to Ruidoso was just what the doctor ordered for all four of them. Tamara and Julie spent the better part of the morning dragging Clay and Terry through all the shops in town until the two men finally had had enough and found a shop that specialized in custom-made saddles. Clay talked the women into continuing their shopping without them while he and Terry looked at the saddles. Taking advantage of the girls' absence, Clay ordered three handmade saddles — a roping saddle for Jack and two matching tooled saddles for him and Tamara, a roping saddle for him and a barrel saddle for her. He had their initials carved on the fenders of both. The saddle maker promised to have all three finished and delivered in six weeks. Clay wrote him a check for half and said he would pay the rest when the saddles were delivered.

Leaving the shop, they met the girls for lunch before going to the races. Finding seats in the Jockey Club, the four of them spent the afternoon betting more against each other than doing any serious gambling. When the final race was run, Tamara had lost twenty-four dollars, Clay had lost forty, Terry eighteen, and Julie — the only winner of the day — had won twenty-six.

"We're the last of the big-time gamblers," Terry laughed as they walked through the parking lot to the pickup.

"Well, at least we bought a couple of bags of feed for some of the horses. The way some of those nags I bet on ran, I think they need some more energy."

They ate supper at the Silver Dollar Restaurant on their way back to Roswell and got back in time to have a brief visit with Jack before heading to the ranch. Once there, they popped popcorn and sat around the living room recapping the day and laughing at each other's antics. It was late when they finally decided it was time to turn in. The next day Clay and Tamara drove to Carlsbad to visit the caverns, and after Terry made sure the boys they'd hired were feeding the ranch cattle properly, he and Julie drove to Clovis to visit some friends. Clay and Tamara left Friday morning for the Del Rio rodeo, stopping in San Angelo to pick up Tamara's horse.

Clay was a little uneasy as they pulled into the rodeo grounds. It felt as if he'd been away for a year rather than three weeks. As soon as he stepped out of the pickup and took in his surroundings, though, the old feeling of excitement came back with a rush. Tamara came to stand beside him. "How does it feel to be back?" she asked.

"It feels great. I really missed this!"

"Well, here comes somebody to give you a real welcome back," she said, pointing in the direction of the arena.

Clay looked up and saw Billy Ettinger coming toward them. "Oh, boy, that's just what I need. Haven't I had enough problems?"

"Hey, Junior, it's about time you quit loafing around and got back to work. I was beginning to think this life had gotten too tough for you and you'd finally quit," Billy jested.

"You mean you were hoping I'd quit so you wouldn't have any competition."

"Since when did you start thinking you were

competition? As a matter of fact, it's been harder since you've been gone. I haven't had anyone to carry my gear bag for me."

Clay grinned. "I bet that was tough for an old codger like you," he smirked.

"I've had about all of this mushy male bonding I can stand," Tamara said. "Why don't you two just shake hands and say hello like normal people?"

Clay and Billy laughed together, then shook hands, each genuinely glad to see the other.

"What did you draw in saddle broncs?" Clay asked.

"Undertow," Billy answered. "What about you?"

"Coors Bandit," Clay responded. "It ought to be interesting. They're both good horses."

"Yeah, but I plan on riding mine," Billy said.

"I've always said, if you're going to dream, dream big."

Tamara rolled her eyes and said, "Here we go again. I'm going to take Charger into the arena and warm him up while you two continue this battle of dimwits."

"Let's go talk to Kenny and Loren. They've been asking about you," Billy said. "By the way how's Jack doing?"

"He's improving every day," Clay answered. "Thanks for the flowers and the card."

"Sure. It was the least we could do. I just wish I'd had time to get by and see him."

"He'd love that. With a little luck, he'll be out of the hospital in two weeks."

"That's great!" Billy said. "He should be back

to traveling with you pretty soon."

"I hope so," Clay responded sincerely.

"I know what you mean. It's not the same without him."

"He's like a woman. You can't live with him and you can't live without him," Clay said, causing Billy to laugh outright.

Chapter Fourteen

Clay had drawn Bayware in the barebacks. Rosining his rigging handle, he watched them run the horse into the bucking chutes. Billy helped him set and tighten his rigging, waiting while Clay buckled on his spurs and chaps.

"Ol' Bayware here likes to lunge hard from the chute, then dip his head and kick high with his rear. If he gets you pulled back off your riggin' on the lunge, he'll lose you over his head on the kick," Billy advised.

"Guess I better keep myself pulled up on the rigging, then."

"Be a good idea if you want to make it to the whistle."

Clay cocked an eyebrow and asked, "Why do you know so much about bareback horses? All I've ever seen you watch is saddle broncs."

"Ol' Bayware here used to be a saddle bronc horse, but he made a better bareback horse because of his bucking style, so Lou changed him over."

"How many times did he throw you?"

With a sheepish grin Billy answered, "Three. One time he whipped me back so hard I thought my back was broken."

"Well, I appreciate you telling me about him, but I'm surprised you did. If I'd gotten thrown, you wouldn't have had any competition in the saddle broncs."

Billy let out a belly laugh. "I won't have any even if you don't get thrown, Junior."

Bayware weighed more than twelve hundred pounds, and most of it was muscle and brawn. Performing just as Billy had predicted, he lunged hard out of the chute when the gate swung open. If Clay hadn't been prepared, the rigging handle would have been jerked right out of his hand. Gripping tight, he managed to keep himself pulled up on his rigging and was ready when Bayware's front feet hit the ground, his hind feet kicking into the air. All Clay could see in front of him was the arena dirt. Bayware had his head buried between his legs, and his body was almost vertical. Just when Clay feared the horse was going to tip over forward, he felt the body surging down and the head coming up. But he didn't have time to consider his good luck — as Bayware's feet hit the ground, he ducked left, throwing himself into the air and twisting his body sideways. Clay dug his spurs into Bayware's neck and waited for his front feet to touch the ground. When Bayware jumped again, Clay raked his spurs along the horse's shoulders, jerking his knees hard and making the rowels on his spurs ring. Three more bucks and Bayware ducked back to the right and sunfished again. Only Clay's skill saved him from being thrown as he gripped with his spurs and locked his right arm into his thigh to stay astride.

The eight-second whistle blew and Clay welcomed the presence of the pick-up men as they moved in beside him. He walked slowly back to the chutes, winded yet elated. The announcer called out his score of seventy-seven as he climbed over the chutes to the platform behind.

"I would have bet my winnings you'd get thrown before the fourth jump," Billy greeted him.

"What winnings?" Clay huffed.

"The ones I'm going to get in the saddle bronc riding."

"Oh," Clay said, grinning, "you mean the winnings you'll get for second place if you don't buck off."

"Yeah, right!" Billy said. "Let's go down to the roping chutes. I told Gary Dean I'd tail his calf for him."

"I'll get my rigging and find Tamara, then meet you there."

Clay and Tamara sat on the arena fence to watch the calf roping. By the time Gary Dean rode into the box, a nine point three was the leading time. Billy stood beside the roping chute keeping the calf pushed up. He would twist the calf's tail to force him out of the chute faster when Gary nodded, a practice sanctioned in most rodeos.

Gary Dean was presently sitting twelfth in the standings in calf roping and sixteenth in steer wrestling. He and Billy often traveled together on weekends like this when neither of their wives was with them. Since Gary pulled a gooseneck trailer with living quarters, it was as if they carried their own hotel along.

Gary was set in the roping box. His well-trained roping horse, Tripper, had his eyes locked on the calf in the chute, his ears up and twitching. Gary made sure the calf was standing straight, facing forward, and pushed all the way against the gate. Then he nodded and hesitated only a millisecond before giving Tripper his head. Lifting his rope over his head, he swung it just three times before Tripper had him in position. He threw his loop like a pitcher throwing a fastball and caught the calf around the neck. Gary jerked the slack from his rope and threw it into the air, stepping off Tripper's right side while the horse slid on his haunches, bracing for the jerk of the calf as it hit the end of the rope. Gary was down the rope and had the animal flanked before it could move. Grabbing the calf's foreleg, Gary looped his pigging string over the hoof and pulled it tight, throwing it out of his way while he gathered up the animal's two back legs, crossing them over the foreleg. With the pigging string Gary made two wraps and a half hitch, or a hooey, as it's sometimes called. Throwing his hands in the air to signal that his run was complete, the clock stopped. The calf remained tied for the allotted ten seconds, and Gary's time was official: a nine point five, not quite fast enough to take first but a good time that would probably win him some money.

Clay and Tamara applauded Gary's run and congratulated him on his way out of the arena. They stayed on the fence to watch part of the steer wrestling. The stock was large and rangy, which put the competition on a different level and made turning the animals and bringing them to a stop a difficult task. Once the steer wrestlers had them turned, they then had to twist the long-horned animals to the ground. If any of the competitors failed to throw his steer as the animal's back legs came off the ground, he was in for quite a struggle. Several of the cowboys missed their opportunity to throw their steer as they brought it around, and one steer wrestler was picked up bodily and carried around the arena before he managed to plant his feet and twist the animal to the ground. The leading time was a seven point four. Gary threw his steer in six point four and held first until the next-to-last steer wrestler threw his steer in six flat.

Clay was already behind the chutes with his bronc saddle when the steer wrestling was over. The specialty act of the evening was Wild Whip McCallahan. Using two large bull whips, the entertainer popped balloons, ripped playing cards in half, and broke a cigarette in his lovely assistant's mouth four times, each time getting closer and closer to her face. His big finale was cutting a steer head out of a large paper square held in a metal frame. Using both whips, he worked with precision skill until he had the silhouette carved out. By the end of his performance, the first six saddle bronc horses had been run into the chutes, then saddles were cinched on their backs.

Billy was the third rider out. Clay was eighth. Clay helped Billy adjust his saddle and buckled on his bronc halter; then they watched the action in the arena. Darren Goebly scored a sixty-nine on Blaster, a coal-black horse that turned it on for the first five seconds, then slowed in the last few seconds to keep Darren's score low. Wendell Cummings scored a seventy-two on Gloria, a roan mare with large black spots on her rump. Gloria bucked straight for three jumps, then stopped, reared, and pivoted. When her front feet came down, she bunched and bucked into the air. She did this four times in a row, with Wendell spurring every jump.

Billy climbed down on Undertow's back, stuck his high-heeled boots in the stirrups and held them away from the horse's sides. With the rein tight in his hand, he turned to Clay and said, "Watch close and you may learn something," and nodded for the gate before Clay could respond.

Undertow hesitated only slightly before spinning out of the chute and thrusting his head between his legs. Hitting on his front legs and kicking hard with his back legs, the dappled-gray horse gave Billy a classic saddle bronc ride. Billy's spurs were over the points of the shoulders each time Undertow's front hooves bit the ground, and he raked them down the horse's side on each lunge, ending at the saddle cantle. Undertow was a rank ride, but Billy's style made him look no rougher than a kid's rocking chair. Fortunately for Billy, the judges were aware of both the difficulty of riding Undertow and Billy's ability. His score, a seventy-nine, handily took the lead.

"They just felt sorry for you because you're so old," Clay said as Billy climbed back to the platform.

"I'll take it any way I can get it," Billy responded wryly. "I just hope you paid close attention and learned something."

"I sure did," Clay said. "I learned that maybe by the time I'm as old as you, I might get some breaks."

Coors Bandit was standing in the chutes with Clay's saddle cinched on his back. A light strawberry roan with large splotches of white, he had a dark patch around one eye and a white patch around the other. "He looks like he got in a fight with an ugly stick and lost the battle," Billy remarked casually as Clay straddled the chute.

"That's funny — I was just going to say Bandit reminds me of you," Clay said, taking the rein in his right hand and easing down into the saddle. He was ready when the gate man took hold of the latch. Nodding his head, Clay braced himself in the saddle. Coors Bandit sulked in the chute, refusing to move. The gate man had begun closing the gate when the horse turned and tried rushing out of the chute, but the opening had closed down and there was barely enough room for him to pass. Clay's left foot caught the end of the gate and pushed him out of the saddle as the roan horse shot into the arena. Landing on his side only feet from the chute, Clay rolled over and groaned. He had landed hard on his right shoulder and banged his head against the ground. He rose groggily to his feet and searched out the judges. They were standing together only a few feet away and he walked over to them. "I get a reride, don't I?" he asked.

One judge, Cliff Abernathy, shook his head. "It looked clean to me," he said.

"Me too!" chimed in Guy Dillon, the other judge.

"He fouled me on the gate!" Clay said adamantly. "You saw my foot hit the chute!"

"He was fouled!" Billy shouted from the platform, and though both judges looked at him, they refused to be swayed by his comment.

"I'm sorry, Clay," Cliff said. "I didn't see it."

"I didn't either," Guy added.

"Aw, come on, fellas. My blind grandmother could have seen that foul! The gate was almost closed when that nag came out! How could you miss it?"

Guy was already moving away. Cliff gave Clay a sympathetic look and said, "Sorry, Clay, but we didn't see a foul. He might have done it, but neither of us saw it."

Clay pulled off his glove and threw it on the

ground in anger. "I'm going to make appointments for both of you to see an optometrist!" But neither man was listening to him. They had already turned their attention to the next rider.

"Bummer," Billy said. "You was robbed."

Disgusted, Clay spat out, "I don't see how they could have missed that! I thought if the gate was closing and the horse came out it was an automatic reride."

"It usually is," Billy said. "But it's at the judges' discretion. Most of them give rerides, but apparently Guy and Cliff want to get the show over with. You need to lodge a complaint and use my name as a witness."

"It's over. I don't think lodging a complaint will accomplish anything. They've always seemed to be fair before. Maybe they just didn't see the foul."

"Yeah, maybe," Billy said. "But if they didn't, they better not be driving. They'll definitely have a wreck before they get out of the parking lot!"

Clay shook off his anger and said, "No, Billy. I guess it's like a missed call at a football or basketball game. Things like that happen." Picking up his bronc saddle from the platform, he threw it over his shoulder, then looked at Billy and asked, "You want to watch the team roping or walk over to the concession stand and see who's hanging around?"

"Let's go to the concession stand. Team roping is like picking your nose."

"How's that?" Clay asked, mildly surprised.

"It's fun to do, but nobody likes to watch."

This brought a peal of laughter from Clay, who replied, "That's true enough, I reckon, but I never thought of it like that."

"That's why you got me, Junior, so I can advise you on the ways of the world and teach you the finer points," Billy said with a hint of a smile.

"It makes me shudder to think of the possibilities," Clay quipped.

After depositing Clay's saddle in the camper, they walked to the concession stand. Several contestants were gathered there, and Clay and Billy were soon involved in conversation, Clay telling Steven Garrett about Jack's condition and how long it would be before the old rancher would start traveling with him again. While they were talking, Tamara was busy exercising Charger in the open area outside the arena gate, and Clay kept glancing in her direction. Her ride on the magnificent animal was like poetry in motion, as if horse and rider were one.

"Don't you think so, Clay?" Steven asked.

"Huh?" Clay responded, startled by the question.

Chuckling, Steven said, "I was just saying how I thought the PBR was pulling most of the best bull riders away from the PRCA, but I can see your mind really isn't on bull riding or rodeo right this minute."

Clay grinned sheepishly. "It's hard to stay focused when you can look at someone who looks that good on a horse," he answered. "But to answer your question, I think there's a chance for bull riders to compete in both. I like the idea that the PBR is offering bull riders a chance to earn more money and I don't blame any man for pursuing the large purses. If you're going to ride bulls, you might as well go for the most prize money you can get."

"That's a good point. I just hate to see the PRCA lose all its good riders, that's all."

"I don't think it will," Clay responded. "It'll lose some, but I think there's plenty that'll do both of them. As a matter of fact, I might try the PBR next year, but I'll still make PRCA shows so I can ride broncs. Now, if they ever start a professional bronc-riding association, I might change my mind."

The team roping was over and the pickup was in the arena unloading the fifty-five-gallon drums that signaled the barrel racing. Clay left the group and walked to the opposite end of the arena. Tamara rode up to stand beside him.

"Got kind of a raw deal in the saddle broncs, didn't you?" she asked.

"The judges must have gone to sleep," Clay replied. "But it's only one ride — I'll make it up. Now it's time for you to strut your stuff. Is Charger ready?"

Tamara patted the horse's neck. "He's ready, all right! All I've got to do is get him around the barrels without hitting one."

Four other women were ahead of Tamara. Cathy Gilbreath turned in a time of sixteen point seven, followed by Toni Witherspoon with a time of seventeen point one. Gail Fisher ran a sixteen point five, and Linda Culbertson ran sixteen point nine. Tamara worked Charger into the alleyway after Gail's run and waited for the arena director to give her the go-ahead signal. When she touched her spurs to Charger's side, the big horse was at full speed in two leaps, heading for the first barrel. Queuing him at the precise moment, Tamara guided him around the barrel, then gave him his head to run all out to the second one. Checking and turning, horse and rider rounded the second barrel and raced to the third. Charger slowed only slightly as he dug in and turned around the drum, leaving little room between Tamara's leg and the steel rim. After he cleared the barrel, he stretched out and ran for all he was worth, crossing the electronic timer to stop the clock at sixteen point one seconds.

Clay let out the breath he'd been holding and whistled loudly as Tamara passed by. He jumped down from the fence and waited for her to bring Charger under control before walking over to her. "They're all still standing!" he said, pointing to the barrels.

"Just the way I like 'em," she smiled.

"Heck of a ride, Tamara! I'm going to get my gear and get ready for the bull riding. I'll see you afterward."

"Don't kick any more chute gates."

"I'll do my best not to," he said, grinning at her.

If Clay could have picked the bull he was going to ride, it would have been the one he'd drawn for that night's performance. Firestorm was a huge Charolais that had been ridden successfully only eight times in the last two years. Many of the cowboys dreaded drawing the rangy bull, but Clay relished the challenge and knew that if he successfully covered him, he would take first place. His only concern was what happened after the ride. Firestorm was notorious for charging unseated cowboys and bullfighters.

Watching the bull enter the chute, Clay was awed by the size of the animal, but what amazed him even more was the agility he exhibited. In another competition, Clay had seen him duck left, then veer right while twisting his body in midair. The rider had lasted only two seconds before being catapulted into the air.

Clay dropped his rope down beside Firestorm, and Billy, using a long wire hook, snagged the tail and pulled it under the bull's belly. Reaching between the chute slats, he handed the rope up to Clay, who ran it through the loop, then positioned it with the handle in the middle of Firestorm's back. Clay was the second rider out. The barrels had been cleared and the bullfighters were in place by the time Clay had his rope set. The first rider, George Bonet, was on Lambchop, a gray Brahma bull with banana

192

horns. It was evident from the beginning that George was overmatched. Lambchop, contrary to his docile name, was anything but tame. Coming out of the chute in a leaping buck, the gray bull corkscrewed and landed parallel to the chutes, leaving poor George hanging off of the side. One more high leap and George was kissing the arena dirt.

By the time Lambchop was herded out of the arena, Clay was on Firestorm's back and Billy was pulling his rope tight. With his wraps made, Clay moved up on his rope and nodded for the gate.

Firestorm was famous for his exit from the chute. Rearing up on his hind legs, he would push off, then arch straight down, trying to force the cowboy forward and over. The bull's timing was impeccable, his back feet hitting the ground while the rider was leaning forward. In one swift move, the bull would lunge upward and throw his head back, catching the poor cowboy full in the face. If the cowboy was lucky, he was merely thrown off the bull's back, but more times than not he was either knocked unconscious or wished he had been.

Clay, prepared for Firestorm's devilish move, forced his body back when the bull started down. When the yellow bull made his second leap, Clay was back away from the massive head as it swung upward at him. With spurs dug into the bull's side, Clay hung tight as Firestorm hit the ground and leaped into the air with a twisting jump, all the time swinging his head backward in an intimidating gesture. When the bull's feet hit the ground, he pivoted on his back hooves, twisting right and dipping his right shoulder in an attempt to draw Clay into the well. Clay barely saw the move coming in time, but managed to shift his weight to the left and throw his free arm back for balance. Even so, he was unprepared when Firestorm swung back to the left with lightning speed. Fortunately the move was into Clay's hand, and he was able to hold himself on the bull's back by sheer strength. Another quick move to the left shifted Clay off center, and he felt himself sliding off of his rope. A swift buck to the right and Clay was sliding down the bull's side. The sound of the eight-second whistle had never been sweeter as Clay opened his hand and prayed for the rope to release.

The bullfighters moved in rapidly to draw the bull's attention away from Clay, whose leg had slipped over Firestorm's back.

Firestorm had Clay right where he wanted him. Swinging his large head, he connected solidly with Clay's back. One of the bullfighters jumped on the bull's back and managed to grab the tail of the rope and jerk hard, freeing Clay's hand. Meanwhile the other bullfighter moved in and distracted Firestorm by slapping him in the face. With his hand free and Firestorm moving away from him, Clay turned and ran for the arena fence, only a few yards away.

You could feel the tension drain from the crowd as Clay climbed to safety. Bruised, but otherwise unharmed, Clay came down off the fence only after Firestorm exited the arena.

Tamara finally felt her heartbeat begin to slow, but she was still having problems catching her breath, which she had held throughout the entire ride, until Clay was walking safely back to the chutes. Now she listened as the announcer called out the judges' combined score and let out a Texas yell that mingled with the shouts of approval from the crowd. Clay's score for the spectacular ride was an almost unheard-of ninety-five. The crowd continued to applaud and shout for Clay until he finally walked into the arena and bowed before the audience.

"You get lucky riding one bull and you think you're something, don't you?" Billy asked with a wide smile as Clay joined him on the platform behind the chutes.

"Lucky is right! The only reason I stayed on that rascal is because I was scared to death of falling off. He wanted to do some major damage to my body."

Billy guffawed. "Whatever the reason, you sure put on one whale of a bull ride. I doubt anyone will top that score — they'll be writing about that ride for a long time to come. You'll probably be interviewed on TNN and ESPN and maybe even get an endorsement from some boot or blue jean company."

"All for one bull ride, huh?" Clay asked.

"Sure! And I'll be your agent. I'll handle all your publicity for only fifty percent."

"What a deal!" Clay responded. "When the companies start calling, you'll be the first one I contact. But for now I'd settle for a large steak and a tall glass of iced tea."

"Now you're talking. Let's go!"

"We'll get loaded up and meet you and Gary at the gate," Clay said, jumping down from the platform and grabbing his gear bag.

Tamara was waiting for Clay by the trailer. When she saw him coming, she closed Charger's trailer gate, then turned to him. "I don't think I've ever seen a better bull ride in my life, or been so scared while I was watching one," she said, putting her hand on his arm.

Clay appreciated her heartfelt words and refrained from making light of the comment. "I understand how you feel. I've never been on a bull like that in my life, and I've never felt that kind of power. I don't know how I managed to make it through that first jump of his. I think the only way I stayed on after that was that I was so scared I couldn't think. I just rode."

"I hope you don't ever draw one like that again," Tamara said with emphasis.

"At least not this week," Clay said, smiling.

Tamara started to give a sharp reply but stopped herself when she saw his smile. "If there's another one this week, I'm going to find myself a calf roper to get hitched to. My heart couldn't handle another of those rides."

Clay laughed and led her to the pickup. "Let's go get something to eat. I'm so hungry my belly thinks my throat's been cut."

Chapter Fifteen

Ginger Loring sat on the leather sofa in her apartment, staring angrily at Jay Crawford. "What do you mean he's gone to rodeos in Del Rio and Brownwood? I thought he had to stay here and take care of the ranch while Jack Lomas was in the hospital. How could he just take off and leave like that?"

"That's what he does, my dear. He makes a very tidy sum of money riding wild bulls and bucking horses."

That got Ginger's attention. "When you say a tidy sum, exactly how much do you mean?"

Jay smiled slyly, knowing he had her full attention and delighting in divulging such information. "I have it on good authority that your cowboy has already earned over eighty thousand this year and should easily top the hundred-thousand mark by the time they go to the big rodeo in Las Vegas."

Ginger's eyes widened in surprise. "You mean he makes that much money riding those disgusting animals?"

Smirking, Jay answered, "That's what I've been told. I did a little checking, since I've never been interested in rodeo and didn't have the slightest idea how much rodeo cowboys make. There's quite a few who top the hundred-thousand-dollar mark every year, and there's one Texas cowboy, Ty Murray, who made over two hundred thousand last year. And that doesn't include endorsements."

"Where did you hear that? In the lounge at the Roswell Inn?" she asked, her distaste obvious.

"No, though I have gotten some good information from the local clientele of that establishment. I happen to have uncovered this particular bit of information at the public library." He grinned at the shocked look on her face. "Don't look so surprised. Through the years, I've been able to glean much of my information from local libraries. If businesses knew how much they could learn about their competition from the resources available there, they'd pay someone to do nothing but stay in libraries, researching other companies. As a matter of fact, that could be a good business if I ever think about going legit. I could hire out to companies to provide them reports on all their competitors."

Ginger screwed up her face. She just couldn't see Jay spending time in a library poring over reference books and compiling information. She was about to voice that opinion when he continued.

"Nah, I couldn't do that. It would drive me crazy — but it may be an angle we could use in the future."

Ginger smiled to herself, then said, "Back to Clay Tory. When does he return?"

"I didn't get an exact time, but the general

consensus was that he'd be back Sunday afternoon."

"Hmmm . . . that means he'll probably be going to the hospital as soon as he gets home. Why don't you stake it out, let me know when he arrives, and I'll be there when he leaves."

"And what reason will you give for being there?"

"I was in a wreck, remember? I'll be there to see a doctor about my sore neck, or something like that. Why don't you do a little more research and find me the name of a doctor who specializes in those kinds of things? Just make sure he's not one our cowboy has been to in the past," she cautioned.

"Good thinking. That's a tall order, though. I don't know how I'll go about it."

Ginger gave him a knowing look. "You'll find a way. You always do."

"You're getting to know me too well," Jay replied. "That scares me."

Ginger arose from the sofa and walked slowly toward him until she was standing directly in front of him. She couldn't miss the hungry look in his eyes. Sinking slowly into his lap, she wrapped her arms around his neck. "Why does that scare you? Are you afraid I might be getting too close to you? That I might be reading your thoughts and I might know what you're going to do before you do it?"

Searching her face, Jay felt for a moment that she actually *could* read his mind. Mentally shaking off that thought, he responded with a sly smile, "Nope, I'm just afraid you might get smarter than me and realize you don't need me."

Ginger was disappointed with his answer — not that she believed it. She had thought for a moment that she had finally found a crack in his cool facade, and she would have liked nothing better than to have him admit it. Nibbling on his earlobe, she whispered, "I'm already smarter than you, but don't let that bother you. I'm not as devious. I still need you to come up with the plans."

Jay responded with a chuckle and buried his head in the nape of her neck.

Clay outscored Billy Ettinger in the saddle bronc riding in Brownwood and delighted in rubbing it in all night. He placed fourth in bareback riding, but bucked off High Lonesome in bull riding. Tamara placed second in barrel racing. She would have placed first, but Charger slipped turning the second barrel. Clay spent Saturday night in San Angelo at the Allen residence. He tried to convince Tamara he should go on to Roswell after dropping her off, telling her he needed to get back as soon as possible to check on the ranch, but she wouldn't hear of it.

"You wouldn't be doing anybody any good if you fell asleep and killed yourself. I promise I'll wake you up early enough so you can get home by noon."

After putting up a weak argument, Clay finally

relented. He readily admitted to himself that he wasn't eager to leave Tamara's company, and he was too tired to drive the rest of the way home. He had called the ranch three times in the last two days. Julie had answered each time and assured him that things were going well. Terry and the boys had everything under control, and Jack was doing better each day.

Clay and Tamara arrived at the Allens' a little after one in the morning. After stabling Charger, they raided the refrigerator, waking Tamara's mother in the process. While she made grilled cheese sandwiches and french fries for them, they filled her in on all the latest news, including Jack's condition. Clay finally climbed into bed at two-thirty, and Tamara promised to wake him at seven.

Clay was dreaming he was standing at the edge of a clear mountain stream watching the water ripple over the smooth stones, when suddenly he was seized by an overwhelming feeling of being drowned. Spitting and sputtering, he came fully awake. Gasping for air, he heard giggling coming from above him. When he opened his eyes he spied Tamara standing over him, holding an empty glass. It took him a moment to realize that the water on his face and the bedsheets had come from the glass.

"I tried three times to wake you up, but you just kept rolling over and telling me to go away. This was the only thing I could think of to get the job done. I didn't want to break my promise."

"Very effective," he said, grabbing her and pulling her down to him. She was willing until she realized he was using her and her housecoat to mop the water off his face. She struggled to break away, but he pulled her onto the bed and rolled her in the soaked sheets. Her gales of laughter caught Cliff Allen's attention as he passed the open door.

"Sounds like you two still have too much energy," he commented. "How about repairing those fences in the holding pasture this morning?"

"Uh," Clay stuttered, looking guiltily at Tamara's father. "Sorry, sir, but I've got to get home."

Both Tamara and her father broke into laughter as Clay blushed. Cliff smiled and winked at his daughter before continuing down the hall.

Still blushing, Clay pulled the covers over his head and groaned. "I can't believe your dad caught us wrestling on the bed like that. He must think I'm some sort of pervert or something, accosting his daughter in his own house."

Tamara laughed hysterically. "We were just wrestling. He didn't think anything of the kind. If he had thought you were a pervert, he would have had the same shotgun with him that he's used on the other men who tried to accost me," she said, still giggling.

By the time Clay showered, dressed, and arrived in the kitchen, Tamara's mother had his breakfast ready, and, to his relief, Mr. Allen was nowhere in sight. Mrs. Allen plied him with sausage, eggs, homemade biscuits, and gravy. He ate until he couldn't eat another bite, and when she tried to feed him more, he shook his head and held up his hands. "I can't eat any more. If I ate like this every day, I'd never be able to haul myself on top of a bronc or a bull."

"I love cooking for someone with a hearty appetite," Mrs. Allen said. "By the way, I've got a package for you to take to Jack."

"If it's some of your cooking, it might not make it to him."

"No, it's not food. I have an old picture of him, Cliff, and Will Hightower that was taken at the Pendleton rodeo. I had it framed and thought he might like to have it."

"I'm sure he'll love it. He sure did appreciate the card you sent him."

"I'm glad to hear he's doing so well. You be sure to tell him that when he gets to feeling better, we expect him to come by for a visit."

Clay promised to bring Jack himself as soon as he was well enough to travel.

Though he left the Allens' later than he'd intended to, Clay tried to hold his speed down. He thought that being well rested and fed made up for the loss of time. When he arrived at the ranch, a little after noon, he found Terry and Julie relaxing in their home.

"Everything's going fine," Terry responded to Clay's questions. "The cattle have plenty of water and hay. I've checked on them every day and haven't found any weak ones. I did doctor a few calves that had pinkeye and brought in one bull that has a hoof problem."

"Have you been in to see Jack?" Clay asked.

"We went yesterday," Julie said. "He's talking more, but he's still using his typewriter. The nurse said they were going to remove it from his room soon so he won't be able to rely on it to communicate. Then he'll have to talk more."

"That makes sense," Clay reflected. "I think I'll run in and see him this afternoon and tell him how I did."

"He'll be happy to see you, but we already told him about Del Rio. He asked, and since you'd told us, we thought it would be good for him to know," Julie said.

"That's okay. I'll fill him in on Brownwood."

"There's some leftover chicken-fried steak in the refrigerator if you want something to eat," Julie offered.

"I'm still full from breakfast. I swear, Tamara's mother is trying to fatten me up."

"You could use some fattening up. You've lost weight in the last few weeks," Julie said, looking him up and down.

"Hmm, maybe that's why my pants are a little baggy," Clay said, grabbing his pants legs and holding them out. "I thought you were stretching them in the wash. I guess I'll have to start eating second helpings, but right now I'm going to head into town and see Jack. I'll eat those leftovers when I get back."

"Tell Jack hello for us," Terry said.

It was still early afternoon when Clay pulled into the parking lot of the hospital. He didn't notice the man sitting in the red Corvette. If he'd turned and looked back before he entered the door, he would have seen the man pick up his cell phone and dial a number, all the while keeping his eyes glued to Clay.

Clay was amazed at the number of new flower arrangements and cards that Jack had received since he'd last been in his room.

"I didn't realize you had that many friends," Clay said jokingly as he read the cards.

Jack smiled, his grin more evenly spread across his face than it had been since the stroke. "How was the rodeo?" he asked slowly.

Clay told him how he and Tamara had performed in both Del Rio and Brownwood, giving him every detail and passing on all the kind wishes from the other cowboys. "Everybody misses you and says to hurry up and get well," Clay concluded.

"I miss them, too!" Jack said.

Clay was about to comment when the door opened and a man in a white coat walked in. Hesitating briefly at the sight of Clay he held out his hand. "Hello, I'm Doctor Miles. I'm in charge of Mr. Lomas's rehab."

"I'm Clay Tory," Clay responded, immediately liking the short, rotund man with the firm handshake and sparkling eyes.

"I came to the hospital this afternoon to finish a bit of paperwork and thought I'd stop by and see Jack. I didn't know he had company. I didn't mean to disturb you."

"Not at all," Clay said. "I'm glad you came by. I've been wanting to talk to you, but I've been so busy I haven't had a chance to come in when you were here."

"I understand. Mrs. James told me you were busy at the ranch, what with the drought and all. She and Jack tell me you also compete in rodeos."

Clay nodded. "Yes, sir, I do. I had to miss a few, but I'm back now."

"Well, you'll be pleased to know that Jack is progressing at a spectacular rate. I've seen very few patients advance as fast as he has," he smiled and patted Jack on the shoulder.

"He said something the other day about going home in two weeks. Is that correct?" Clay asked.

"Yes, I told him if he keeps improving at the rate he has been going, it's very possible that he can go home week after next. Of course, he'll have to come in three times a week for rehab, but I've found that patients mend a lot faster if they're able to spend more time in their home environment."

"That's the best news I've had in a long time," Clay responded with joy.

"I have a feeling you'll have your hands full once he gets home," the doctor said, grinning at Clay. "But he's going to have to take it easy and not push himself too hard. We don't want him to overdo it and have another stroke."

"You don't know our cook and housekeeper," Clay said. "He won't be able to sneeze without her knowing it."

Both Clay and the doctor looked at Jack and laughed when they saw him frown and nod his head vigorously.

The doctor chatted with Clay a little longer before telling Jack that he would see him in the morning. A few minutes later, Clay was about to leave as well, when he remembered the present Tamara's mother had sent to Jack. He'd set it aside when he came in. Handing it now to Jack, he said, "Mrs. Allen sent this to you. She thought you might like to have it."

Jack fumbled with the wrapping paper and held the picture before him. A wide smile lit up his face as he stared at the picture. "Pendleton Rodeo," he said, and Clay could see the memories come flooding back to light up his eyes.

"I want to hear all about it when you get home," Clay said. "I'll see you tomorrow." He bent down and kissed Jack on the top of the head. "Don't give the nurses too hard a time."

Walking past the nurses' station and down the hall, Clay pushed open the large glass door and turned toward his pickup. Lost in his thoughts, he didn't see Ginger Loring approaching him until she spoke.

"Hey, cowboy, did you get your fence fixed?"

Clay, stunned by her question, was taken

aback by her sudden appearance, and his pulse raced at the sight of her. She was wearing a thin pullover tucked into a pair of snug-fitting black jeans that accentuated her figure to the utmost. "Uh, yeah, it didn't take too long. How's your car?"

"I'm still driving a rental. They haven't finished hammering out all the dents yet, but they assured me it'll be as good as new when they're through. I'm still skeptical."

"And how are you doing?" Clay asked. "Did it take long to work out the soreness?"

Ginger giggled at the thought. "I was so sore for three days that it hurt to brush my teeth."

Clay laughed easily. "What brings you up to the hospital on a Sunday afternoon?"

"I came in the other day to see Doctor Linman for a checkup. I was having a little trouble with my neck after the accident, and I wanted to make sure it was nothing serious. I left my Day-Timer here and was just coming to pick it up. Are you here visiting your friend Jack?"

"Yeah, I just got back into town from a rodeo and came for a visit."

"How did you do at the rodeo?" she asked with feigned interest.

"I did all right. I won't know for sure until I see the final results later in the week."

"Do rodeo cowboys make much money doing what you do?"

"Some do. It depends. I've done okay the last couple of years," Clay said modestly.

"Do you have an investment portfolio for your winnings?" she asked innocently.

Clay was caught off guard by her question. "Uh, not really. I've got most of it in a savings account at the bank and the rest in an interest-bearing checking account."

Ginger frowned and clucked her tongue, then smiled sweetly. "You really ought to invest your money in something that will earn you more interest. Why don't you come by my office tomorrow and I'll show you some ways your money can work for you?"

Clay had meant to say he would be too busy but he found himself asking, "What time tomorrow?"

"How about eleven o'clock? We can look over a few options and see what might be best."

"Eleven sounds fine," Clay responded. "I'll see you then!"

Ginger giggled again. "Do you know where my office is?"

"Uh, come to think of it, I don't have the slightest idea," Clay replied with a self-conscious grin.

She took a card from the small handbag she was carrying and handed it to him. "The address is right there. My phone number is there too, so if you get lost, call me."

Clay laughed and said, "I think I can find it. I'll see you tomorrow at eleven."

"Tomorrow at eleven!" she confirmed and continued toward the hospital entrance. He watched her walk away, admiring the view. Jay Crawford smiled as he watched Clay from his vantage point in the parking lot. "She's got him hooked!" he said to himself.

Clay arrived in town at nine-thirty the next morning. He had told Julie and Terry that he needed to pay some bills and pick up more mineral blocks for the stock, both of which were true, but both of which could have waited. He had promised Julie he'd be home in time for lunch, since she was cooking his favorite meal — fried chicken. By ten-thirty he had been to the feed store, picked up the mineral blocks, paid the electric bill, and made a deposit at the bank. He drove down Main Street to kill time, waving at several acquaintances and checking his watch every two minutes. Finally he pulled into the parking lot of the one-story office building at the address on the card Ginger had given him. He considered waiting a few moments before going in, but looking at the dark-tinted windows of the building, he knew people would be able to see him and that was an even more uncomfortable feeling. He entered at the front door and was met by a perky receptionist who smiled and asked how she could help him.

"I have a meeting with Ginger Loring. My name is Clay Tory."

"If you'll have a seat, Mr. Tory, I'll tell Miss Loring you're here."

Clay waited fifteen minutes before Ginger appeared. It was just long enough to make him think she was busy, but not long enough for him to become bored.

"Hi!" she greeted him, breezing into the office. She had taken great pains in selecting her attire that morning. She wore a white silk blouse cut low enough to be enticing without being vulgar. Her skirt was forest green, fitting tight about her hips and ending only three inches above her knees. She knew she'd chosen well by the way Clay's eyes traveled her full length as she stood before him.

"Hello," he said. "I'm a little early. I had some errands to do this morning, and I got through sooner than I thought I would."

"That's fine," she said, taking him by the arm and leading him into her office, pleased that he had shown up early. That proved he was eager to see her again. "I was just finishing up some paperwork. I'm sorry I kept you waiting."

He waved her apology away as she guided him to a chair. He expected her to take the high-backed chair behind the desk, but instead she pulled the empty chair beside him around and sat facing him, crossing her legs as she leaned forward and rested one elbow casually on her knee.

"Let's talk about types of investments first. Then we'll talk about your financial goals, and after we've determined those, I'll put together several investment plans and we'll meet again to discuss which ones suit you the best."

"Sounds good to me," Clay said, letting his eyes linger on her exposed legs.

Chapter Sixteen

The meeting lasted for more than an hour. Clay answered her questions honestly, trying to keep his eyes from straying to her neckline or her creamy legs while she took notes on the pad perched on her knee. Several times during the meeting, Ginger slowly uncrossed and crossed her legs, watching Clay out of the corner of her eye to measure his reaction. She wasn't disappointed.

After she wrote down his response to her last question, she closed the cover on the pad and said, "I think that will give me enough to work with." She glanced at her watch and exclaimed, "My goodness, I didn't realize it was so late! Let me buy you lunch?"

Clay hesitated, knowing he was late and would be in trouble with Julie. "I would love to, but Julie's already cooked lunch and she's probably waiting for me by now."

"Can't you call her and tell her you can't make it? I'd love to take you to lunch. It's the least I can do after treating you the way I did the day of the accident."

"Shoot, I think you acted pretty civilized under the circumstances."

"I acted like a snob. I should have called and apologized, but I was too embarrassed."

"There was no need for you to apologize," Clay said firmly. "I'm just glad there was no permanent damage, from either the wreck or the horseback ride."

Ginger laughed, blushing at the thought. "I was beginning to wonder for a couple of days there. I wasn't sure I'd ever be able to sit in a hard chair again."

It was Clay's turn to laugh. "I guess I'd better be going," he said. "Thanks for the lunch invitation. I'll take a rain check if that's all right."

Ginger was disappointed, but she knew Clay had made up his mind. By persisting further she could overplay her hand. "I'm sorry you can't stay. We'll need to get together later this week to look over investment plans. How does Thursday afternoon sound?"

Clay grimaced. "Can't do it on Thursday. I'm leaving early that morning for Flagstaff, Arizona. I've got a rodeo there Friday and one in Grand Junction, Colorado, on Saturday. I won't be back until late Sunday."

Ginger couldn't hide her disappointment this time. For just an instant Clay thought he saw anger flare in her brown eyes, but it vanished as quickly as it had appeared. She smiled quickly, hiding her thoughts, and said, "I forget about your rodeos, but that's where you make your money, isn't it?"

"Yep, and I imagine you find it hard to believe, but it's the greatest way to make a living there is."

"I'll take your word for it," she said, making a face.

"How about we get together next week and see what you've put together?"

"That'll be fine," she responded. She didn't really want to wait that long, but she didn't know what else to do without making him suspicious. "Why don't we make it a week from today — next Monday?"

"It's a date," Clay said. "I'll even let you buy me that lunch."

"You're on, cowboy," she said.

Though Clay could tell Julie was upset at his arriving home late for lunch, she said nothing. The pots and pans banging on the stove top and the lack of conversation were a dead giveaway. Clay knew better than to tell her he'd been meeting with Ginger Loring, though by her attitude he suspected that she somehow knew. He'd merely told her that he'd been meeting about the finances of the ranch and let her assume it had been at the bank.

Clay ate half his meal before cautiously attempting conversation. "Is Terry checking on the cattle in the holding trap?"

"Uh-huh," was the only response he got.

"Is he going to the north pasture after that?"

"Uh-huh."

"Are you going to stay mad at me all day?"

"Uh-huh."

Clay finished the rest of his lunch in silence while Julie cleaned up the kitchen. Carrying his plate to the sink, he rinsed it off, then picked up his hat and started out. At the door he turned back and said, "I promise I'll be home in time for supper. I'm going back into town to see Jack tonight."

Julie just turned her back to him and put another pan in the sink.

Clay met up with Terry in the pasture where they kept the sick cattle. After determining how many could be moved to the pastures with the other cows, they rode to the north pasture to check the herd there. The tanker truck was three-quarters empty and due to be filled the next day. Most of the cattle were lying under any shade they could find, chewing their cuds.

"That's a pretty sight," Terry said. "Before, they were spending all their time walking from water tank to water tank, trying to get enough to drink. Or wandering the range trying to find something to eat. I've got to hand it to you. You've really made a difference in the way these cattle look."

"*We've* made a difference!" Clay said. "This couldn't have been done without your and Julie's help. I might have come up with the idea, but we all made it work."

"I had my doubts there for a while," Terry confessed. "And I wasn't real sure I was going to survive the ordeal! But we got it done, and the proof of success is right here."

Lost in thoughts of his own, Clay barely heard Terry's last words. He turned his horse and started toward the ranch. He waited for Terry to fall in beside him, then asked, "You've been married to Julie for five years now. Do you ever look at other women?"

Stunned, Terry looked suspiciously at Clay, wondering what was behind the question. He started to speak, then hesitated, unsure of how to answer. Finally, after some reflection, he said, "If you mean is that all I do, is look, the answer is of course. I don't know many men that don't look at a good-lookin' woman from time to time. It's kind of like lookin' at a fine horse. I can admire it, but I ain't gonna steal it. But, tell me, why are you askin'?"

Clay cleared his throat. "If I tell you, you got to promise me not to say a word to Julie."

"Whoa! Do you know how hard it is to keep a secret from that woman?"

"Yeah, I know, but this time you got to."

Terry shook his head in despair. "I'll do the best I can. What's this about, anyway?"

"You remember Ginger Loring, the girl that wrecked her car?"

"Sure," Terry said. "Who wouldn't remember someone like her?"

"That's what I mean," Clay replied. "I ran into her again yesterday, when I went to visit Jack. She was at the hospital. She's in investments, and we got to talking about how I was investing my money, and before I knew it, I had a meeting with her today to discuss better ways to invest my winnings."

"And?" Terry asked.

"And I couldn't take my eyes off of her the whole time. I tried, but it was impossible. I even tried to think of other things to distract myself, but it didn't work."

"What kind of things?" Terry asked.

"You know Hanna Burnbaugh?"

"You mean Two-Ton Hanna that works down at the Dairy Palace?"

"That's the one," Clay said.

"Yeah, I know her."

"Well, I tried to imagine her in a two-piece bathing suit lying beside a swimming pool."

"Oh, that's disgusting," Terry said, shuddering. "And what happened?"

"Every time I pictured Hanna, she turned into Ginger."

"Whew!" Terry breathed. "For a minute I was afraid you were going to go somewhere my mind couldn't handle."

Clay chuckled. "I know what you mean. But back to what I was talking about, I almost feel like I'm cheating on Tamara every time I look at Ginger. But of course, I don't have the same feelings for her as I do for Tamara."

"What kind of feelings do you have for Ginger?" Terry asked with a sly smile.

"I don't really know. It's like drawing a bull that's never been rode. It scares the daylights out of you, but you want to go ahead and try it anyway."

"Wow!" Terry exclaimed. "You really do have

a problem. If I was you I'd stay as far away from that girl as I could."

"That's the rub. I don't want to stay away. I want to see her again. I like the feeling of excitement I get when I'm around her. I felt it the first day I met her."

"I'll ask you one question," Terry said after careful thought. "Would you give up Tamara for her?"

"No!" Clay replied adamantly, then looked wide-eyed at his friend.

Terry nodded. "You've either got to forget this girl or chance losing Tamara. And I think you know which one best suits you and your future."

Clay didn't respond to this last remark. How could he argue with what he knew to be true? Riding in silence, he thought about Terry's words and wished now that he hadn't ever met with Ginger.

"I've got one more meeting with her next Monday," Clay said in a voice so low that Terry almost didn't hear him.

"You don't have to go," Terry replied bluntly.

"I know, but I am."

Terry shook his head and clucked his tongue but said no more.

While Clay was at the hospital that evening visiting Jack, Ginger was in her apartment having a lengthy discussion with Jay Crawford.

She had told him about her meeting with Clay

and how she had failed to entice him to lunch. "I think our cowboy is going to be harder to manipulate than you thought," she said. "And unless we can find a way to keep him in town for a while, we may not be able to pull this off. He travels to a rodeo every week."

Jay had to admit he was surprised that Ginger's charms hadn't worked immediately on Clay, but then he had always had a tendency to judge other men by his own reactions. "I may have met someone the other day that can help us find a way to keep Clay Tory in town."

Ginger raised an eyebrow, but Jay waved away her question. "You do have another meeting with him?" he asked.

"Yes, but I don't think it's going to net the results we're after. If we're going to get our hands on that land, we'll have to trick him. I've been thinking about how to do that and I might have an answer."

"Oh?" Jay questioned, cocking an eyebrow. Usually he was the one that came up with the plan and Ginger offered variations. "Let's hear what you've got."

"I'm going to put together a financial plan that he can't refuse," she stated simply.

"That's it?" Jay asked. "What's so great about that?"

"What's so great about that, Mr. Crawford, is that he'll have to sign several pages. I'll convince him it's a standard contract and there's no need to read every page. I'm sure you can come up with a one- or two-page contract that will give us the rights to that land. I'll slip that in with the financial contract and he'll sign all the pages. Simple but effective."

Jay smiled thinly. "I am impressed. That's a great plan." He stood up and paced the floor, his mind churning as he considered all the angles. "Coming up with a one- or two-page contract that's binding is going to be the hard part. I'll have to get in touch with Dresden Ellis, the attorney we used in Boston, and see if he can draw one up that'll be binding in Texas. I've got all the survey tracts of the Lazy L from the courthouse. Maybe that'll be enough. When's your next meeting with your friend?"

"Next Monday," Ginger said.

"Do you think he'll sign the contracts then?"

"That's what I'm shooting for," she responded.

"I'll have to work fast," Jay said, more to himself than to her. "I'll go call Dresden right now." He kissed her quickly and said, "Good job, Gin. You keep this up and I'll let you do all the planning."

Ginger frowned as he hurried into the bedroom to use the phone. She didn't know why but Jay's compliment didn't please her.

Things at the ranch had been going along smoothly. The boys were still helping out with the feeding. Jerry and Larry had their routine down, alternating days hauling water to the cattle. Terry's cousin Shawn had shown his natural leadership and was in charge of feeding the cattle each day. Clay decided things were running well and suggested that Terry and Julie take a few days off as a vacation. "You've earned it. I know Julie would really appreciate getting away for a few days," Clay was saying to Terry as they drove back to the house after checking the hay supplies, "and there may not be another chance if we don't get some rain soon."

"I don't know," Terry said hesitantly. "I wouldn't feel right about leaving the ranch unattended. You'll be gone until Sunday. That'll leave only the boys here to take care of things."

"And they'll do a great job. Look, Tamara and I are leaving in the morning. We'll be back late Sunday. Why don't you and Julie leave Friday or Saturday and plan on coming home the middle of the week?"

"Well," Terry began, "Julie's been saying she'd love to take a few days and go to El Paso. She's been wanting to go shopping in Juarez. There's a shop down there that sells beautiful Mexican blankets, and she wants some for the house."

Clay saw his opportunity and took advantage of it. "It's settled, then. You two go to El Paso and enjoy yourselves. Things will be fine here."

Since Clay and Tamara were going west to Flagstaff, she would meet him at the ranch on Wednesday afternoon. Julie was so excited about her coming that she spent the entire day cooking and cleaning. She kept the men chased out of the house and refused to let them walk on her clean floors. She even made them go into town for lunch, giving them a list of items to buy and bring back with them. And when Tamara did arrive, Julie kept her in the kitchen talking for hours before she allowed Clay to take her in to see Jack.

Clay and Tamara left Thursday morning for Flagstaff. Terry made sure the boys were all straight with the care of the cattle and the chores that needed to be done before he and Julie left for El Paso Friday afternoon.

Clay was doubly excited about this weekend. First, he and Tamara would be together doing what they both loved to do, and second, Dr. Miles had told Clay that he could probably take Jack home early next week. Clay had seen the restlessness in Jack's face and knew he was ready. His speech improved greatly with each passing day and he was now completing whole sentences with little or no stuttering, though he would have to pause and catch his breath occasionally. Julie had volunteered to drive Jack in to therapy three times a week if Terry and Clay could fend for themselves at lunchtime. They had both assured her that they would manage fine.

Clay had been driving at a leisurely pace throughout the morning, knowing they had plenty of time to reach Flagstaff before nightfall. He and Tamara had enjoyed the time to them-selves. They had been discussing their plans for the next couple of days when Clay brought up the subject of their future together. "You know, we've been engaged for several months now and I was wondering the other day if maybe we shouldn't set a wedding date?"

Stunned, Tamara stared at him wide-eyed. "You sure have made a change! You ran backward when you thought I was trying to corral you."

Clay smiled as he remembered the time he'd mentioned buying her a pre-engagement ring. "I just hadn't had time to think about it. Now that I've had time, I think we should make plans, that's all. Ginger was telling me the other day that planning is the key to a successful future."

Tamara eyed him coolly. "And who is Ginger?" she asked suspiciously.

Clay realized his error immediately and tried to brush past it quickly. "She's a lady that's looking into some financial investments for me."

"Uh-huh," Tamara said, not reassured at all. "Is this the same Ginger that had the accident at the ranch?"

"Julie told you about that, huh?" Clay asked, feeling like a mouse caught in the feed bin.

"She told me she wasn't too crazy about her. That she felt this Ginger was a little high and mighty and looked down her nose at us common folk."

"She's not like that. Julie just saw her at the wrong time. She'd just been in an accident and was shaken up. She's really a nice person and really knows a lot about investments. She's looking into some investment opportunities for me to help me earn more money. That's what got me to thinking about us. I want to make sure we have something to carry us through if hard times come."

"Are you sure investments are all you're interested in?" Tamara asked, watching him closely. "Julie tells me this Ginger is very beautiful."

Clay chuckled, trying to make light of her comment. "There's only one woman who's beautiful to me, and that's the one I got with me right now." He figured a little white lie wouldn't hurt.

Tamara scooted closer to him, reassured by his statement, but she wasn't going to let him off lightly. "You better not be telling me a story. Julie promised me she'd keep an eye on you. If I hear you're seeing too much of Ginger, I'll have Julie add a little strychnine to your food."

"I'm not too sure she doesn't already," Clay said with a smile. "For some reason I sure can get her riled without really trying."

"Hmm, maybe you don't try hard enough not to rile her," Tamara quipped.

Clay reflected on that for a moment, then nodded. "Could be."

Chapter Seventeen

Jay Crawford sat in the Red Cloud lounge in the Ramada Inn. He ordered another gin and tonic for himself and a beer for his guest. They had been chatting for the last half hour, mostly about Roswell and who really controlled the wealth and thus ran the city and county. Jay had met the young man several days before and, after learning his name, had struck up a casual friendship. It had occurred to him that this man might in some way be useful to him in his quest to acquire Jack Lomas's ranch, but it wasn't until Ginger mentioned the possible need to keep Clay Tory in town for a while that he thought of his new acquaintance and how he could be used.

"So, are you up for making a little extra money?" Jay asked.

The man gave him a hooded look. "Depends on what I have to do."

Jay laughed. "Don't worry, you won't have to kill anybody. I may need a little night work done. You know, like cutting a few fences and running some cattle off, tampering with a few water tanks. Nuisance stuff that would keep someone worried, but nothing violent. I don't want the sheriff's office looking too closely."

The wicked smile on the man's face answered Jay's question. When he asked, "Who's the target?" Jay knew he'd chosen right.

"An old rancher that you know well — Jack Lomas."

The smile vanished from the man's face, replaced by an evil sneer. Jay almost gasped as the man's eyes bored into him, but he retained his composure and asked, "Am I to assume, then, that you are willing to assist me?"

"You assume right. And if the time comes when you need to inflict some pain on either Jack or Clay, I'll be glad to see that it's taken care of."

Jay gave the man a guarded look. "I hope it doesn't come to that, but if it does, understand one thing — I call the shots. I say who, how bad, and when."

"I don't have a problem with that, as long as I'm paid for my trouble."

"You'll be paid," Jay said. "Leave me a number where I can get ahold of you. I'll be in touch soon."

Both Clay and Tamara fared well in Flagstaff. Clay was sitting second in bareback riding after making a great ride on DoubleTree, a coal-black horse with wild eyes. DoubleTree reared in the chute and fairly walked out on his back legs before pushing off into the air. Landing stiff-legged, then flexing at the knees and jumping forward, he cleared the ground by six feet and landed two lengths away. Each time DoubleTree hit the ground, Clay's head banged hard into the horse's backbone, jarring his neck and making lights explode behind his eyes. Clay's spurs sang with each jump, showing he was in control the entire ride. Only Grady Shuster's ride on a horse that had been ridden just twice during the season kept Clay from taking first place, but he felt confident his score would hold where it was.

He was the first rider out in saddle bronc riding and scored a seventy-eight, which held first place through all the other riders.

Tamara turned in a sixteen point three in barrel racing and was winning at the end of her event as well.

Crackers, a large Hereford bull, proved to be more of a match than Clay had bargained for. Crackers had made it to the national finals the last three years and had thrown many a good cowboy to get there. His normal bucking style was to come out of the chute and spin hard to the left. The tight, quick spins tended to move a rider off his bull rope and into the well — the area inside the spin — but once the rider came off his back the red-and-white bull merely stopped bucking and stood waiting for the gate to open and allow him access to the holding pens. Many a cowboy thanked his lucky stars for the docile beast. Clay had watched the first six riders buck out and knew he had to beat a score of seventy-three to take the lead. He also knew there were some top riders in the next evening's performance and that he would have to score in the low eighties to place. With that in mind, he was determined to give it everything he had.

The first jump out of the chute, Crackers went to his left as Clay had anticipated, but instead of going into a tight spin, he threw his head back to the right and followed with his body. Caught off guard, Clay almost lost his seat and managed to dig in only with his right spur to hold himself upright. But it wasn't to be. As Crackers spun quickly into Clay's hand, Clay could feel himself being pulled away from his bull rope and down into the well. Trying in vain to hold himself in position, Clay dug his right spur into the bull's side and gripped the rope harder, trying to lift up each time the bull's feet left the ground. It took Crackers only two quick spins to unseat his unwanted burden. As soon as Clay's feet touched the ground Crackers stopped dead in his tracks, allowing Clay to reach up and unwrap his hand from the handle of the bull rope amid the audience's laughter, which added insult to injury. Tamara couldn't help but tease him as they loaded Charger into the trailer and started for Grand Junction.

"It must have been terrifying to be strapped to that wild beast."

Clay grinned. He could feel the heat rise from his neck into his face as he turned red. "I can't help it if he just stops, but it sure is embarrassing."

Tamara cracked up. "At least you provided the comic relief for the evening. Maybe you and Crackers can work up an act to entertain the audiences."

"Very funny," Clay remarked dryly. "You better not plan on sleeping on the way to Grand Junction."

Tamara giggled again.

Terry's cousin Shawn was responsible for scheduling the feeding in each of the pastures as well as monitoring the water tanks. He checked daily to make sure there were no sick cattle that needed to be moved to the doctoring pasture or any calves with pinkeye that needed to be cared for immediately. Since Clay and Terry had entrusted him with the responsibility of looking after the ranch in their absence, he had taken the job seriously, handing out assignments to the other three boys on an even basis. Each of the others had accepted his leadership without question, and the four had worked well together. Saturday morning, Shawn had given himself the assignment of feeding the cattle in the north pasture, since it was the farthest from the house and took the longest to complete. Gilbert and Thomas were feeding the cattle in the west pasture and would be gone long before Shawn finished. His brother Timmy was home helping their father build pens on their spread. Shawn was driving the ranch pickup and had his horse loaded in the stock trailer behind, since after feeding he planned to ride the fences. There were two or three spots in need of repair, and he wanted to get to them before the cattle found them.

Before he could reach the large trailer that was filled with hay, the cattle heard the sound of the truck engine and came running, surrounding the truck and trailer. Shawn had to move slowly to keep from hitting any cattle as they reluctantly parted to let him pass.

Stopping a short distance from the hay trailer, Shawn unloaded the horse and un-hooked the trailer, then backed the truck into the small enclosure by the side door of the big storage trailer. The enclosure prevented the cattle from pulling the bales of hay off the back of the truck while it was being loaded. Once he had the hay off the truck, he closed the storage trailer's door and drove out of the pen. It took a few minutes to work his way through the herd of cattle that blocked his path. Past the cattle, he sped forward to get well ahead of them, hooked the two bungee cords to the steering wheel to hold the truck on a straight course, shifted into low gear, and stepped out. The truck rolled along at a slow pace and Shawn stepped up on the rear bumper and climbed to the top of the stacked bales of hay. The cattle quickly closed the gap between them, bawling their delight. The calves ran and bucked, butting each other playfully as their mothers chased after the sweet-smelling hay.

Shawn cut the two wires on each of the bales of hay and scattered the blocks along the ground as the pickup continued its slow forward progress. After he had thrown out all the hay, Shawn hurried back to the storage trailer for another load. It took three pickup loads to feed all the cattle. Then Shawn put on his chaps and spurs, stepped into the saddle, and rode along the line of cattle, counting each one. By the time he reached the end of the line, he knew several head were missing, so he rode back, counting again. By the time he reached the end, he had determined that close to two hundred head were missing. Letting his gaze sweep the pasture, he tried to figure out where they might be. Since he'd been feeding, he'd come up short only one other time, but just by six head and they'd been over a rise heading toward him when he found them. If two hundred were missing, that was a different story altogether. He decided to hit the fence line on the west side, which was closest to him, and ride it north. This was the weakest section of fence and the one that he had been planning to check today anyway. Kicking the horse into a long trot, he hit the fence and turned along it, glancing around occasionally in hopes of spotting the cattle coming toward him. He rode most of the west fence and found no breaks where cattle could have gotten through. He was almost to the northwest corner, which was the part of the pasture closest to the county road, when he saw the break. When he got down and inspected the ground, he could plainly see the tracks where the cattle had crossed. His first thought was that the cattle had broken through a weak spot in search of greener grass, but when he inspected the ends of the barbed wire, he saw that they were broken evenly. Each strand of barbed wire is actually two wires twisted together. When they break, one usually breaks off longer than the other. This fence consisted of five strands of barbed wire, and each one was the same length. Shawn knew they'd been cut.

Remounting, Shawn rode a wide semicircle around the gap in the fence. A short distance away he picked up the tracks of two horses, showing plainly in the dry, dusty ground. Someone had driven the cattle through the cut fence. He stopped back at the gap and considered his alternatives. He could go back to the ranch and call for help, or he could trail the cattle to see where they'd gone. This section of Jack's pasture bordered the Flying R ranch. Shawn had never been on this part of the ranch, but he knew the owner, Gregory Randolph, and he knew Randolph wasn't part of this. It was a tough decision for the seventeen-year-old to make, but the responsibility that went along with ranch work made a young man grow up fast. Taking his horse through the gap, he decided to trail the cattle and see where they were being taken.

Two hours later, Shawn was riding warily into what he believed to be a box canyon. The trail had been easy to follow over the dusty prairie. He had dropped over the rim a short time before and noticed that the walls of the canyon were getting steeper. Half a mile into the canyon, his horse's head came up suddenly, ears flicking forward, nostrils blowing. Patting the horse's neck, Shawn spoke softly to him and listened intently. The faint sound of bawling cattle came to him. He urged the horse forward and felt his stomach muscles tighten. Were the men who had stolen these cattle still with them? Had more men joined them? If they were there, what would he do? He had no weapon, and he felt sure they would. Sweat dripped from under his hatband and ran down his face, but he ignored it as his eyes roamed the walls of the canyon looking for any place that could hide a man. The sounds of the cattle grew stronger, and Shawn knew he was getting close. Thirty yards ahead, the canyon turned sharply to the right, blocking his view. Pulling his horse to a stop, he slowly dismounted and tied the animal to a scrub oak. He knew he was taking a chance by going ahead on foot. If there were men there and they spotted him, he might not make it back to the horse in time, but he wanted to get a peek at the situation before riding in.

Hugging the wall of the canyon, Shawn worked his way up to the point where the wall turned right and peered around the corner. He could see only partway up the canyon, but he could still distinctly hear the bawling cattle. Easing himself further around the corner, he kept his back to the rough rock and scanned everything in sight. He strained to hear the sound of voices, but couldn't hear anything over the din of the cattle. He eased forward even more and found himself looking straight at a makeshift pen that ran the entire width of the canyon. Beyond the fence he saw the two hundred cattle bunched tightly together in the small enclosure. The solid, steep walls of the box canyon made it a perfect holding place for cattle. But Shawn wondered why they were being held here. He knew it was a long way to any major road where the cattle could be loaded for transport, and any direction they were driven would take them too close to houses and increase the chance of being detected.

Shawn wondered if the men who had done this were holed up somewhere close by. He worked his way back to his horse, mounted, and headed down the canyon again. About a quarter of a mile back he'd seen a trail leading to the top. Before he did anything about the cattle, he wanted to make sure no one was around.

Topping out of the canyon, Shawn looked around the open prairie. He could see nothing that would raise suspicion, nor did he see a place that could hide anyone. As he rode the rim of the canyon, he half expected to see someone coming toward him at any moment. The horse beneath him felt his nervousness and responded in kind, flicking his ears forward and backward.

Shawn rode to the end of the canyon and looked down on the penned-up cattle below. Anger coursed through him as he saw now what he hadn't been able to see from below. At least twenty head of good cows were lying dead in the entrapment. The small confines forced the other cattle to stand on the swollen bodies. He saw one calf standing atop what he guessed was the poor animal's dead mama. His anger built to the point where he wished the men responsible for this cruelty would appear, so he could vent his rage immediately but it was apparent that they were nowhere close.

Shawn's first inclination was to pull down the fence holding the cattle, but after serious consideration, he realized the sheriff would have to be called out to inspect the scene. Getting his bearings, he decided it would be closer to ride on to Randolph's headquarters than to go back to Jack's house. Putting the horse in a long trot again, he headed for the Flying R.

Three hours later, Shawn was back at the canyon with Ben Aguilar and Dennis Holt, Randolph's foreman, and two of his hands. Ben and Dennis drove out in a four-wheel-drive pickup, while Shawn and the two ranch hands rode their horses. Since the horses could take a more direct route, they all arrived at about the same time. Upon seeing the water-starved animals in the pen, one of the Flying R ranch hands let out a string of expletives that left little doubt as to what he'd do if he ever got his hands on the men responsible for such an act of cruelty.

Ben Aguilar scowled as he looked down at the cattle. "Whoever did this did it for spite, not to steal."

"But who would hate Jack or Clay that much?" Shawn asked.

"That's the question, isn't it?" Ben replied.

After another half hour of searching for evidence, Ben finally gave the go-ahead to tear down the fence and release the cattle. Shawn and the two Flying R hands threw their ropes over the fence, dallied around their saddle horns and put spurs to their horses. The fence gave way with little resistance and opened a large gap. At first the cattle shied away from the opening, but they soon realized that it meant freedom and as one they charged through it and into the open canyon, leaving behind the twenty-odd carcasses and about fifteen other cattle that were too weak to run. Dennis volunteered to move the weak animals to water about a mile away while Shawn and the other two hands herded the rest of the cattle back to the Lazy L range. Ben promised to look at the broken fence where the cattle had been driven through and do everything he could to find out who was responsible for this, but Shawn knew that with so little to go on, there wasn't much chance of that happening.

It was after dark when Shawn drove up to the ranch house, tired, dusty and downhearted. He had thought about calling Clay on his cell phone, but he knew there was nothing Clay could do at this point, and there was no use worrying him.

Chapter Eighteen

On Saturday morning the Colorado sky was clear and cloudless, but by noon dark storm clouds blocked out the sun, and shortly thereafter they opened up to pour their contents on the residents and visitors of Grand Junction. Clay lay on the bed in his camper and listened to the almost musical rhythm of raindrops beating against the metal roof. "If only it was doing this in Roswell," he said out loud. He and Tamara had arrived in Grand Junction early that morning. Charger was stabled close to the arena, and Tamara was in room 354 at the Ramada Inn. Travel-worn, Clay had slept like a baby in the camper parked in the hotel lot. The first gentle drops of rain had awakened him from his peaceful slumber, and now, peering out the window, he watched the rain fall harder and harder. Tonight's performance would be a sloppy one. He hoped the rain would at least stop before the rodeo began. He saw Tamara walk out on the second-floor balcony and look toward the pickup, and he shook the curtains to let her know he saw her. She waved back and looked up at the sky. Clay lay down on the bed and rested, listening to the steady drum of the rainfall and wishing once again that it was falling on the drought-ridden prairie in New Mexico.

The rain slackened by three in the afternoon,

but the skies remained overcast and a light rain continued to fall. By rodeo time the rain was little more than a drizzle. Though every effort had been made to drain the water from the arena, large pools remained in several spots. The mud was ankle-deep and sucked at the feet of anyone who tried to walk through it. Tamara had resigned herself to the fact that she wouldn't be winning the barrel racing in Grand Junction. A time of sixteen point four from the previous night was winning.

"I'm not about to take a chance on Charger slipping in that mud and injuring himself. I'll take him slow and easy. It'll be good for him to lope through the barrels for a change." Though she put up a good front, Clay could tell she was disappointed at the turn of events. Her spirit, like his, longed for the chance to compete.

"I don't mind the barebacks or the saddle broncs in this kind of weather, but I sure do dread riding bulls. It's hard for the bullfighters to maneuver, and it makes running almost impossible."

"Maybe Triton will do like Crackers did," Tamara remarked with a slight smile.

Clay chuckled. "I've seen him buck before. He ain't nothin' like Crackers. He enjoys using those horns of his."

The rain kept many people away from the rodeo that night and the stands were only half filled, but the rodeo went on anyway.

Clay sat on the rail behind the chutes, wearing

his yellow rain slicker and plastic hat cover to ward off the rain. Plastic bags covered bareback riggings on horses in the chutes. Clay had his rigging in place on Tonto, a red-and-white paint horse in chute number three. Tonto was a good draw, but the rain and mud could affect the way he performed. The rain also added a degree of danger that was a worry in each of the contestants' minds. The chances of a horse or bull slipping and falling on a contestant were greatly increased, and things were also harder once a cowboy was on the ground.

Clay was lost in his thoughts when someone suddenly grabbed his arm and almost jerked him off his perch. He jumped and almost swore until he saw who it was. Billy Ettinger peeked out from under the brim of his hat and grinned broadly at Clay.

"Great day for ducks, isn't it?" Billy said, looking at the dark sky.

"Where you been?" Clay asked. "I thought I'd see you in Flagstaff."

"I was going to enter there, but I decided to go to Gillette, Wyoming, instead. They were offering a little more added money."

"How'd you do?"

"Bucked off a horse that I should have ridden. Got my spur hung in the cantle and blew a stirrup."

Clay grinned and said, "It seems like that's always the way it goes. You change your plans, thinkin' you're going to improve your situation, but things never work out."

"That's the truth. I was going to enter a rodeo in Montana instead of this one, but I changed my mind at the last moment, and look what happened. Who'd you draw in this event?"

Clay nodded toward the paint horse in the chute. "I got ol' Tonto there."

"Could have done worse. Who's winnin' it?"

"Joe Eustace with a seventy-nine."

Billy looked out over the arena and shook his head. "Going to be hard to beat that in this arena."

"I thought about just loading up and heading back to New Mexico, but I figure, what the heck, I might as well give it a try."

The first rider in the barebacks was ready to go. Billy and Clay moved up the chute to watch the ride.

Ray Watson was on Cloudy Day, a chestnut sorrel with four white stockings. Cloudy Day hit the arena with all four feet, splashing water and mud in all directions. Clay saw both judges turn away from the horse and rider to prevent being splattered. It was hard to judge a rider if you couldn't see him, but it was obvious to all the cowboys watching that Cloudy Day wasn't giving it his best. His hooves created a sucking noise each time he leaped in the air, and water and mud showered in all directions when he came back down. Ray rode to the whistle and dismounted on the back of the pick-up man's horse, close to the chutes. It was a sight to watch him walk the short distance. As he negotiated his way around the deeper pools of water, his boots stuck in the mud with each step and he had to hard to free them.

"I love indoor arenas," Billy said, watching Ray try to remove the thick layers of mud clinging to his boots.

Clay nodded and watched Gill Anderson come out of chute number two aboard Lock-knee. It was almost a repeat of the previous ride, except Lock-knee tried to turn back several times and almost lost his footing. The rain had started up again in slow, steady sheets, and the already slick mud was becoming slicker. Gill also made it to the whistle, and both he and Ray scored in the low seventies, which meant they were out of the money.

With a feeling of dread, Clay removed his slicker, wiped the water off Tonto's back with a towel, removed the plastic bag from his rigging handle, and took his seat on the horse's back. Working his gloved hand into the rigging, Clay pulled his hat down tighter on his head with his free hand and nodded for the gate to open.

Tonto ran out of the chute, then his rear hooves slipped sideways as he bucked in the other direction, taking Clay in two directions at once. From that point on, it was a wild ride. The paint's feet slipped and slid in all directions as he leaped into the air time after time.

Clay almost smiled to himself as he raked his spurs along Tonto's shoulders once again. Old

Tonto was a mudder — a horse that loved to perform in the mire. Apparently in his element, Tonto splashed about, leaping high and twisting each time his feet hit the ground. Several times Clay could feel the horse's feet almost slip out from under him, but every time he caught himself and continued his wild spree.

The rain-soaked crowd knew they were witnessing a great ride and cheered Clay and Tonto on, and Clay barely heard the whistle above the din.

Sliding onto the back of the pick-up horse, Clay was smiling in satisfaction as he remembered what Jack had told him on several occasions: "Never make a ride on a horse until you climb on his back." Those words came back to haunt him now when the announcer called out his score — a seventy-eight. It was good enough for second place for the moment.

"You've got to be the luckiest person I've ever met," Billy said as Clay came to stand beside him. "I've watched Tonto buck out several times before, but he's never turned it on like that. Who'd have guessed that sorry nag liked the mud?"

"I sure wasn't counting on it!" Clay remarked. "I'd already made up my mind I was leaving here empty-handed, but I may just make a little yet."

The rain slackened again as the bareback riding ended. Clay's score held to take second place. The rodeo officials had called in a local dirt contractor, who showed up with a large tractor that had a heavy drag and a big roller. They stopped the rodeo for a half an hour while the tractor and roller worked the arena into better shape, dragging the standing water out and compacting the earth to squeeze the water out of it. By the time they were finished grooming, the arena, while not in great condition, was much better. The calf roping and steer wrestling went without incident, and the times posted for each event were close to or better than the ones of the previous evening. The drag and roller had worked.

"Looks like we have a rodeo after all," Clay remarked to Billy and Tamara as they huddled beneath the awning of the concession stand.

"I'm going to watch the other barrel racers ahead of me before I make up my mind about whether I run Charger or not," Tamara said.

There was another pause as the large equipment was moved in once more to work the ground. Clay and Billy stood behind the chutes, their saddles already cinched down on each of their horses. Billy would be the first rider out and Clay would be fourth. Billy had drawn Copper Top, a red sorrel, and Clay had drawn a large buckskin called Yellow Dog. Both horses were top buckers and evenly matched.

The groundskeeping equipment moved out of the arena, and all attention turned to the bucking chutes. Billy was ready, and Clay stood over him, to lend a hand if needed. Billy was set and nodded his head to the gate man. It was a different story in the saddle broncs. With the ground packed down by the heavy roller, the horses were able to buck in their normal fashion. Copper Top bucked straight for two jumps, then planted his front feet and pivoted to the right. In a lightning-quick move that comes only from experience, Billy dropped his left spur from Copper Top's shoulder to his side and dug in to hold himself in the saddle. As soon as the sorrel horse leaped forward, Billy's spur was back in rhythm. Copper Top bucked two more jumps, then ducked to the right again, and once more Billy had his spur in the horse's side. After three more jumps, the whistle blew. Billy pulled on the rein with both hands and waited for the pick-up men to move in. His score of seventy-seven put him in first place.

"Looks like the arena's pretty firm," Clay said when Billy came back.

"I didn't feel Copper Top slip once, and he bucked as hard as the last time I rode him."

They watched the next two rides before Clay climbed into the saddle. Billy was still winning and didn't mind rubbing it in. "Second place is a seventy-three," he said with a mischievous smile. "If you try real hard, you might beat it."

"I'll do my best," Clay assured him with a tight grin and nodded for the gate.

Yellow Dog spun out of the chute, jumped one full length, planted his feet, and snorted hard. Bunching himself, he leaped into the air and kicked out with his back feet. Clay used the rein and saddle swells to hold himself in the saddle as he spurred the buckskin. Yellow Dog bucked four jumps down the arena, then started a right-hand turn, jumping and kicking out with each buck. His four-point landings vibrated the ground beneath him and jarred every bone in Clay's body. Bucking twice to the right, Yellow Dog suddenly changed tactics — instead of leaping forward, he vaulted straight into the air and kicked out sideways with his back feet, twisting his body and trying to throw Clay off balance. Digging in with his spurs, Clay pulled hard on the rein and squeezed with his knees, holding himself upright through the twist. Yellow Dog hit the ground, swung his head to the left, pivoted on his front feet, and swung his body around in a fast twist that would have un-seated Clay, had he not seen it coming and dug his spur into the horse's side. Yellow Dog pulled two more quick twists, then jumped straight ahead, trying to throw Clay off once more, but Clay kept time with the horse's moves until the whistle blew. On the ground and walking back to the chutes, he had to smile when he heard his score announced — a seventy-seven to tie Billy's score. If that score held through the remaining riders, Clay and Billy would split first and second.

"I think the judges felt sorry for you 'cause I been beatin' you so bad lately," was Billy's remark as he and Clay carried their saddles back to their pickups.

"I sure hope so," Clay replied. "It's about time they noticed me. I was beginning to think they were all related to you or something."

"They're not all related to me. Just half of 'em. The other ones I have to pay off," Billy said with a smug smile.

Clay threw his saddle into the camper and said to Billy, "I'm going to go watch Tamara's run. I'll be up by the arena gate."

Billy waved and Clay hurried back to the arena, arriving in time to find Tamara warming up Charger outside the gate.

"Have you decided whether or not to run him?" Clay asked as she stopped Charger beside him.

"So far the ground seems to be holding up pretty good. They brought the roller in just before the barrel racing. I think I'm going to let him run."

They watched three more barrel racers make their runs, then it was Tamara's turn. Charger pranced into the alleyway, feeling the excitement and tension that communicated itself from rider to horse. Turning him in a full circle to the right to ensure that he was in the right lead, Tamara gave him his head and let him run. Checking just before the first barrel, Charger gathered himself, flexed his neck, and turned around the barrel, leaving just a fraction of an inch between horse, rider, and barrel. With little guidance, the big horse dug his back feet into the packed earth and pushed off, racing toward the next barrel. Mud

247

flew into the lower stands as Charger planted his feet and slid into the second barrel, bending his body around and digging in for traction. Tamara tucked her left leg in tight to the horse's side and felt the rim of the barrel brush her pants leg. Around the second barrel, horse and rider stretched out, racing for the third barrel. Charger slowed only slightly, digging in with all four feet and turning his massive body around the barrel. Glancing down, Tamara saw that in turning he had gotten so low that the top of the barrel was even with her hips. Fearing that his feet were going to slip out from under him, she almost made the mistake of reining him up but caught herself in time, realizing that to do so could have catastrophic results. Trusting her horse, she felt him begin to rise as he came around the barrel and pushed off, gaining top speed in two jumps and crossing the timer line to stop the clock at sixteen flat and take the lead by four-tenths of a second.

"Wow! What a run!" Clay said exuberantly as Tamara brought Charger to a stop outside the arena.

"Did you see how low he got on that third barrel?" Tamara asked breathlessly.

"I sure did! I thought he was going to fall for a second there," Clay said.

"So did I, but he pulled it out and ran the fastest time we've ever run."

"Apparently it's the fastest time anyone's ever run in this arena," Clay responded when he heard the announcer say that Tamara's run had just set a new arena record.

Tamara was on cloud nine as she cooled Charger down. Clay wondered how long the broad smile she wore would remain in place. And to think that she almost didn't run at all. Tonight was sure turning out to be full of surprises, he thought.

The arena was prepared by the drag and roller one more time before the bull riding began. The rain had stopped shortly after the steer wrestling, delighting all those in attendance. The arena was in good shape, and Clay had drawn a top bull. Clay and Billy stood in the arena watching the first bulls buck out. The first four rounds went to the bulls, with none of the riders able to make the eight-second whistle. Jeremy Clark, the fifth rider out, scored a seventy-one on Bogus, a black, horned bull that went into a right spin, then switched back to the left and finished by leaping into the air for three bucks, twisting his body with each one. Jeremy tried to use his spurs for extra points, but he had to dig in and hold on to keep up with Bogus's changing tactics.

Triton was in chute four. Billy helped Clay get his rope set while the next three bull riders rode out, only one making a qualified ride. Clay sat on Triton's broad back while Billy pulled his rope tight for him. Clay scooted up on his rope and nodded for the gate. Triton swung his huge head out the gate, his body following with a twist and leap that took him into the air, carrying Clay ten feet from the chutes. His front feet landed first, and his head and shoulders were already moving to the right and into Clay's hand. As the bull's back feet came down, his body twisted to the point where his head and tail were almost touching for an instant before he leaped into the air once again. Clay felt his left shoulder drop as the bull's feet touched down, and his right spur was jerked free from Triton's side. One more powerful leap and Clay's hand was literally jerked loose from the rope and he went flying through the air, landing hard on his neck and shoulders. Rolling, he came instantly to his feet, fighting through the haze of pain that threatened to overwhelm him. He was only six feet from the arena fence, and in two strides he was up the mesh wire and sitting on the top rail, where he lowered his head and waited for the nauseating pain to subside. Ever so slowly, the pain in his neck and shoulders began to lessen. He looked up and saw that Triton was still in the arena. The big bull was standing with his head up, nostrils opening wide, eyes shining brightly as he sought a new target. Each time the pick-up men moved close to him, he charged their horses, causing the frightened animals to retreat. Both bullfighters tried to draw his attention toward the open gate leading to the holding pens. To Clay it looked as if Triton wasn't through gloating over his victory and wanted to strut his stuff for the crowd. It took the bullfighters and the pick-up men several more attempts before they finally convinced the bull to stop his grandstanding and exit the arena. Clay climbed down from the fence and stood for a moment to let the wave of dizziness pass.

"You all right?" Billy asked, watching Clay's wobbly climb over the chutes.

"I think I will be if my head quits hurting."

"You took quite a spill out there. Looked like you were shot out of a cannon, the way you came flying off."

"Feels like I was shot out of a cannon and hit a brick wall."

"You got any pain pills?" Billy asked.

"I got some aspirin," Clay responded. "I may take the whole bottle."

"I got some mild pain relievers a doctor gave me last time I hurt my ribs. I'll give you a couple of them in case you get to hurtin' too bad. They aren't too strong, but I wouldn't recommend driving if you take 'em."

"I think I'll be okay. I'll get Tamara to rub my neck and shoulders with some theragesic," he said, wincing as he reached down and picked up his bull rope.

Concern showed on Tamara's face as Clay and Billy walked toward her. "That was a nasty spill," she said. "Are you okay?"

"My neck and shoulders hurt and I've got a headache, but I think I'll live. You still have that tube of theragesic you carry with you?"

"It's in my bag. I'll get it," she said.

Clay groaned when he bent over to unbuckle his chaps. He sat on the bumper and pulled each of his boots up onto his knees to remove his spurs. By the time he had all his gear in the bag, Tamara had found the tube of ointment.

"I've got to get going," Billy said. "I'll see you next week in Albuquerque."

"I'll be there if my head doesn't come off before then," Clay said, trying to smile.

"Might help your riding if it does," Billy said. "I think sometimes the swelling up there throws your balance off."

Clay gave him a thin smile. "I don't think it was Triton that gave me this headache. It was your constant prattle that caused it."

Billy guffawed. "I'll see you later. Y'all be careful and don't step in nothin'."

"See ya," Clay replied.

Tamara rubbed Clay's neck and shoulders with the ointment, then ordered him into the camper.

"I'll drive!" she said. "You take these aspirins and lay down."

Clay didn't argue, knowing he couldn't drive with his head, neck, and shoulders aching like this. They were staying another night in Grand Junction and leaving early in the morning. He was asleep by the time Tamara got Charger stabled, and he didn't wake up until the next morning when she knocked on the camper door. His head was clear and pain-free, but his neck and shoulders were stiff and sore. By the time they ate breakfast and picked up Charger, it was after eight. Clay let Tamara drive, and he sat on the passenger side, trying not to move and groaning each time he did.

Chapter Nineteen

Tamara and Clay arrived back in Roswell late Sunday afternoon. Tamara had already agreed to spend the night at the ranch rather than go on to San Angelo. She was eager to visit Jack and see how he was doing. Clay slept a good part of the trip home, but he was still under the weather when he stepped out of the pickup.

Terry and Julie were still away on their trip, and there was no one at the ranch when they got there. Tamara sent Clay on into the house while she unloaded Charger and cared for him. When she returned, Clay was soaking in a hot tub of water and Epsom salts. Half an hour later some of the soreness had ebbed from his muscles, and he could move a little easier. They were about to leave the house on their way to see Jack when the phone rang. Clay instantly recognized the voice on the other end of the line as Ben Aguilar.

"Hey, Ben, what's up?" Fear gripped Clay's heart as thoughts of something happening to Jack or Julie and Terry flashed through his mind.

"Oh, not much. I was just wondering if you were going to be coming into town to see Jack this afternoon," Ben answered in a casual tone.

"Yeah, we were just walking out the door. Why is something wrong?"

"Nothing serious. Why don't I stop by and see

you at the hospital in about an hour or so?"

"That'd be fine," Clay said.

"Good. I'll see you there," Ben said and hung up the phone.

"What did Ben want?" Tamara asked as Clay replaced the receiver on its cradle.

"He didn't say," Clay responded with a puzzled look on his face. "He said it wasn't anything serious and that he'd stop by the hospital in about an hour and tell me."

"Hmm, that's odd. If it wasn't serious, why didn't he just tell you on the phone?"

"Good question. I guess we'll find out when we see him," Clay said as they walked out the door.

Each time Clay visited Jack, he was astonished at the progress the old rancher had made since his last visit. This time he was even more surprised than usual, as Jack greeted them in what was very nearly his old voice, with no trace of his previous stuttering or slurring of words.

"Boy, it's good to see you two," Jack said happily as they came into his room. Jack was fully dressed in his usual long-sleeved cotton shirt, blue jeans, and boots. Instead of sitting in bed like he usually did, he was sitting in the large chair with his feet propped up on a footstool that the nurses had apparently rounded up for him. His room was filled with fresh flower arrangements, and there was a new pile of cards and letters.

"You look too fit to be in a hospital," Tamara

said, giving him a hug.

"I'm being released for good behavior tomorrow," Jack said with a broad smile.

"That's great!" Clay whooped. "I'll just have to move those boarders out of your room before you get home."

Jack chuckled, and Clay noticed that his right hand and arm were still bent and he held them close to his stomach, using his left hand to reach for the drink that sat on the table by his chair.

Tamara and Clay told Jack about the two rodeos they had been to and how they'd placed. "I've bucked off the last three bulls I've been on," Clay said. "It's really frustrating. I make a ninety-five ride on Firestorm and then buck off bulls that I shouldn't have any trouble riding."

"Sounds like you've picked up some kind of bad habit. Why don't you call Lyle Jones and have him come out and watch you ride a couple of times? He's a good one for spotting bad habits and helping to work them out," Jack said.

"That's a good idea. I'll call him tonight and see if he can come over later in the week and give me a hand. Shawn's been wanting to try Torpedo. It'll be a good opportunity for him to try his hand."

"I'll be there to watch, too," Jack said.

"I'll pick you up in the morning, then," Clay said with a grin.

"I'll be waiting with bells on," Jack said, returning his grin.

Tamara kissed him on the cheek. "I expect

you to come spend some time with us as soon as possible."

Clay had forgotten all about Ben Aguilar's phone call until he and Tamara stepped outside the hospital and saw the sheriff sitting on one of the stone benches.

"Hey, Ben," Clay greeted him. "Why didn't you come on in?"

"I thought I'd give y'all a little time together. I'll step in and see the old codger before I leave. Besides, it's you I really need to see, and I didn't want to upset Jack."

"What is it?" Clay questioned, noting the frown on the sheriff's face.

"There was a problem at the ranch while you were gone," Ben began. "Someone moved about two hundred head of cattle from your north pasture and held them in a trap on the Flying R, in a box canyon pen that was big enough for only half that many. No food, no water. Twenty-three head died, and there's still some weak ones being held at the Flying R. Shawn's the one that found them missing and trailed them to the trap. Whoever did it cut the fence and drove them hard to the canyon, then just left them there."

Clay was dumbfounded. "Any idea who it was?" he asked.

Ben shook his head. "We couldn't find anything that would give us a clue, or a reason why. If they were trying to steal them, they picked the wrong ranch to drive them to. There's no way they could have gotten out undetected."

"This doesn't make any sense," Clay said. "I can't see why anybody would want to drive two hundred head of cattle into a trap and leave them with no food or water."

"That's what's got us stumped. We can't figure out why they did it. It took too much work for it to be a prank — and what did anyone have to gain? If somebody did it to get at you or Jack, why did they go to all that trouble? They could have done a lot of other things that would have required a lot less effort and gotten better results."

Clay frowned at the thought. "What do I need to do now?"

"Nothing really except pick up the few head of cattle left on the Flying R."

"I'll stop by there tomorrow and make arrangements to haul them home," Clay said.

"I hated to be the one that had to tell you about this, but I thought it would be better if I did it rather than Shawn."

"He's a good kid," Clay said.

"Yeah, he is," Ben agreed. "Kinda reminds me of another kid I used to know."

Clay grinned. "I wonder what ever happened to him?"

"I hear that after he made my life miserable for a while, he hooked up with an old rancher. Turned out the old rancher and this kid had a lot in common. They were both so cantankerous and ornery that they stayed together just to aggravate each other."

"Sounds like a fairy tale to me," Clay said with a sly grin. "Except you left out the part of the villain. I believe he was some stiff-backed sheriff that forced the two together, then stood back to watch."

Ben chortled. "Well, despite my obvious bad judgment, you got a nice kid working for you, and he deserves a lot of credit for the job he's done."

"He sure does," Clay said. "And I've got a pretty good idea what I can do to show him my appreciation. He's been wanting to learn how to ride bulls and saddle broncs. I'm going to have Lyle Jones come out to the ranch and help me out with a problem I've got. I'll see if he'll spend a little time with Shawn, get him started. And I know a couple of guys on the amateur circuit that would be glad to take him to some rodeos."

"Oh, boy," Ben said, "now there'll be another rodeo hand to watch out for. I'm going in to visit Jack while I still have some of my senses about me. I think I'll reconsider running for sheriff next term. I might even move to Montana."

Clay and Tamara chuckled all the way to the pickup.

Tamara left for San Angelo early Monday morning, though Clay tried his best to talk her into extending her stay for another couple of days.

"You know I would," Tamara said, "but I

promised Dad I'd go to Dallas with him to-morrow."

"I know," Clay responded dejectedly. "You going to call in our entries for Albuquerque and Phoenix?"

"I'll call 'em in Wednesday morning. We want Albuquerque Friday night and Phoenix Saturday night, right?"

"That's it," Clay affirmed. "And you'll be here Thursday afternoon?"

"I'll be here. Tell Julie not to go to any extra trouble."

"That's like telling a horse not to eat, but I'll pass along your message."

When Tamara's pickup was out of sight, Clay climbed into his truck and drove to the Flying R. He found Dennis Holt in the barn overseeing the shoeing of several horses.

"I've been feeding each of your cows about four gallons each day. They're lookin' better, but they're still weak. They'll need at least two more weeks of steady feeding before they're healthy enough to turn back with the herd."

"I appreciate what you've done, Dennis. I'll pay you back for the feed."

Dennis waved his hand in dismissal. "You'd have done the same for us. I wish I could get my hands on the men that did this. I'd teach 'em a little Western justice."

Clay knew what he meant, feeling the same way himself. "I'll come pick them up this after-noon. I'm bringing Jack home from the hospital this morning."

"Yeah, me and the wife went by to visit him the other day and he told us he was being released. He's done real good."

"He sure has. I'm ready to get him back home. I think he'll feel a lot better once he's back on the ranch, but I don't want to tell him about this for a while."

Dennis nodded. "I won't say a word."

Clay left the Flying R and drove into Roswell, straight to the hospital. Jack was already dressed in his jeans and boots. His hat was lying on the table beside him. He was sitting in the chair, waiting expectantly, his suitcase packed and at the door.

"Have they released you yet?" Clay asked.

"I'm waiting on the doctor. He said he'd be here first thing this morning, but he hasn't shown up yet."

"I'll go ask one of the nurses if they know when he might be coming in," Clay said, stepping back into the hallway.

There were three women sitting at the nurses' station, none of whom Clay recognized. After only a moment one of them looked up and noticed him.

"Can I help you?" she asked in a friendly voice.

"Yes, do you know when Doctor Miles will be in?"

Turning to look at a clipboard on the desk, she flipped a couple of pages and ran her finger down the list, stopping at the doctor's name. "He's scheduled to be on rounds now," she said. "Would you like me to page him for you?"

"No, that won't be necessary. I'm sure he'll be by shortly. Thank you."

Clay returned to Jack's room to report. "He's somewhere in the hospital. I imagine he'll be here soon."

"I hope so," Jack said. "I'm ready to get out of this place. If prison is worse than this, I sure as heck don't ever want to go there."

It was another hour before Dr. Miles made it to Jack's room. "Well, well," he said, looking at Jack's packed suitcase, "I see our patient is ready to be released. What's the matter, Jack? Didn't we treat you well enough?"

Jack shook his head. "I'm just tired of the food here. I may take a couple of these nurses home with me, though."

The doctor chuckled. "They're going to miss you around here. You've gotten to be one of their favorite patients." Turning to Clay, he said, "He keeps them entertained with stories of his days on the rodeo circuit."

"I imagine most of those tales are somewhat embellished," Clay said with a grin.

"He's told quite a few about you as well," the doctor said.

Clay directed a questioning look at Jack, but Jack just grinned at him.

"You hungry?" Clay asked as he loaded Jack into the front seat of the pickup.

"I could use some real food," Jack answered.

Clay had questioned the doctor at length about what Jack could eat, and the doctor had given him a typed list of foods he recommended, as well as those that Jack should stay away from.

"I don't know if the Cattlemen's Cafe has any food on the list," Clay said.

"I don't care what's on that list. If I don't get some steak in my body soon, it's going to rebel and start eating my innards."

"Now, Jack, you heard what the doctor said. You have to stay away from red meats as much as possible. They're a big part of the reason you had a stroke."

"Could be," Jack responded. "But if I got to quit eating steak, I might as well be dead anyway. Now let's get going."

Clay argued all the way to the restaurant, but to no avail.

Meanwhile, on the other side of town, Ginger Loring looked at her watch once again and realized that Clay Tory wasn't coming. One part of her fumed at being stood up, while another part was relieved. She had the documents ready for Clay's signature, including a two-page contract that would give Jay Crawford control of all the land that made up the Lazy L ranch. It was buried in the middle of several other pages that made up an investment contract for a small part of Clay's savings. They would invest just enough of his money to make him feel comfortable while still making him a good profit. She thumbed the pages while staring at a painting of the skyline of New York City, and wondered if she should abandon this whole thing, including Jay, and go back there now. Get a fresh start. There was something about this deal that didn't feel right to her, and the further she went, the worse she felt. The buzz of the intercom startled her, and she reached quickly for the button.

"Mr. Crawford is on line one for you," the receptionist said.

"Thank you, Christine," Ginger replied and pushed the button for line one.

"He didn't show," Ginger said before Jay could say anything.

"Any idea what happened?" Jay asked.

"None. I tried calling him at the ranch, but all I got was the answering machine. I left a message telling him to call me, but so far he hasn't. You don't think he's on to us, do you?"

"Relax. There's no reason he would be on to us. Something probably came up at the ranch and he couldn't get away. It's not like he's missing out on a million-dollar deal by not showing up. I'll go by the hospital and see if he's been there today and call you back."

"If he calls, should I try to get him to come in today?"

There was silence on the line while Jay thought about her question. After a moment he said, "No, see if he can meet you later in the week. We need him to fall for you, remember? It's going to take a while for us to get everything in place after he signs the papers, and we may need his un-knowing assistance. Make sure when you set up the meeting that it's at a time when you can take him to lunch. You'll have a better chance of working your magic in that setting."

Ginger sighed. "Gotcha. Let me know what you find out at the hospital."

Chapter Twenty

On Thursday afternoon Tamara drove into the ranch yard just as Clay and Terry rode up. They'd been out checking on the cattle in the sick pasture and moving several head into the west pasture with the large herd. While Clay and Terry were unsaddling their horses, Julie and Jack returned from town. Jack got out and yelled at Tamara, "It's about time you were gettin' here, young lady! Julie's done cleaned the house three times and cooked everything we got in the refrigerator."

Tamara ran to him and gave him a big hug. "It's good to see you home, Jack!"

"It's good to be here," he said, then lowered his voice. "Except Julie's tougher on me than those nurses in the hospital. At least they'd slip me a piece of roast beef or some taters every now and then. She won't even let me eat a piece of dry hamburger meat. How about you and Clay take me into town tonight and buy me a steak?"

Tamara laughed and shook her head. "I'm not about to take a chance like that. If Julie found out, she'd skin me alive."

"What's he tellin' you?" Julie asked, coming around the pickup with a sack of groceries in one arm.

"I've just been tellin' her how good you been takin' care of me," Jack said, winking at Tamara.

"Yeah, I'll bet," Julie said, then hugged Tamara with her free arm. "Terry, you and Clay grab the rest of the groceries out of the pickup when you come in."

Jack took Tamara by the arm and started for the house. "Have you seen the things Clay's done for the cattle?"

Tamara nodded. "He showed me last time I was here."

"I think I underestimated that boy's intelligence. He's smarter'n I gave him credit for."

"Well, let's don't tell him. It'll just give him the big head," Tamara said with a twinkle in her eye.

"I agree," Jack said, chuckling.

Clay and Tamara left early the next morning. Clay had told Terry what had happened while they were gone and warned him to keep a sharp eye on the cattle. Shawn now had a full-time job at the Lazy L. To reward him for his good work, Clay had bought two starter bulls from Lyle Jones. Both Clay and Lyle had worked with Shawn some, giving him instructions and yelling encouragement as he rode. Clay had ridden three bulls while Lyle looked on. By the third one, Lyle had his problem worked out. It had been a matter of Clay dropping the shoulder of his free hand too low, which caused him to lose his balance.

While Clay and Tamara were on their way to Albuquerque, Ginger Loring and Jay Crawford

267

were sitting in Ginger's office, talking in hushed tones.

"I don't know why he didn't meet with me this week. He said he was too busy and didn't have time. He said he'd call next week and set up a time to meet," Ginger said.

"I think the problem may be the woman he's with. I hear she's really something," Jay commented.

Ginger shot him an angry look. "And who told you that?"

"Two men I met in the bar a couple of weeks ago. They saw them together at the Cattlemen's Cafe."

Ginger felt something close to jealousy stir inside her, but she fought it down, wondering why she felt this way. Her brow wrinkled in thought, and Jay hid the smile that threatened to break on his face. He hadn't missed the anger that lit up her eyes.

"If this woman is the problem, we may have to remove her from the equation," Ginger said, with a sly smile on her lips. "Are they going to another rodeo this week?"

"They left this morning," Jay replied casually.

Ginger gave him a look to show that she was impressed. "And they'll return on Sunday?" she asked.

"That's what I hear. They've gone to Albuquerque first, and they'll be in Phoenix on Saturday."

"Hmm. I think I may pay Clay Tory a visit

Sunday afternoon."

Jay raised his eyebrows in question, but remained silent as he watched the wheels turning in her mind.

"I thought you had a plan to keep him in town," Ginger said, staring at him.

"It's still in the works. Our man had a little accident on his last escapade. Seems he fell off a horse and hurt his back. We had to postpone our other plans, but I think we'll be back in business soon. As a matter of fact, I'm meeting him this afternoon to discuss our next move. If it goes as well as I hope, I think it will keep Mr. Tory around for a while." He looked at Ginger and continued, "And if you could create a bit of tension between him and this woman, it might be just the icing on the cake."

Ginger smiled. "And what a sweet icing it will be!"

Later that afternoon, Jay met with his acquaintance. The plan they had originally devised was now ready to be carried out.

"It'll be a little tougher since the manager is back, but I think it can be done. If you want, I can cause a little harm to come to either him or the kid," the man sitting across from Jay said.

"No!" Jay stated emphatically. "Like I said before, somebody gets hurt and the law won't stop searching until they find who did it. Right now they're not going to look real hard for someone who's moved a few cattle or vandalized a few items. If the time comes when I need someone hurt, I'll let you know, but if it happens before I give the word, the money stops. Do you understand?"

Hard eyes stared back at Jay and slowly the man nodded his head. "I'll start things rolling again tomorrow night."

"Why not tonight?" Jay asked impatiently.

"Because the help I need won't be available until tomorrow, that's why!" the man answered in an insolent tone.

"All right," Jay responded, feeling the tension rising between them. "Let me know when it's done."

"You'll know," was the man's short answer. Then he got up and walked out. Jay stared at his retreating back until he disappeared. He wondered again if he could control him long enough to pull this off.

Terry and Shawn drove through both large pastures Friday morning, checking all the cattle. The water was in good shape, but the supply of hay was getting low. Clay had made a call last week and ordered two tractor-trailer loads from his contacts in Colorado. If there were no delays, they were due to arrive at the end of next week, which would be just in time.

Jack was sitting at the kitchen table going over the ranch records for the first time since he'd gone into the hospital. Julie was cooking lunch and running the calculator for him when he needed something added. Suddenly he let out a mild expletive. "Dadgum that boy," he said angrily.

"What?" Julie asked, concerned by the look on Jack's face.

"Clay!" Jack exclaimed. "He hasn't used a dime out of the ranch account to pay for all these expenses, which means he's been using his own money. Bring me the phone, please."

Julie set the phone on the table and Jack dialed a number he apparently knew by heart. Julie turned back to the stove to stir the pinto beans, but kept her ear tuned to Jack's conversation.

"Jim Collins, please," Jack said gruffly. "Jack Lomas," he said, then waited for half a minute, his foot tapping the floor with impatience.

"Jim, Jack Lomas!" Julie heard him say. "Thank you. It's good to be home. Yes, I'm doing much better, thank you. Look, the reason I'm calling is that I was just going over the ranch accounts and found that Clay hasn't used any of the money for expenses, and I wanted to make sure you'd followed my instructions." Jack remained silent for a few moments as he listened to the attorney on the other end speak, then finally said, "I see — and he did go to the bank and sign the papers. You're sure? Uh-huh. Okay. Thanks, Jim. No, that's all I needed. Thank you. 'Bye."

Julie glanced quickly at Jack and saw the frown he still wore.

"That hardheaded whelp! I ought to take a bull whip to his backside," Jack snapped angrily.

"What on earth did he do?" Julie asked, surmising what had happened but not understanding Jack's anger.

"I set up accounts at the bank for him to use if anything ever happened to me, and that insolent young buck ignored them and used his own money. I know those trucks, the tanks, and all the feed he's bought have run up quite a bill, not to mention what he's had to pay for water. I'll bet he's used a sizable chunk of his bank account to cover all those costs."

Julie chuckled, prompting a glare from Jack. "Just what do you find so funny, young lady?"

"You two are so much alike it's not even funny. You sit here getting mad because Clay won't use your money and Clay's so proud that he uses his money instead of yours. Why don't you just find out how much he's used of his and replace it with yours?" she asked innocently.

Jack's head jerked up in surprise, then he chuckled. "That's an excellent idea. All I need are the receipts for all the expenses," he said thoughtfully.

"They're in the folder in the desk in the living room," Julie said. "I'll get them for you, but don't you dare tell him I told you."

"I won't. I'd like to go to the bank this afternoon — if you don't mind taking me?"

"I'll be happy to!" Julie said with a mischievous smile.

Clay called late Saturday afternoon to update everyone on the Albuquerque rodeo. He had missed his bareback horse out and received a no-score, but he was sitting third in saddle broncs while Billy Ettinger was winning it. He had made a successful ride on his bull, scoring a seventy-six, which was good enough for fourth place, but he didn't think it would hold. Tamara was in first place in barrel racing. They were in Phoenix, resting before the night's performance.

"Well, cowboy up and ride hard," Jack said. "We need the money to replace all the groceries Julie cooked up while Tamara was here."

Clay laughed loudly on the other end and said good-bye.

That afternoon, after Jack got back from town, Terry drove him around the empty pastures to look at the water tanks and windmills. "If we could get a good rain before the first of November, this grass would come back," said Jack. "It'll be a while before the groundwater is high enough for the windmills to have enough water to pump again, but the runoff would fill enough of the dirt tanks to hold the cattle until it did come back."

"All we need is rain," Terry agreed. "The weatherman says we got a slight chance in the next week."

"We need more than a slight chance," Jack said. "We need a miracle, and tomorrow I'm going to be in church praying for one."

"That's the best place to be," Terry agreed. "Julie and I'll be there with you."

Jack nodded his appreciation and looked out over the brown prairie. "We need to start weaning calves in about another three weeks. I don't know where we're gonna put 'em. We ain't got a pasture with enough water to hold 'em."

"We'll think of something," Terry said. "At least we got cattle to worry about weanin'."

Jack nodded. "That's a fact. If it weren't for you and Julie and Clay, all the cattle would have been sold off at a big loss by now. I just hope we don't have to do that anyway. I've talked to some of the other ranchers in the area that had to sell. They didn't get nothin' for their herds. They'll be lucky if they can hold out long enough to re-build."

"We'll hold out," Terry said with conviction.

"By the grace of God," Jack whispered.

On Saturday morning, while the three boys fed the cows, Terry and Shawn rode both pastures, checking the fences and making sure there were no breaks in them, repairing any they found. It took them most of the day, and both of them were bone-tired when they got back to the house late that afternoon. Terry and Julie had fixed up their extra bedroom for Shawn to stay in until Jack and Clay could get him a trailer of his own. Turning in early that night, neither dreamed what would be waiting for them the next morning when Jerry came speeding up the driveway air horn blaring and dust swirling around his rig as he set down on the air brakes.

Going to the door in just his jeans, Terry, still half asleep, wondered what in blazes was happening.

"You better get dressed and get over to the

west pasture!" Jerry yelled from the window of the truck. "Somebody's played the devil with the water tanks, and there's thirsty cattle bawling their heads off!"

Jack was standing at the door of the house with his pants unbuttoned and only an undershirt on. "What in thunder happened?" he shouted, not hearing Jerry's explanation.

"Nothing," Terry shouted back. "Shawn and I'll take care of it." He rushed back into the house, yelling for Shawn to get dressed. "Julie, hurry up and get up to the house and head Jack off before he insists on going with us."

Terry and Shawn were out of the house and down the lane in less than five minutes after Jerry woke them. Jack was still trying to get his boots on when Julie came rushing in. "Now, just where do you think you're going?" she asked.

"I'm going with Terry and Shawn to find out what in blazes is going on. What was that fool hollerin' about, and why was he blowin' that dad-blamed horn?"

"You just settle down," Julie said in a voice of authority. "Terry and Shawn have already left to find out what the commotion is all about. They'll fill you in as soon as they get back. I'm sure it's nothing. I'm going to get breakfast started. Why don't you go ahead and take a shower and shave that stubble off your face? Maybe they'll be back by the time you're through." Her take-charge attitude had a calming effect on Jack, and he nodded and walked toward the bathroom.

When Terry and Shawn drove up to the water tanks in the west pasture, they couldn't believe their eyes. All four tanks were completely empty. Gaping holes were knocked in each one. The ground showed where each one had spilled its contents on the dry soil. The plumbing that connected the tanks to the tanker had been totally destroyed, as well as the hoses used for filling the vessels. Somebody had taken an axe to everything in sight — even two of the tires on the trailer had been cut. Thirsty cattle bawled out their plea for water.

Terry jumped back into the pickup and Shawn followed. Driving as fast as he dared, Terry headed for the north pasture. With his window rolled down, he knew before he got there that the scene would be the same. The sounds of the cattle reached his ears long before he arrived at the water tanks. It was indeed the same, including the tires on the trailer. Surveying the destruction, Terry wanted to rant and rave, but he knew he had to act fast or the cattle would start walking in search of water. And thirsty cattle didn't stop at fences, they would walk through them in all directions and it would take weeks to round them up — at least those that didn't die of thirst first. Jumping back in the pickup, he drove to the west pasture as fast as he could. Jerry was still there, awaiting instructions.

"Can we use this tanker to haul water?" Terry asked as he pulled up beside Jerry.

"I don't know. I didn't see any holes in it, but it's got two ruined tires. Let's take a look."

After a thorough inspection they found that the hoses used for filling the tanker had been cut, but Jerry knew where he could get some more. The only serious damage was the tires.

"Can you get it to town like this?" Terry asked.

"Sure," Jerry said. "Empty like that, the other tires will hold the weight."

"Good. I'm going to call Brian Calloway and have him meet you with two tires. Do you know where his place is?"

"Yeah, I've had plenty of tires mounted there."

"I'm going to get some metal and tar and start repairing the tanks. We've got to get water to these cows fast or they're going to start walking, and when they do we'll lose a lot of 'em."

"Hold on," Jerry said. "If we got to get water to these cattle in a hurry, I got a better idea. Let's get to a phone and let me make a call. I know a fella that can probably have us a couple of loads of water here within the hour."

Terry almost hugged the truck driver, but instead he just asked, "Are you sure?"

"I'd bet your last dollar on it," Jerry said with a grin.

Chapter Twenty-one

True to his word, Jerry arranged for two tankers to be at the pastures in about an hour. He had called Carl Grey and explained the situation in terse words. Carl promised that he'd get the trucks rolling in fifteen minutes.

"They've got to drive to the wells and fill up, then come here. It'll take them a little over an hour to get here," Jerry said. "Meanwhile, I'll take the tanker in and get the tires replaced if you'll call Calloway's and have someone meet me there."

"I'll do that," Jack said, having heard Jerry's conversation. "Terry, you and Shawn get the tar from the barn. That metal we got to repair the windmills should work to cover the holes. Drill two holes in each piece and then use nuts and bolts to pull them down tight against the sides of the tanks. Put the tar in between to seal them."

"Good idea," Terry said, grabbing his hat and motioning for Shawn to follow him.

They had two tanks repaired in each pasture by the time they heard the trucks coming. Julie had saddled two horses and hauled them to the pasture where Terry was working. Jack had ridden along to survey the damage, despite Julie's objections. Shawn went with one of the tankers to the west pasture, and Julie and Jack followed, leaving one of the horses for Terry. As soon as the cattle were watered, he would ride the pasture to make sure none of them had strayed. Shawn would do the same in the west pasture.

Clay and Tamara arrived home late in the afternoon to an empty house. Clay was about to call the hospital to see if something had happened to Jack when he heard the pickup coming up the drive. Walking outside, he saw the trailer behind the pickup that Terry was driving and Shawn following in the other pickup. Tamara came to stand beside him as he waited.

"You missed the excitement," Jack said as he stepped out of the pickup.

"What excitement?" Clay asked, suddenly concerned by everyone's disheveled look.

"I'll let Terry fill you in," Jack said, "but let's go in the house and sit down. I'm too tired to stand out here."

Clay was shocked speechless by Terry's account. He sat without speaking for several moments. At last he found his voice. "Did you call Ben?"

"We haven't had time," Jack said. "Besides, there's nothing he could do. There weren't any tire tracks or anything else that could be traced. We looked."

"How are the cattle?" Clay asked.

"They're fine," Terry replied, weariness tinging his voice. "There were only about forty head that had strayed. Shawn and I found all of them and moved them back to water."

"Y'all did a great job," Clay said. "Shawn, that's twice you've helped save our cattle. Thanks."

Shawn blushed at the compliment. "I was just doin' my job," he replied.

Clay smiled at him. "And you're doing it great." Turning to the other four sitting at the table, he asked, "Can you think of anyone that might have a grudge against Jack — or me, for that matter — that could be behind this?"

No one said anything as they all thought about his question. There was not much chance to answer, for at that moment they heard the sound of a car coming up the driveway. Clay rose and went to the door. Surprised and bewildered, he watched Ginger Loring pull to a stop and get out of her car.

"Hey, cowboy, I figured if I was ever going to see you again, I'd have to come out here."

As Clay stood dumbfounded, Tamara came to stand beside him. Glancing first at Tamara, then at Ginger, he felt like a snared rabbit. Ginger's smile remained on her face as she came up the walk toward them.

Clay finally found his voice. "Hey, Ginger. I'm surprised to see you out this way. I figured after your last trip you'd shy away from this part of the country."

Ginger gave a short laugh. "You know what they say about the snake that bit you. You got to come back to see it."

Tamara hadn't said a word thus far, but Clay could feel the tension. "Ginger, this is my fiancée, Tamara Allen. Tamara, this is Ginger Loring, the lady that had the wreck down the road a ways."

Tamara smiled, but Clay could tell it was forced. Ginger's manner was easy and pleasant as she held out her hand in Tamara's direction. "Pleased to meet you. I've been eager to meet the woman that captured this cowboy," Ginger said.

"Pleased to meet you," Tamara responded coolly.

"Come on into the house," Clay said, feeling a strong need to have someone else between these two.

Ginger smiled and walked through the door that Clay held open for her. Tamara let her go in first, then followed closely behind, putting herself between Clay and Ginger.

"I hope I didn't come at a bad time," Ginger said over her shoulder.

When Clay hesitated, Tamara spoke up. "Actually it isn't the best time. Someone vandalized all the water tanks and trailers that are used to water the cattle. It's been a rather hectic day around here. Clay and I just got back from Phoenix and haven't had time to get caught up on all that's happened."

Ginger's hand flew to her mouth. "Oh, my goodness! Why would anyone do such a thing?"

"We don't know," Clay said, hurrying to

answer. "We were just discussing that."

"I have come at a bad time. I'm sorry," Ginger said, stopping in the living room. "I just wanted to show you the investment plan I put together for you, but it can wait. Why don't you come into the office when things settle down a bit and I'll show it to you then?"

"That's probably a good idea," Clay agreed. "How about Wednesday morning?"

"Sounds good to me. Say around ten o'clock?"

"I'll be there unless something else comes up," Clay said with a tight smile.

"I'll show myself out. It was nice meeting you, Tamara," Ginger said warmly.

"It was nice meeting you too," Tamara replied, but her voice lacked the warmth to make it sound true.

Clay watched Ginger walk to her car before returning to the kitchen. Tamara and Julie both eyed him coolly as he walked in, and Terry wore an I-told-you-so look. Jack was the only one whose expression Clay couldn't read. He took his seat at the table and said, "What's for supper?" It was the wrong question at the wrong time. The nasty looks he received from Tamara and Julie coupled with the disbelief on Terry's face convinced him he would be better off keeping his mouth shut. He sat staring at his boots and tried to bear the silence that engulfed the room.

It was the next morning before Julie or Tamara would speak civilly to Clay. Julie cooked his breakfast and asked him what his plans were for the day.

"I guess I better get some plumbing and get those tanks back on automatic. Then I'll have to see to getting the other tanker repaired."

"I've got to take Jack in this morning for his therapy. There's some stew in the refrigerator. You and Terry can heat it up for lunch."

"Thanks," Clay said. "I'm glad to see you're talking to me."

Julie gave him a tight smile. "I'm sorry. It's just that I don't like that woman, and I was upset when she showed up here yesterday."

Clay didn't know what to say, so he didn't say anything.

Jack came into the kitchen, already showered and dressed. Julie set a bowl of oatmeal and two pieces of wheat toast in front of him, ignoring his scowl. "I'd give half this ranch for a plate of fried eggs and three strips of bacon," he said, frowning at the bowl of oatmeal.

Clay chortled and finished the last bite on his plate. Julie had gone to change clothes. He and Jack were alone.

"Looks like you put a bur under a couple a gals' saddle blankets yesterday," Jack stated, giving Clay an innocent look.

"Yeah, and I wish I knew what I did to put it there. I didn't invite Ginger out here. She just showed up. They acted like I brought my mistress in to meet my fiancée. I don't understand women."

Jack chuckled. "Boy, don't no man under-stand women, and if a man claims he does, he's the biggest liar there is. But one thing I do know about the female species is that they've got a sixth sense about things. I don't know nothin' about this Ginger, but if she's got those two women upset, you can bet there's something to be upset about."

Clay reflected on Jack's comment, then said, "There's nothing there! She had an accident on the road, and now she's helping me invest some of my winnings. There's nothing else."

Jack put another spoonful of oatmeal in his mouth and said nothing until he'd swallowed it. "I got a peek at her yesterday. She's a good-lookin' filly."

"And?" Clay asked, expecting Jack to say more.

"And nothin'!" Jack said. "I was just sayin' she's a good-lookin' filly, that's all."

Clay got up from the table, stomped to the kitchen sink, and rinsed off his plate, being none too gentle as he did. He set the plate in the drainer, then walked out of the kitchen without another word.

Jack's frown deepened as he stared at the half-eaten bowl of oatmeal.

Tamara awoke to the slam of the screen door as Clay stalked outside. He admitted he was as angry with himself as he was with Jack for hitting so close to the truth. Walking down to the barn, he tried to sort out his thoughts. The sight of

Ginger yesterday had made his pulse race, but was it just her beauty or was there something else? Comparing Ginger to Tamara, he knew Tamara was the one he loved, the one he wanted to spend the rest of his life with. If a woman like Ginger could stir him like this, though, was he really ready to settle down? Would he be able to resist temptation and remain true to one woman?

Tamara found him still at the barn when she went searching for him. "I'm sorry I got mad at you last night. I realize you didn't invite that woman out here, and I shouldn't be getting angry with you, but I didn't like her. I know I shouldn't be that way — I don't even know her — but I got the feeling she's after more than helping you with your investments."

Clay was surprised by her statement. His first inclination was to deny it, but he stopped himself and said, "I don't know what she's after, but I do know I love you and I wouldn't trade what we've got for a thousand of her kind," and at that moment he knew that what he said was true.

Tamara stepped close to him and looked him straight in the eye, then kissed him tenderly. "I couldn't stand losing you. I don't think there's anything happening between you and her, but that doesn't mean I like her or trust her, so I'm asking you to stay away from her, for my sake."

"I've got one more meeting with her Wednesday to see what she's put together. After that I won't see her again. I promise." He could tell Tamara didn't like it, but she nodded her assent, willing to bend a little.

Clay stayed at the house until Tamara left, then went to meet Terry in the west pasture. Terry had already bought the plumbing supplies they needed, and he and Shawn were busy fixing the automatic float valves. It took the rest of the day to finish hooking up the tanks in both pastures. Larry had shown up earlier and taken the trailer into town to have the new tires put on. Finished at last, Clay and Terry leaned against the pickup while Shawn checked the tanks for any leaks.

"You know, whoever's doing this is waiting until I'm out of town. I get the feeling they're out to even a score, but I can't think of anyone that would have this big a score to settle with me."

Terry chuckled. "The way I figure it, it could be anyone that knows you."

Clay smiled at Terry's humor. "We may have to do some planning of our own to see if we can put a stop to it."

"Got any ideas?" Terry asked.

"I got the beginning of one, but right now it needs some fine-tuning. I'll let you know when I have it all together."

"I can't wait," Terry remarked snidely.

"Let's get back to the house. I need to call Carl Grey and thank him for his help. I don't know what we'd have done if he hadn't hauled that water for us."

"That's a good friend you got there," Terry said.

"A good friend Jack's got. I've come to learn he's got a powerful lot of friends."

"That's because he's always been a friend to others. There's not many around these parts that don't owe Jack at least one favor."

"I reckon I owe him more'n any of 'em," Clay said. "I thank the good Lord every day that Ben Aguilar got Jack to take me in."

"I reckon he owes you too," Terry replied. "That old man would have dried up and blowed away like sand if you hadn't come along when you did."

"We just got to take care of him so he stays around for a long time."

"I'll drink to that!" Terry replied.

The two loads of hay showed up the next day. Clay had hired two extra hands to help unload it. One load was put into the vans in the pastures and the other in the barn at the ranch. Clay drove into town Wednesday morning for his meeting with Ginger Loring. Julie had been silently upset, but she had fixed his breakfast anyway and told him she was taking Jack in later for his therapy.

Clay arrived at Ginger's office a few minutes before ten o'clock. For some reason, he wasn't as eager to see her as he had been the last time. He had to wait only a few moments before she came out of her office. She was wearing a tight-fitting light blue blouse with the top button undone and a short white skirt that fit snugly around her trim waist. Clay, walking behind her to her office, couldn't help but notice her seductive walk. It occurred to him that she was purposely accentuating her moves for his benefit. When he realized this, he suddenly found that his desire for her had waned, and he now knew what it was that had made her alluring to him in the first place. It was the age-old problem faced by men — they wanted what they knew they couldn't have, but once it was within their grasp, they no longer desired it.

Ginger had him sit in the same chair he'd occupied during their previous meeting, and again she pulled the other chair around to face him. Sitting down and taking a folder from the desk to her left, she crossed her legs and watched out of the corner of her eye for Clay's reaction. She was disappointed to see that he didn't even look down, but instead studied the painting on the wall behind her. She opened the folder and pulled out a stack of papers.

"I've put together what I feel are some diversified investments that will allow you to increase your holdings, while at the same time keeping that investment relatively safe." She went on to explain each of the investments to him, how much capital he would have to put up, and what kind of return he could expect if the economy remained stable. All during her presentation, she kept watching him, expecting him to glance at her legs or the opening in her blouse, but not once did his eyes stray from her face. When she had finished the presentation, she took the papers and placed them in a neat stack on the desk.

"So, what do you think?" she asked.

"Sounds impressive," Clay responded.

"Good!" Ginger said, smiling. "All I need is your signature on these forms, giving me the right to invest your money as I've outlined, and a check for fifteen thousand. Then your money will be on the way to working for you." She handed him a pen and moved the documents closer to the edge of the desk.

Clay picked up the stack of papers and glanced at the one on top. "I learned from a very wise man never to sign my name on anything until I've had a chance to read it completely. I'll take these home with me and read them over. If I have any questions, I'll get back with you. If everything's like you said, I'll sign them and drop them back by with the check."

Ginger's breath caught in her throat, and her mind raced for a way to stop him. "Here, let me put them in a folder for you. I have special ones for clients."

Clay reached over to the desk and picked up the plain manila folder that the papers were originally in. "This will do just fine," he said. "I should be able to look these over by the first of next week. I'll give you a call." He smiled and held out his hand, not noticing how pale her face was.

Ginger was a nervous wreck when Clay left.

She immediately tried to call Jay Crawford, but was unsuccessful in reaching him. As she paced the floor in her office, she waited, almost praying he would call. She had already called every place where she thought he might be and left messages for him to call as soon as possible, emphasizing how urgent it was that she talk to him.

Jay Crawford was smiling to himself as he walked into the Red Cloud lounge. He had just returned from meeting with Tony Madiro, a man who had flown out from Chicago only this morning and was very interested in buying development property. He had shown Madiro what he could of the Lazy L, and had explained the development opportunities to him. "Being only sixty miles from Ruidoso, you could build a retirement village for wealthy clients. The climate here is suitable. They'll be close to ski resorts, gambling casinos, horse racing, and it's only a short drive to Mexico. You could build a mall here for the residents, and with all this land you could set up hunting and fishing resorts to attract outside wealthy clients."

Madiro had been impressed to the point that he was asking for a price. Jay had already set a figure in his mind, but had increased it at the last moment. "Two million," he said casually. "Ten percent down locks you in."

The man said nothing, but Jay knew he was pleased with the price. He promised to call within a week to let him know what his partners thought about the deal. "If they like it, I'll have my attorney draw up the papers. How soon will you have title to the land?"

"Should be within the week," Jay told him.

Taking his usual seat at the bar, Jay looked around at the other three patrons, none of whom he knew. The waitress brought his drink without him having to order. She smiled and said, "Hey, Jay, what've you been up to?"

"Just trying to make a buck," he said, smiling back at her.

She was about to turn away when she stopped and said, "Oh, by the way, someone named Ginger called. She wants you to call as soon as possible. Said it was urgent."

The smile left Jay's face. "Did she say what it was about?"

"No, only that it was urgent that you call."

Jay took a five-dollar bill from his pocket and threw it on the table. "Thanks, Paula." She watched him hurry out, his drink untouched.

Ginger wasn't looking out the window when Jay sped up, parked in his space, and hurried to the apartment. Whirling around as the door swung open, she began to verbally attack him. "Where have you been? I've been trying to reach you since noon!"

"I was with a client, showing him the Lazy L. I feel fairly certain we've got a buyer if you got the documents signed," he said.

Ginger looked distraught. "He wouldn't sign them. As a matter of fact, he took them home with him, including the two pages giving us the rights to the ranch."

"He did what?" Jay fairly shouted. "How could you let him get out of your office with those papers? Do you know what will happen when he reads them? He'll have the law on us so fast we won't know what hit us!"

Ginger chewed her lip nervously. "Maybe we should pack up and get out of here before he does."

Jay was pacing the floor now, his brow wrinkled in thought. He stopped and said, "No, we wouldn't get far before they caught us. We've got to get those papers back."

"How are we going to do that?" Ginger cried.

"I don't know yet, but I'll think of something."

"It's got to be done soon," Ginger said, "before he has a chance to read them."

"He's leaving day after tomorrow for Abilene. If he hasn't read them by then, we may have a chance to get them back. There won't be anybody in the house but the old man. I've got a contact that might be able to get them. I still don't understand how you could let him take them out of the office."

"He just did it. I never dreamed he'd do something like that. I thought he'd sign them in the office. There was nothing I could do without making him suspicious."

"We have to get them back, and then we have to figure a way to get Clay Tory's signature on them."

Ginger looked at him like he was crazy.

"There's no way we can get his signature on them! We've got to get those papers and cut our losses."

"I've got too much invested in this to quit now. There's more than one way to get a signature. If he won't do it willingly then we'll just have to persuade him in some other fashion."

Ginger started to say something but stopped. She didn't like the look in his eyes.

Chapter Twenty-two

Thursday morning after breakfast, Clay got Terry and Shawn alone at the barn. "I've got a plan to catch whoever vandalized our water tanks and took our cattle."

"I'm not sure I want to hear this," Terry said sarcastically.

"It's not the most foolproof plan, but if we put our heads together, we ought to be able to cover most of the bases. I stopped in town the other day and picked up two more cell phones. Now, here's the plan." He laid it out for them, explaining what he wanted them to do. The hardest part was going to be keeping Jack out of it. Terry would fill Julie in later, but only because there was no way for him to do what he had to without her knowing.

"We'll start tonight. It's going to take some acting on our part in case they're watching the ranch — and I'm pretty sure they are. We'll start the show around six o'clock. Terry, make sure all the other boys are gone by five today and that they won't be back. Any questions?"

They both shook their heads. Shawn wore an eager look on his face, but Terry looked more like he was going to be ill. Slapping him on the shoulder, Clay said, "Cheer up, Terry, it's going to be all right."

"So you say," Terry replied forlornly.

They spent the rest of the day going about business as usual. Clay drove into town and called Tamara at three o'clock in the afternoon.

"Hello, Clay," she answered when her mother called her to the phone.

"Hey, angel, I've missed you," Clay said, dreading to say what he had to tell her.

"I miss you too. I can't wait for you to get here tomorrow. What time will you be arriving?"

Clay hesitated for a moment, then answered, "That's why I'm calling. I'm not coming."

"Why not?" Tamara asked in alarm. "Is Jack all right? Has something happened?"

"Jack's fine," Clay hurried to reassure her. "The reason I'm not coming is because of what's been happening at the ranch the last two weekends while I've been gone. We're going to try to stop it."

"How are you going to do that?" Tamara asked, alarm and skepticism in her voice.

"We've got a way," Clay said. "Don't worry, we're not going to do anything foolish. We just want to find out who it is and then let Ben take care of them."

There was a moment of silence on the other end, and Clay wondered what she was thinking. He didn't have to wait long to find out. "Clay, are you sure this doesn't have something to do with that woman — Ginger?"

"What do you mean?" Clay asked, puzzled by her question.

"I mean, are you sure you're not missing the rodeo so you can be with her?"

Clay felt anger well up inside him but fought to control it. "Tamara, I'm not staying here to be with Ginger. I've told you, she doesn't mean anything to me. I love you," he said forcefully.

"I don't see why you don't let Ben handle this thing, then," she replied angrily.

"Look, Tamara, I've got to find out who's doing this, and the only way I can do it is to catch them in the act. Ben doesn't have the manpower to post deputies out here. I'm sorry I have to miss going with you, but this has to stop. Now quit worrying about me and Ginger. There's nothing going on. I promise. I'll call you tomorrow night at the hotel, all right?"

"I guess," Tamara responded without emotion.

"I love you," Clay said.

" 'Bye," came the reply from the other end before the line went dead.

Clay slowly hung up the phone, feeling his anger rising — not at Tamara but at the person or persons who were the reason he wasn't going to be with her.

At six o'clock that evening Clay, Terry, and Shawn were sitting in the kitchen drinking iced tea and talking to Jack and Julie. Pushing his chair back from the table, Shawn remarked, "I reckon I'll be heading out to Dad's. I'll be back in the morning."

"Tell your pa hello for me," Terry said, rising

from the table as well.

Clay stood up and said, "I'll feed the barn stock tonight."

The three walked outside together, and Clay spoke in a quiet tone. "I'll see you in the morning."

Shawn got into his pickup and drove out of the yard. Clay and Terry headed to the barn without looking back.

Later that evening, Clay loaded his camper as usual, putting his clean clothes and gear in their usual places.

He spent a restless night, going over in his mind all the things that could go wrong with his plan and working out alternatives in case something did.

At ten o'clock that same evening, Jay Crawford was in the Red Cloud, listening to the man who sat across from him.

"He's going to Abilene tomorrow and Waco Saturday. He loaded up his pickup earlier this evening," the man said.

"This one ought to be like taking candy from a baby," Jay said. "Is everything ready for tomorrow night?"

"It's ready. I've got two men watching the house and two more watching the road leading into the ranch. After the two attacks we've made so far, they're liable to be a mite suspicious."

"The thing on our side is that they don't have

enough hands to watch all the places," Jay said. "And the sheriff's department doesn't have enough deputies to patrol all the county roads. Just remember, the important thing is to get those papers back. The fires ought to draw everyone away from the ranch, giving your man plenty of time to get in and get the goods."

"You do realize that setting those hay vans afire could touch off a prairie fire?"

Jay shrugged. "I don't care if it does. It might help speed things along."

Clay's alarm clock was set for five o'clock. When it went off, he felt as if he'd just fallen asleep. Showering and shaving, he grabbed a quick bite to eat, said goodbye to Jack, and drove off. The sky in the east was just beginning to show light when he hit Highway 380 and turned east.

At six-thirty, Shawn drove his pickup into the yard and parked in the shed attached to the barn. He often parked there so his truck would be out of the way. He and Terry saddled horses and rode south. Half an hour after they had gone, two figures lifted the tarp in the back of the pickup and climbed stealthily out of the back, slipping into the barn through a side door.

Clay sat on a bale of hay in the coolness of the barn and spoke to the man sitting on a five-gallon bucket across from him. "We'll be waiting here until this afternoon when they go to feed, so we might as well get comfortable and relax."

"I just hope that after we've gone to all this trouble, they show up," Darrin Corbett stated. Clay knew Darrin more by reputation than as a personal acquaintance. When he had called Lyle Jones to solicit his advice, Lyle had recommended Darrin and had even called him to request his help. Darrin was more than happy to lend a hand — or a huge body, Clay thought as he looked at Darrin's impressive physique. The man stood only six feet tall, but his broad shoulders, mammoth biceps, and barrel chest made him an imposing figure.

Under the cover of darkness the night before, Terry and Julie had carried an ice chest full of drinks and sandwiches to the barn. Clay popped the top on one of the soft drinks and leaned back against the stack of hay. His thoughts turned naturally to Tamara, and he frowned, recalling their last conversation. He wished he could have convinced her that he wasn't remaining at home so he could be with Ginger Loring, and he wondered for the hundredth time why she believed he was. She would be leaving soon for Abilene, and he regretted that he would not be there with her, but he had to stop whoever was creating these problems. He had to know who was behind it, and why.

Shawn and Terry returned after noon. Unsaddling their horses, they walked into the barn, ignoring the two figures stretched out on the hay. Clay had warned them that there was a good chance someone was watching the house and everything had to look as if he'd left for Abilene. When he'd left this morning, he'd driven fifteen miles east on Highway 380, checking his sideview mirror constantly to be sure he wasn't being followed. Then he turned onto a gravel driveway and drove half a mile before reaching a ranch house that belonged to Pat and Lori Axtell. Shawn and Darrin were already there waiting for him.

By three o'clock Clay was pacing up and down in the barn, his patience wearing thin. Darrin lay sleeping on the hay. Clay envied him.

By the time five o'clock came, Clay was a bundle of nerves. Terry opened the large sliding doors and backed the pickup in to begin loading it with the sacks of feed. This was the only deviation from the daily routine that they would make. It was the only way Clay could think of to get him and Darrin in the truck unnoticed. Cinder blocks were placed in the back and plywood over the top. It was a tight squeeze for Darrin to get underneath, and Clay barely had enough room to fit in beside him.

"I'm glad we ain't got far to go," Darrin said as Clay's elbow accidentally dug into his ribs.

Terry and Shawn stacked the feed so that none of the plywood showed. Only someone looking closely would be able to tell there was more than feed in the back of the pickup. Terry threw two folded tarps on top before he drove out of the barn and waited for Shawn to close the sliding door.

Clay clenched his teeth the entire way. Each time a tire hit a rut or bounced over a rock, the metal floor of the pickup bed dug into his spine. Squeezed tightly between the tire well on one side and Darrin on the other, with his nose only inches from the plywood above him, he had no room to maneuver to a more comfortable position. It seemed to take forever to reach the trailer in the west pasture. Clay would stay at this one, since it was closest to the county road and the place someone would most likely hit first.

Terry backed into position and waited for Shawn to open the large door. They unfolded one of the tarps, making sure that half of it remained in the pickup on top of the sacks of feed. The other half was pulled inside the trailer and laid on the floor, but not before one of their passengers had managed to slip out from beneath the plywood and into the trailer. Terry and Shawn then unloaded several sacks of feed onto the part of the tarp that had been put on the floor of the trailer, then covered them with the other half. Next, they loaded several bales of hay onto the pickup and began their daily routine of feeding the cattle.

Inside the trailer, Clay peered out through a small hole in the side. His range of vision was limited, but he'd found several holes in the side of the trailer from which he could survey his surroundings. He watched Terry and Shawn put out the hay and felt sorry for Darrin, who was still trapped in the narrow confines of the plywood-

and-cinder-block construction. He owed the man a huge debt. He hoped all this would be worth the trouble they had gone through. His intuition told him something was going to happen tonight. He settled down to wait.

When the hay had all been put out, Terry drove away carrying his passenger to the north pasture. He dropped Darrin off in the same fashion as he had Clay. He'd made sure to leave enough loose hay in the pickup to hide the plywood. After he and Shawn were through feeding the cattle, they returned to the house.

Jack was waiting for him when he drove into the yard. "Did you get your packages dropped off?" he asked innocently.

Terry's mouth dropped open in utter surprise, causing Jack to chuckle. "I may have had a stroke, but I haven't gone brain-dead." He added, "What's the plan?"

Finding his voice, Terry quickly explained what Clay had in mind. When he'd finished, Jack remained in thoughtful silence for several moments before speaking. "I don't see anything else that can be done. It's risky but if they both keep their heads about 'em, they should be all right." He chuckled again and said, "I sure wish I could have seen Darrin get under that plywood."

"I didn't think we were ever going to get him out. Shawn and I were beginning to believe we were going to have to hook a chain to the trailer, tie it around his neck, and drive off to get him loose. If anyone was looking too close, they probably wondered why it was taking us so long to get the tarp laid down."

"So now we sit and wait and see what happens?" Jack asked.

Terry took the portable cell phone from his shirt pocket and set it on the table. "Yep, now we wait," he said.

Chapter Twenty-three

Darkness closed in over the prairie like a soft blanket. Clay slipped silently out of the trailer and moved stealthily beneath it until he was hidden behind the wheels. He pulled Jack's old .45 pistol from his waistband and set it on the ground beside him. He was already weary of waiting, but he knew it might be several more hours before anything happened, if at all. While inside the van, he'd had time to think about his last conversation with Tamara. At first he'd been angry, blaming her for being upset with him, but the longer he thought about it, the more he could see why she was angry. He couldn't deny that he'd been attracted to Ginger. It may have even gone beyond attraction, and he suspected that Tamara had sensed that. Julie knew it as well. He could tell by the way she had acted. Jack had told him that women could sense things. He knew he would be angry if he thought Tamara harbored feelings for another man. How could he expect her to feel any different? And the fact that he'd tried to hide it from her had only made it worse. He made himself a promise that as soon as this was over he was going to take a trip to San Angelo and get things straightened out between them.

Clay tried to put Tamara out of his mind so he could concentrate. From his vantage point he could survey the surroundings for a hundred yards in all directions. To the north about fifty yards away lay the water tanks, and beyond them was a line of scrub oaks and then open pasture. To the east and west there was only open land, and to the south the terrain sloped down toward the gate. This was the direction Clay surmised they would come from when they came. They would probably park down the road and come in on foot. The question was, How many would there be, and what was he going to do when they arrived?

In the north pasture, Darrin was hunkered down beneath the trailer the same as Clay. His field of vision wasn't as clear as Clay's, but there was only one way the attackers could enter, unless they wanted to climb through some rough country to get there. If they did that, they'd make a lot of noise before they got to him. No, they'd probably come from the north side, since it was closest to the road and open country, so that's where he concentrated his watch. Darrin patted the .357 Magnum sitting on his lap and smiled.

Ten o'clock came and went. Clay glanced at the luminous dials on his watch once more. It was ten minutes to eleven. He yawned and looked out over the cattle, most of them lying down and chewing their cud. As his eyes scanned toward the south, his head suddenly came up. Something had moved out there. Something that hadn't been there just a moment ago. Letting his eyes move slowly from left to right, he picked up three figures coming toward him in the dark. They were spread out, with about thirty feet between them. Pulling the cell phone out of his pocket, he hit the button he'd programmed in earlier to dial Terry's phone. It rang only once before Terry answered.

"Yeah?" was all Terry said.

"They're here!" Clay whispered.

"Gotcha!"

Clay hung up the phone and set it aside.

Terry had no more than disconnected when the phone rang again.

"Yeah?" he responded again.

This time it was Darrin saying, "They're here!"

"Gotcha!" Terry repeated. He hung up the phone and dialed the sheriff's office. Jack watched, his face expressionless. When Terry hung up again, he grabbed his hat and started for the door.

"Hold on," Jack ordered.

"I've got to get up there, Jack!" Terry cried.

"I said hold on!" Jack bellowed, rising from the chair and walking to the hall closet. He reached in and pulled out his .30-.30 deer rifle. "I'm going with you — and I'm not going to argue."

Julie had been sitting at the table but now rushed into the living room. "Jack, you —"

"Hush, young lady! That's Clay up there, and I'm going, even if I have to fire the both of you. I still run this place." He turned to Terry and motioned him outside. "Let's get going!"

Julie could only watch them drive away.

Clay continued to track the men as they approached. He counted four of them now. One was circling wide and coming in from the direction of the water tanks. All four seemed to be coming directly toward him. At first he'd thought they were going to try to wreck the water tanks again, but now he could see they were making their way toward the hay trailer.

The four men came together and stopped twenty-five feet away. They talked in hushed tones and Clay could make out only a few words, not enough to figure out what they were up to. Taking advantage while their attention was turned away from him, Clay eased himself toward the end of the trailer, the .45 held tightly in his hand. Suddenly a light flared in the midst of the group and Clay saw one man holding a match to a torch held by another man. By the light of the fire, Clay could see the men's faces. He didn't recognize the three standing beside the man who held the torch, but as his eyes came to rest on that one, the breath caught in his throat and he gasped involuntarily. All heads turned in his direction. Thinking quickly, he stepped out from beneath the trailer and brought the gun up, cocking the hammer as he did. The ominous click made three of the men straighten in alarm, but the man with the torch only smiled.

"Hello, little brother," Randy Tory said.

"Long time no see. But then, you weren't real anxious to see me, were you? You never even came to visit me in prison."

Clay looked at the younger of his two older brothers. Both had done time in prison for kidnapping him and Jack, as well as dealing in stolen property. "Where's Warren?" Clay asked, wondering where his other brother was.

"Oh, he got time off for good behavior. They let him out a little over a year ago. I hear he's got himself a job over in Arizona somewhere."

"So, it was you causing all the problems," Clay said. "Why? We didn't do anything to you. You and Warren and Pa were the ones that kidnapped Jack and me. You feel like you got to get even because we didn't go along with your plans and you got sent to jail?"

Randy threw back his head and laughed. "Do you think that's what this is all about?"

"Isn't it?" Clay asked.

Randy laughed again. "You never were too bright, little brother. This doesn't have anything to do with what happened back then — although I'll admit I gladly took the job when I found out who the victims were."

"Why, then?" Clay asked.

"I don't know why," Randy said. "All I know is a man paid me to have some cattle run off and these water tanks torn up, and tonight we're going to burn your hay trailers."

"No, you're not!" Clay spat. "You drop that torch. Now!"

"Or what?" Randy asked. "You'll shoot me? I don't think so. I don't believe you got the guts."

Clay brought the gun up level and aimed it at his brother's chest. "If you believe that, then you're the one that's not too bright, Randy. Now drop it!"

The other three men started backing away from Randy, but he remained in place, the smile still on his face. One of the others spoke. "Look, this thing's gotten out of hand. You said there wouldn't be anybody around. I didn't bargain for this."

"Shut up!" Randy barked. "This is my little brother. He's not going to shoot anybody."

No sooner had the words gotten out of Randy's mouth than the echo of shots reached their ears.

Clay let a smile come to his lips. "Looks like your friends met Darrin. That was his .357 Magnum you just heard. I hope those weren't close friends of yours."

As one, the three men broke and ran, heading toward the road. Only Randy and Clay remained. Randy still held the torch. He turned to watch the three fleeing men. Clay never took his eyes off him, still aiming the gun at his brother's chest.

Randy watched the men for a few seconds, then turned back. As he did, his arm dropped, but instead of releasing the torch, his arm continued its movement. He intended to throw the torch, but stopped as the earsplitting sound of the exploding .45 shell brought him up short. He stared at Clay in disbelief.

Clay once more aimed the barrel of the .45 at Randy's chest. He had sensed Randy's intention and fired into the air. Fortunately that had worked.

"Drop the torch now, Randy, or the next shot won't be in the air."

Randy let the torch fall to the ground. "You really would shoot me, wouldn't you?"

"You're absolutely right," Clay said. "Now put your hands in the air and turn around."

Randy's smile returned. "I don't think so, Clay. You see, I didn't like it too much in that prison, and I sure don't plan on going back. So if you want to stop me you're going to have to shoot me." As he turned away, Clay called out to him.

"Who was behind this?"

"I don't know his name. He never told me, but he drives a Corvette, a bright red one with a personalized license plate that says BADBOY."

"Why did he hire you?" Clay asked.

Randy started walking away. "Like I said, he never told me."

Clay watched until the darkness enveloped Randy completely. Only then did he lower the pistol. His hand was shaking as he went to pick up the cell phone.

Pressing Terry's number, he held the phone to his ear and waited.

"Hello," Terry answered.

"Terry, this is Clay. Can you pick me up?"

"I'm down at the gate now. Ben and his deputies are here. They got three fellas tellin' them they were just out for a drive and decided to go for a stroll. I'll be there in a minute. Wait, Ben wants to talk to you."

"Clay, I got three gents down here that claim they didn't do anything, and two of my deputies have four others captured on County Road 125 telling them the same thing," Ben said when he was on the line.

"Terry's on his way to get me. I'll be down there in a minute," Clay replied.

It took another two hours to get all the stories straightened out and an accurate account of what had taken place. Darrin had waited under the trailer until the man carrying the lit torch started walking toward him. He then stepped out from under the trailer with his pistol aimed dead center at the man and yelled, "Hold it right there or I'll blow a hole through you big enough to stuff this trailer in."

The man had stopped in his tracks, turning white as a ghost. Seeing Darrin standing there holding that hogleg, his three friends turned and ran like scared rabbits, leaving him to fend for himself. He dropped the torch and ran after them. Darrin aimed the gun in the air and fired off three quick rounds, bellowing with laughter as he watched them pick up speed. The two deputies waiting in the bushes by the parked car swore they'd never seen four men as frightened

311

as the ones that came running out of the Lazy L pasture that night. When the four recognized the deputies for what they were, they practically begged to be arrested.

While Terry drove to the north pasture to pick up Darrin, an upset Ben Aguilar questioned Clay about what happened. "I gather this was your idea?" he asked angrily.

"Most of it," Clay admitted.

"Why didn't you tell me about this, instead of taking a stupid risk like that? You could have gotten yourself and Darrin killed. Do you realize what kind of danger you put yourself in?"

"I knew I had to stop them from doing any more damage, and that's what I did."

"All you did was to stop the hired muscle," Ben said angrily. "The person behind this is still free."

"He might be free, but at least he knows we won't stand idly by while he destroys the ranch," Clay shot back just as angrily.

Ben threw up his hands in disgust. "Can you identify these as the men that tried to burn the trailer?" he asked, pointing to the three men standing by his car.

"They're the ones," Clay answered.

"Is this all of them?"

Clay looked away and said, "That's all."

Jack saw the expression on Clay's face and knew there was something he wasn't telling. He wanted to get Clay off to himself and question him, but Terry arrived with Darrin just then, so

Ben took Clay to see the other four men, who were begging the deputies to keep that crazy man away from them.

Ben had to question Darrin to find out what had happened with the other four hired men. "I just shot into the air to let 'em know my gun was really loaded," Darrin insisted. "They had this idea of burning the hay trailer, and I didn't see as that was too good an idea, seein' as how dry it is."

Ben was fit to be tied by the time Darrin finished. "I'll be back to talk to you two tomorrow," he stated, ordering the deputies to take the seven men to the courthouse. "I may think of something to charge you with," he said in a parting shot.

Terry and Darrin rode to the house in the back of the pickup, giving Jack an opportunity to talk to Clay. "You didn't tell Ben everything, did you?"

Clay knew better than to try and fool Jack. "My brother Randy was one of the men out there tonight. He was the one who was going to throw the torch on the trailer."

"Why didn't you tell Ben?" Jack asked.

"I wanted to, but for some reason I couldn't."

"I can understand that," Jack said.

"I didn't even know he was out of prison. He told me Warren got out some time ago and is working in Arizona."

"I know," Jack said.

Clay could only stare in surprise at the old rancher.

"Ben called me and told me about him getting out. Told me Warren had been a model prisoner and had gotten time off for good behavior. I helped him get a job on a ranch down there. I remembered how he could have warned your father that night in the barn, but he didn't. Randy was a different story in prison. He was always in trouble, nothing serious, but enough that he had to serve his full time. Ben called me about two months ago to let me know that he'd been released. I didn't think he'd come back here, and I certainly didn't think he'd try to get revenge."

"He didn't," Clay replied. "He was hired by someone."

"Who?" Jack asked.

"He didn't know the man's name, and I didn't have time to question him. All he said was the man drove a red Corvette with a personalized license plate that said BADBOY."

"We need to tell Ben," Jack said.

"We can't. If we do, I'll have to tell him about Randy, and I can't do that."

Jack gave Clay a sympathetic look but didn't say anything. Clay certainly didn't owe Randy anything, but Jack understood how it was. Clay wasn't going to turn his brother in.

Chapter Twenty-four

It was Jay Crawford's turn to pace the floor. The phone call he'd been waiting for was an hour overdue. Ginger sat on the sofa, chewing her nails.

"What if he didn't get the papers?" Ginger asked.

"He'll get them. He has to," Jay responded nervously.

But by 2:00 A.M. the call still hadn't come. Ginger's nerves were worn to a frazzle. She was exhausted, but she couldn't sleep, so she sat on the sofa idly thumbing through a magazine. Jay sat on the opposite end staring into space. Glancing at the phone on the coffee table for the thousandth time, he jumped to his feet and shouted, "I can't stand this anymore! I've got to get out of here!"

"Where are you going?" Ginger cried.

"I don't know, but if they've been caught, you can bet they've told the authorities about us."

"We don't know that," Ginger said. "And who is 'they'? I thought there was just one person getting the papers."

"There is," Jay responded, "but that's not all that was happening tonight." He gave her a scathing look and said, "Since you haven't been able to keep your cowboy in town, I've had some men creating problems that would keep him here. I thought if I could make him stick around for a couple of weeks you'd have time to lure him into your web. Besides, we may need him here when we sell the ranch, just in case we need his signature on something else."

"What kind of problems have you been creating?" she asked, looking at him apprehensively.

"Running off a few head of cattle, wrecking his water tanks. And tonight they were going to burn the trailers where he stored the hay."

Ginger's hand flew to her mouth. "Do you realize what you could have done? This country is so dry you could have started a prairie fire that would be impossible to put out."

"Who cares?" he shouted. "By the time our investors took control and started development, it would all be grown back again."

"But think of all the innocent families that could have been burned out. You could have ruined a lot of these ranchers around here."

"Since when did you develop a conscience? Who cares about these dumb hick ranchers?"

Ginger gave him an icy stare. "I may like to make money, but I'd never totally destroy somebody to do it."

Jay gave an evil laugh. "Oh, really? And just what do you think we would have been doing to Clay Tory and Jack Lomas when we took their ranch away from them?"

"It never would have gotten taken away,"

Ginger shot back. "You know as well as I do that the courts would have blocked the sale and given the ranch back to Jack and Clay eventually. All we wanted was the money from the buyer. We weren't going to destroy anybody."

Jay stomped to the door. "You can stay here and feel sorry for these backward hillbillies if you want to, but I'm going to find out what happened. If I even suspect the law's looking for me, I'll be out of here like a shot."

"And what about me?" Ginger asked, already suspecting what the answer would be.

Jay gave her a jeering smile. "You can stay here and cry for your poor ranchers. You've gotten weak, Ginger. That means you've lost your edge, and therefore, my dear, you're of no use to me anymore. You're on your own." He walked out, slamming the door behind him.

Ginger stood staring at the door, expecting to feel shock, grief, or devastation, but none of those emotions came to her. She only felt betrayed and angry. Turning, she headed for the bedroom. Tomorrow she'd decide what to do.

Andy Cordova waited until the two county sheriff's cars drove off in the direction of town and the pickup truck went in the other direction before coming out of his hiding place. He carried the papers tucked in the waistband of his pants. He had watched Jack and Terry leave in the pickup — a piece of luck, he'd thought at the time. A short while later Julie had left the main

317

house and headed for her trailer. He had taken advantage of the house's being empty to make his entrance. He had a good description of the papers he was looking for, and it took him only ten minutes to find them in Clay's room and exit the house, undetected.

He had hurried down the drive, expecting to find the car waiting for him, but when he got to the road it wasn't there. Trying not to panic, he began walking toward town, staying close to the bar ditch. If a car came by he would hide in the ditch until he could see who it was. He had been walking for close to an hour when he saw the reflection of headlights just over a rise. He jumped into the ditch and lay flat. He waited for five minutes, but the headlights didn't come. Then he stood up, walked toward the rise, and stooped down. When he peered over the edge, he could see the vehicles parked in the road, but the glare of the lights prevented him from seeing who it was. Deciding not to take a chance, Andy crouched in the ditch and waited. He heard two more cars arrive. He could make out the men moving around, but he couldn't recognize any of them. He felt certain that things hadn't gone as planned, and he wasn't about to walk into an unknown situation.

He remained in the ditch until he heard the cars begin to start up and leave. He peeked out and saw one of them coming toward him, so he dropped flat, blending in with the earth. He waited until the pickup was out of sight before standing up. The only car remaining was the one he and the others had driven out here. It was parked on the side of the road, apparently waiting for a tow truck to come haul it into town.

Andy checked the driver's-side door, knowing it wouldn't be locked. Benito had never fixed it. Who would steal this piece of junk anyway? he thought. They had taken the key but that wasn't going to stop him. Looking around to make sure no one was about, he ducked under the dashboard and, with the aid of his cigarette lighter, found the wires he needed. Using his penknife, he cut three wires and stripped the insulation from the ends. In short order he had the ends twisted together and touched them to a single wire that he held separately. He smiled as the starter engaged, and he soon had the car headed toward town.

But where was he to go? He and Benito shared a small house on the south side of the city, but if the police had Benito, they might come looking for him. No, he'd better find another place to stay until he was sure he wasn't being hunted. Driving the back streets to avoid being seen, Andy parked the car in an abandoned shed four blocks from his cousin Jesse's house and walked the rest of the way. He would spend the night there and find out what happened to the others in the morning.

Clay was up early Saturday morning helping Terry and Shawn feed the cattle. He and Jack

319

drove through the holding pastures and checked on the sick cattle. "We haven't had this few cattle in the sick pen in a long while. You boys been doin' a good job," Jack said, giving Clay a warm smile.

"If we don't get some rain pretty soon we're going to have to start selling stock after all. We didn't do anything but postpone it for a little while," Clay said glumly.

"No, that's not all you did. You added at least two hundred pounds each to all the calves, which will mean a higher price at market. You also gave us some breathing room. If we have to we can find a buyer up north. But I have a feeling we ain't gonna have to. I have a feeling we're going to get some rain in the near future."

Clay grinned and said, "I never knew you were a fortune-teller, Jack."

Jack chuckled. "I'm not. But whenever I get a feeling like this, it's usually right."

"I wish you'd get a feelin' for who tried to burn our hay trailers," Clay said.

"If I could do that, I sure wouldn't be ranchin'. I'd be sellin' my talents to the police."

"Not you, Jack. Ranching is the only thing you were ever meant to do," Clay said.

"I reckon it is," Jack agreed. "I guess that's what the good Lord did with all the fools he made and didn't know what to do with."

As tired as he was, Clay had planned to sleep late Sunday morning, but Jack had different ideas. "Get up!" he yelled, throwing open the door to Clay's bedroom. "I haven't been to church in over two months and it's been longer than that for you. We're going this morning!"

Though Clay was glad to be in church and see many of his friends, his mind kept wandering to the previous night's events and to his brother. He wondered who could have hired those men to burn the hay trailers. He went over the list of people he thought might do something like this. It was a short list, and he eliminated each one in turn. He knew no one who drove a red Corvette, but for some reason there was a nagging in the back of his mind that he had seen one lately. He couldn't remember where, but the thought refused to leave his head.

Jack took Clay, Terry, and Julie out to eat after church. The talk was kept light during the meal and on the drive back to the ranch. Terry and Julie went to their house, and Clay and Jack retired to the main house. When Clay walked in, he noticed the light blinking on the answering machine. He pushed the Play button and listened as Ben Aguilar's voice came from the recording.

"Jack, Clay, this is Ben Aguilar. I need you to come into the office this afternoon if you can. Sorry to have to do this on a Sunday, but I just received some evidence this morning that I need you to look at. I'll be here until about four o'clock. Call me if you can't make it in."

"What do you reckon he's found?" Jack asked.

"I don't have any idea, but I ain't got nothin'

else to do. How about you?"

"Nothin' that can't wait a while. Let's go see what he's got," Jack said, turning around and walking out the door.

Clay drove to the Chaves County courthouse and parked in Jack's favorite spot — one of the spaces marked RESERVED FOR SHERIFF'S DEPT. Ben was in his office when they entered.

"Have a seat," he bade them.

"What's this all about?" Jack asked.

Ben picked up a manila folder and handed it to Clay. "Does this belong to you?" he asked.

Clay took the folder and opened it. Recognizing the contents, he gave Ben a startled look. "Where did you get this? It was in my bedroom on my dresser!"

"Have you read these papers?" Ben asked.

"Not yet," Clay said. "I haven't had time."

"Jake Montoya called me this morning. Seems one of his nephews found these last night and was telling his cousin about it. The cousin called Jake. Jake had a convincing talk with his nephew and together they brought the papers to me. You really need to look at the fifth and sixth pages of that contract."

Clay opened the folder and began thumbing through the pages. He let his eyes scan over them, then handed each one to Jack.

Ginger Loring looked in the mirror at the dark circles under her eyes. She had spent a sleepless night trying to decide what course of action to take and hadn't gotten out of bed until almost noon. While the bathtub filled with hot water, Ginger picked out the clothes she was going to wear. Holding up the white slacks, she chose a pink blouse with high collar and button front and smiled to herself. "I might as well look good if it's going to be my last day as a free woman." She knew now what she had to do.

Jay Crawford drove around behind the Lucky 7 bar and parked close to the back door. Only three other cars were in the parking lot on that Sunday afternoon, and Jay recognized none of them. This was the fourth bar he'd been to since noon, and so far he hadn't gotten a clue as to where Randy Tory was. All eyes turned to look his way as he entered through the back door. Stopping just inside, he waited for his eyes to adjust to the dimly lit interior. He made out a man and a woman sitting at one of the tables. Another man sat on a stool playing one of the electronic video games, and another man was at the bar. The man at the bar looked familiar to him, so he walked over and sat on the barstool next to him.

"Hot day out there, isn't it?" Jay asked.

"Sure is!" the man answered.

"Let me buy you another beer," Jay offered and wasn't refused.

A few beers and a lot of small talk later, Jay had learned no more than he already knew. Seven men were in jail, and Randy Tory was nowhere to be found.

He paid the tab and left the bar. It was two o'clock in the afternoon, and he was no closer to finding out if Clay Tory still had the contracts.

"So, she was trying to get the ranch?" Clay said, handing the folder back to Ben. "If I'd signed those pages would they have been able to sell the Lazy L?"

"If she had a buyer lined up already, she could have. Of course, we could have gotten an injunction against the buyer to stop him from taking possession until we could get a hearing to determine the legalities. I couldn't say whether or not it would hold up in a court of law, but I'd venture to say it would. You do have power of attorney and that means you have the right to sell the Lazy L. It's a good thing you didn't sign."

"But isn't what she did illegal?" Clay asked.

"It's illegal if you can prove it. She can always claim she was planning on making you an offer and already had the documents drawn up. They just got mixed up with the other contract. That's why you were smart not to sign them when she tried to get you to." He paused and thought for a moment. "What I'm trying to figure out is the link between this" — he pointed to the folder — "and what's been happening out at the ranch. I have a feeling it's all connected."

"I'd bet on it," Jack said. "It's the only thing that makes sense."

Ben looked directly at Clay and held his gaze

for several moments before he said, "One of our guests that we picked up the other night revealed some interesting news. He told me the man that recruited him for the job was named Randy Tory. You wouldn't happen to know anything about that, would you?"

Clay returned Ben's gaze. "No, I wouldn't."

Ben shrugged. "If I get any more information I'll call you."

Jack started to rise, but Clay remained seated. "What are you going to do about Ginger Loring?" he asked.

"As soon as I get an address, I'm going to have her brought in for questioning," Ben said. "I doubt she'll tell us anything, but at least she'll know we're aware of her attempted scam. We can arrest her if you want to press charges. If we find her today she wouldn't be able to make bail until tomorrow. A night in jail might make her more willing to cooperate."

Clay contemplated the suggestion, then said, "I'd be willing to press charges." He turned to look at Jack, and Jack nodded his assent.

"I'll get the papers for you to sign. It won't take but a moment," Ben said. He stepped out of the office, leaving Clay and Jack alone.

"You sure you want to press charges against her?" Jack asked.

"Why wouldn't I?" Clay asked defensively.

"I thought you might have some special feelings for her," Jack replied, his face solemn.

Clay shook his head. "No, I don't have any

special feelings for her. She tried to trick me into signing over the ranch to her. I think she deserves to be arrested and put in jail, and if she's responsible for all the things that have happened in the last few weeks, then I want to see her prosecuted."

Jack nodded. "We'll have to wait and see."

Ben returned with the paperwork and, after going over the fine points, showed them where to sign. Clay signed his name without hesitation, and slid the papers to Jack. When all the signatures were in place, Ben called in one of the deputies and handed the papers to him. "Have you come up with an address for Ginger Loring yet?"

"1125 Green Street, apartment 2-A," the deputy answered.

"Good. Issue a warrant for her arrest and send a car over to pick her up."

"Yes, sir!" the deputy answered and left to carry out Ben's orders.

Turning back to Jack and Clay he said, "I'll call you if we get any information worth pursuing."

Jack and Clay took that to mean they were no longer needed or wanted there. "Let's go, Clay," Jack said, picking up his hat and placing it on his head. "There's nothing else we can do until they find her."

"What are you going to do about Randy?" Clay asked.

"I really don't have anything on him," Ben

said. "Unless you want to press charges against him as well."

"No," Jack said before Clay could answer. "I don't think he'll be around here anymore."

"Good enough for me," Ben answered. "If I get any word on his whereabouts, I'll let you know."

"Thanks," Clay responded, relieved to know there would be no charges filed against Randy. He knew that if things had been different, Randy would have burned both hay trailers. But he was still his brother, and he didn't want to see him back in prison.

Chapter Twenty-five

Jack and Clay had little to say on the way home, both of them content to keep their thoughts to themselves. Clay turned up the driveway to the house and was almost in the yard when he saw the Ford Mustang in the drive. Parking beside the car, Clay gave Jack a look of bewilderment.

"That's Ginger Loring's car," he said. "I wonder what she's doing here?"

"I reckon we're about to find out," Jack said. "Are the keys in the ignition?"

Clay looked in through the passenger window and shook his head. "Nope. She must have them with her."

"Well, let's go see what she wants," Jack said, starting up the walk toward the house.

Whatever the two men expected to see when they walked into the kitchen, it wasn't the scene that presented itself to them. Ginger was sitting in one of the kitchen chairs, a washcloth pressed to her face. Julie sat facing her, holding her hand and patting it in a comforting manner.

Jack looked at Clay with a startled expression, but Clay could only stare at the scene before him, dumbfounded by what he was seeing.

Terry sat at the opposite end of the table holding a half-empty cup of coffee. He gave Clay a weak grin but didn't say a word.

When Julie looked up and saw the two men, she came to her feet and spoke. "Clay, Jack, Ginger has something to tell you. She came out here hoping to find you home. I didn't know where you had gone."

"We've been at the sheriff's office," Clay responded angrily, looking at the woman who had tried to swindle him.

Ginger looked up at him with red-rimmed eyes. "I suppose you know all about what I tried to pull, then?"

"Yeah, we know," Clay spat out. "And there's a warrant out for your arrest." He had expected that bit of news to startle her, but she only nodded as if she'd expected it and continued to look him in the eye.

Julie stepped forward and put her hand on Clay's arm. "Clay, give her a chance to explain. She came out here to tell you what she'd done. She could have cut and run, but she didn't."

Clay looked at Julie as if she'd lost her mind. Julie, who just a few short days ago was mad at him for meeting with this woman, was now defending Ginger. "How do I know she isn't here trying to save her own neck? You realize she's the one that's been behind all these things that have happened in the last few weeks. She almost had our hay set on fire. Do you know what kind of damage that could have caused?"

"I wasn't responsible for any of those things," Ginger said. "It was Jay Crawford. I didn't even know he was doing them until last night."

"Who's Jay Crawford?" Jack asked.

"He's the man who masterminded the plan to steal your ranch." She hesitated for a moment, then spoke quietly, "He's my partner. *Was* my partner," she corrected.

"What do you mean?" Clay asked brusquely.

"He left this morning. When his contact didn't call, he figured they'd been caught, and he cut out."

"Does he drive a red Corvette with a personalized plate?" Clay asked.

"Yes, he does!" Ginger answered. "How did you know?"

"The man he paid to burn our hay was my brother. He told me the man that hired him drove a red Corvette."

Ginger's surprise was genuine. "You mean your brother was going to burn your hay? But why?"

"It goes way back," Jack interjected. "Do you know where this Jay Crawford was heading?"

"No, I don't. He just walked out this morning, saying he was leaving and that I wasn't useful to him anymore."

"Because you didn't get me to sign the papers?" Clay asked in an insolent tone of voice.

"No, because I didn't agree with his tactics. I told him it was crazy to risk starting a fire as dry as things were. It could have ruined a lot of ranchers in the area. He said I was weak and he didn't need me."

Clay's anger diminished slightly. "I don't understand what he hoped to gain by what he did. Why did he drive off the cattle, vandalize our water tanks, and try to burn the hay?"

"He was trying to keep you in town for a while. Keep you from traveling to rodeos on the weekends."

Surprised by her answer, Clay asked, "Why?"

"I was supposed to charm you and get you to sign over the ranch. I couldn't do that if you were traveling every week. And especially if you were traveling with Tamara." She gave him a small smile. "I know now that I never stood a chance. You were interested for a little while there. I could see it in your eyes, but never enough. I knew that the last time we met in my office. I wonder if Tamara knows how lucky she is?"

Clay was surprised by her answer and her honesty. "What are you going to do now?" he asked her.

"I'm going to town and turn myself in. I'm tired of all this."

"Can you give us any idea where we might find Jay Crawford?" Jack asked.

Ginger shook her head. "He might still be around town. He hates to lose. One word of warning — watch your backs. He has a buyer interested in your ranch, and he may still believe he has a chance to get it."

Clay and Jack exchanged worried looks.

"I'd better be going. I don't want to be on these roads after dark and besides, if I get to the jail too late I might miss the evening meal." She

331

smiled at her attempt at humor and walked out.

Clay stood there for only a moment before hurrying after her, calling her name as she reached her car. "Ginger, wait a minute."

She turned and looked expectantly at him.

"Thank you for coming out here. Like Julie said, you could have run, but you didn't."

"Hey, cowboy, I never ran from anything," she said with a wide smile, then looking deeply into his eyes, she added, "I meant what I said in there. Tamara is a lucky woman. If she doesn't treat you right, you look me up. I won't be hard to find — I'll be the one behind bars."

"I don't think you'll be spending much time in jail. Just tell them what they want to know and they'll go easy on you."

Ginger smiled again. "Take care of yourself, Clay, and take care of Jack. I hear he's quite a man."

It was Clay's turn to smile. "He sure is!"

Without another word, Ginger drove away. Clay watched until her car was out of sight. For some reason he felt like a weight had been lifted from his shoulders. Smiling, he walked back into the house.

Later that evening, Clay called Tamara's home. Mrs. Allen told him she had come home but had already left for Dallas and would be gone until Wednesday.

"Is there a phone number where I can reach her?" he asked.

"She didn't leave me one. Did you two have a

fight or something? She's been as cross as a grizzly, but she won't tell me what's wrong."

"We had a misunderstanding," Clay answered. "That's why I need to talk to her. If you hear from her, will you ask her to call me, or get a phone number where I can reach her?"

"I'll try, but she's like her father. When she gets upset she won't talk to anyone until she's got it out of her system."

"Do you know if she's entering the rodeos in Enid and Durant?"

"No, she didn't say."

Clay sighed. "Thanks, Mrs. Allen. I'll try to call her on Wednesday."

"All right, Clay. If I hear from her I'll try to get a number where you can reach her."

"Thank you," he said.

Clay was in low spirits when he walked into the kitchen. Julie was busy preparing supper while Jack and Terry made plans to start weaning the calves. All three of them noticed his mood, but it was Julie that commented first. "Did you get hold of Tamara?"

"She wasn't home, and her mother didn't know how to get in touch with her," Clay replied gloomily.

"I gather you two had a spat," Julie said.

Clay nodded. "She thought I was staying home this weekend so I could be with Ginger. I tried to explain to her what was happening, but she didn't believe me."

"She'll come around. Don't you worry. She's

just a little upset right now, but as soon as she has time to calm down and think about it, she'll forgive you and everything will be back to normal."

"But what has she got to forgive me for? I didn't do anything!" Clay exclaimed.

"That's not the point," Julie said. "She thinks you did and therefore, you did. So make sure you apologize and let her forgive you."

Clay looked perplexed and Jack chuckled. "Boy, you just heard woman's logic from a woman. It don't matter whether you were wrong or not, you've been tried, judged, and found guilty. So swallow your pride, apologize, and tell her how much you love her, or you'll never get another minute's peace."

Clay couldn't help but smile. "In other words, it doesn't matter what I do, I'm guilty."

"Now you got the picture," Terry said. "We men have been wrong ever since Eve took a bite out of that apple, and we'll be guilty until the end of time."

Julie turned to her husband and smiled. "That's the reason I married you, honey. You're smarter than you look."

The next morning things seemed to be back to normal. Clay and Terry spent the morning working on the hay baler in the barn. Jack came down occasionally to give them advice and see how they were coming. They stopped for lunch around noon and were back at work when Julie called Clay to come to the house.

"A deputy just called and wants you to meet Ben at the north pasture. He said Ben has learned something and is on his way there now."

Since Julie was taking Jack in to rehab, Clay left Terry working on the baler and took the ranch pickup to meet Ben. He wondered as he drove what Ben could possibly have found. It took him half an hour to cover the dirt roads to the north pasture. Julie hadn't told him where Ben wanted to meet him, but he guessed it would be at the water tanks. When Clay got there, he didn't see Ben or his car anywhere. He knew the sheriff would be coming in off the county road, so he parked where he could see him coming. Turning off the engine, he leaned back in the seat and pulled his hat low over his eyes, letting his thoughts stray to Tamara's lovely face and green eyes. Soon a thought came to him. As he sat there relaxing, the plan grew and took shape until it was a full-fledged strategy with all the points thought out, ready for implementation. Clay was so intent on his thoughts, he didn't hear the sound of footsteps approaching the truck and didn't see the man until he tapped Clay on the shoulder. Alarmed, he snapped out of his reverie with a start to see a man standing there holding a gun, and it was pointed at him.

"Hello, Mr. Tory. I'm glad to see you could make it. Now, how about stepping out of the pickup? And keep your hands where I can see them. I wouldn't want to shoot you before we've had a chance to conduct a little business." He reached over with his free hand and opened the latch on the door.

Clay gently pushed the door open, keeping his hands in view. "Jay Crawford, I presume," he said as he stepped down from the pickup.

"You must have talked to our Ginger," Jay said.

"She told me all about your scheme. She also told me you were the one who hired my brother."

Jay Crawford laughed. "I can't take credit for the entire scheme. Ginger had her finger in it as well. As far as hiring your brother, that was a stroke of luck I hadn't counted on. Where is he, by the way?"

"I don't have a clue," Clay answered.

"I never heard from him after the night they were supposed to burn the hay trailers. What happened, anyway? I mean, you left for one of your rodeos, and the old man and hired hand were at the ranch house. So how did you foil such a good plan?"

"It wasn't that difficult," Clay said, staring hard at Jay.

Jay chuckled. "You're pretty arrogant, aren't you? I suppose you're wondering what I'm doing here. Well, Mr. Tory, I've got too much invested in this venture to just run off and leave it, so you're going to have to sign these papers." He pulled them from his back pocket and set them on the hood of the pickup. "I've still got a man interested in paying me a nice sum for this property."

Clay glanced at the papers and said, "Those papers are worthless. Do you honestly think you have a chance of getting the Lazy L?"

"You don't seem to understand. I don't want your stupid ranch. All I want is the money that someone is willing to pay because they think I have the deed to the ranch. By the time they figure it all out, I'll be far away. Now sign the papers."

"And what happens to me after I sign? You can't just walk off and leave me alive, can you?"

"Well, that does pose an interesting question. If I leave you alive, you'll head straight to the sheriff, and he could make enough inquiries to cause me problems. I've never killed anyone, but I don't believe it's all that difficult. I am an excellent shot. One bullet to the heart or the head and it will all be over. But first I need you to sign those papers. If you refuse, I'll have to shoot you in the kneecap, and I'm sure that would be most painful. So be a good sport and sign."

"I'm afraid I can't do that," Clay spoke with resolve.

"Then you leave me no choice," Jay said, aiming the pistol at Clay's knee.

Clay didn't flinch as Jay sighted down the barrel of the gun. He expected to feel the impact of the bullet at any moment, but was determined not to give in to Jay's demands. He was staring so intently at Jay that when he heard the gunshot, he jumped. But instead of feeling the pain of a bullet tearing into his knee, he saw Jay stagger sideways as blood spurted from his shoulder.

The echo of the gunshot died away as Randy Tory walked out from behind the tanker trailer, the barrel of his pistol still smoking. Crawford had dropped his gun and was holding his shoulder, blood oozing through his fingers.

Clay, stunned by the sudden turn of events, could only stand and stare, first at his brother, then at Jay Crawford. Randy walked up to them and kicked the fallen gun out of Crawford's reach.

"Looks like he wasn't finished with you, little brother," Randy said, keeping his pistol aimed at Jay.

"You!" Jay shouted. "I thought you were long gone. Why didn't you contact me after you botched things up?"

"I kinda got to thinkin'," Randy said. "All the time I was in prison, doin' time, I blamed my brother Clay here, and Jack Lomas. But the truth of the matter is, I didn't have nobody to blame but myself. I could have refused to go along with my old man's plans, but I liked the easy money too much. When you told me who it was we were going to be hurting, I jumped at the chance, as you recall. But the other night when I came face-to-face with Clay, I realized I'd been blamin' the wrong person for all my troubles. I stayed hid out and kinda kept tabs on things for a few days. I figured you wouldn't give up so easy so I followed you. It wasn't too hard, what with you drivin' that bright red Corvette. A word of advice — next time you try to pull a scam, don't drive something that makes you stick out like a sore thumb."

Jay, still holding his bleeding shoulder, glowered at Randy. "What do you plan on doing now?"

Randy took the pistol he was holding and handed it to Clay. "I'm going to head down to Arizona and see if I can get on with my big brother, I hear he's doin' right well."

Clay took the pistol and, without taking his eyes off of Crawford, said to his brother, "I owe you my life. He was going to kill me."

Randy smiled. "He sure was. For a moment there I had to fight with my conscience to keep him from doin' it. You've always been a pain in the butt. But I reckon since we're still kin I couldn't let him shoot you."

"I appreciate the sentiment," Clay said, grinning at his older brother.

"I'm bleeding to death here," Jay said irritably.

"I reckon I better get going," Randy said. "I want to be a far piece down the road before this joker starts talkin' to the sheriff." He lifted a hand in farewell and started to walk away but Clay called to him.

"Hey, Randy, wait a minute." Turning to Crawford, he motioned with the pistol. "Give me your car keys."

Jay's eyes widened in surprise. "I will not! I paid almost thirty thousand bucks for that car. I'm not about to just hand it over to you and this ex-convict."

Clay cocked the hammer on the pistol. "Mister, you were about to shoot me in the knee just a few minutes ago. Now I figure it's my turn to return the favor. If by the time I count to three those keys aren't in my hand, I'll blow a hole in your left kneecap. One . . . two . . ."

Jay was fumbling in his pocket with his left hand, trying to locate the car keys. Fishing them out, he held them in his palm, but Clay shook his head and held out his hand, waiting for Crawford to throw them to him. He caught them and tossed them to his brother. "If you're going to put some distance between you and Roswell, you might as well go in something that'll get you there in a hurry."

"Thanks, little brother," Randy said. "I've always wanted to drive one of these."

Clay watched him walk away, then motioned Crawford into the back of the pickup. "You're going to make me ride in the back?" Crawford whined. "I've got a hole in my arm and I'm bleeding to death."

"I know," Clay responded. "I don't want you getting blood on my seats. Now get in back and sit down. And remember, if you try anything I'll put another hole in your rotten hide."

It was a surprised trio that came out of the house in answer to the horn blowing as Clay came up the drive. Clay briefly explained what had happened while Julie found antiseptic and bandages for Jay's shoulder.

When Ben and one of his deputies arrived at the ranch a short time later, he listened to Clay's explanation and Jay Crawford's cries of outrage about his car being taken.

Clay pleaded ignorance, claiming he had no idea what the man was talking about. Ben listened patiently to Crawford's accusations to the contrary, then giving Clay a dubious look, he escorted his prisoner to the patrol car. After putting Crawford in the backseat with the deputy, he spoke quietly to Clay. "I have no doubt that what he's saying is true, but I'll wait until tomorrow to put out an APB on Crawford's car."

Clay smiled at the sheriff. "Thanks, Ben. I figured it's the least I could do, since he saved my life."

"At least it's over," Ben said. "With the confession we have from Miss Loring, we have enough evidence to indict Mr. Crawford on several charges. You'll probably have to testify."

"Just make sure the trial's not at the end of the week, or the first week in December during the finals," Clay said lightly.

Ben rolled his eyes and got into his car. "I'll see what the courts can do to accommodate you. I wouldn't want the state of New Mexico to interfere with your schedule."

"Mighty nice of you," Clay said, still grinning at the sheriff.

Jack stood on the walk waiting for Clay. "I gather Ben didn't buy the fact that you didn't know anything about Randy taking Crawford's car."

"Nope, but he did say he'd wait until tomorrow to report it," Clay said.

"You know, Ben's all right for someone that saddled me with a pain-in-the-side runt."

"Yeah, I can almost forgive him for forcing me to come live with a hardheaded old coot that's used me like slave labor and made my life miserable."

"I think the only thing we agree on," Jack said, "is that Ben's not that bad of a sheriff."

"Looks that way," Clay replied.

"Good. Let's get in the house, then, before we get wet."

"Get wet?" Clay asked in amazement. Then he noticed how dark it had suddenly become. Looking at the sky he saw the ominous thunderheads that had moved overhead and laughed with joy as the first splatter of raindrops began to fall.

Chapter Twenty-six

The rain continued through the night and all day Tuesday, soaking the dry, thirsty land. With several weeks of warm weather left, the grass would have a chance to replenish itself. The runoff would be caught by the dirt tanks in the pastures, allowing Clay to move part of the cattle out of the two pastures. This would be done over the next few weeks, but for the moment it was time to rest.

Clay called Tamara Tuesday night and learned that she was coming home the following day. When he explained to her mother that he wanted to come see her, she encouraged him to come the next day. He left early Wednesday morning, his gear bag and clothes packed in the camper. Regardless of the outcome of his visit with Tamara, Clay planned on making the Enid and Durant rodeos. Listening to the sweet sound of the windshield wipers as he drove through the rain, he thought of what he would say to Tamara when he saw her. He prayed she would be willing to listen to him.

When Clay pulled up to the Allen house, he was relieved to see Tamara's pickup there. With a great deal of trepidation, he climbed the steps to the front door and pushed the button for the bell. It was Mrs. Allen who answered, smiling warmly at him, as she ushered him into the house.

"She's upstairs in her room. Why don't you go on up? Just knock before you enter," she said.

Clay slowly climbed the stairs to the second floor. He thought about the last time he had been there and how things had changed so much in such a short period of time. Standing in front of her closed bedroom door, he hesitated, then raised his hand and knocked. He held his breath until he heard Tamara say, "Come in."

He opened the door slowly and peeked in. Tamara was sitting at her dresser brushing her hair. Her reflection in the mirror made his heart skip a beat, and he paused to stare at her.

Looking up, Tamara caught sight of Clay and stopped brushing in midstroke. Her expression didn't change as she looked at him in the mirror.

"Your mother told me to come on up," Clay said, trying to break the silence between them.

Tamara remained quiet, continuing to stare at him.

"I know you're mad at me, and I know you think I stayed home because I wanted to be with Ginger. But you're wrong. I admit she piqued my curiosity and made me think about our relationship, but that only made me see how much I love you, and that no other woman could ever take your place."

Tamara turned slowly to face him, her expression still unreadable. "How do I know that what you say is true? How do I know there won't be someone else who makes you question our relationship and makes you wonder if you really love me enough?"

Clay didn't speak for several moments, thinking about her question. "The only way you'll know that is through time. The same way I'll know that there's no one else who could take you from me. We have to trust each other. That's what I'm asking you to do now — trust me. I love you and I want to spend the rest of my life with you, but if you don't trust me enough to know that I'm telling you the truth, then I guess we didn't have what I thought we had."

Tamara let her gaze fall to the floor. "I've been feeling all mixed up since the night you called to tell me you weren't coming. On the one hand, I want to believe that woman meant nothing to you, but on the other, I can't help but feel you wouldn't have called me at the last minute to tell me you weren't coming if it hadn't been for her."

"In a way it was her," Clay said, wanting to get everything out in the open. "She was involved in the problems we were having at the ranch." Noticing the anger that flared in Tamara's eyes, Clay hurried to continue. "She wasn't responsible for what happened. The man she was with planned them. She didn't know anything about it."

"What man?" Tamara asked.

"Jay Crawford." Clay went on to explain the events of the past few days, including the part about his brother. When he finished, Tamara was staring at him wide-eyed.

Hesitantly she said, "Then you did stay home to catch the people that wrecked the water tanks and ran the cattle off?"

Clay nodded. "I wasn't lying to you."

Tears began to well up in Tamara's eyes, and she began to dab at them with a tissue. Clay sat on the edge of the bed facing her. "Don't you think it's time we put this behind us and got on with our plans?"

Tamara looked at him through her tears and nodded. "I'm sorry, Clay. I've been a fool, and you're an even bigger one for putting up with me."

"Being a fool is sometimes the best defense. Jack's been using it for years," Clay said, giving her a big smile.

Laughing with joy, Tamara wrapped her arms around Clay's neck and hugged him tightly. "I love you," she whispered.

"I love you too," he whispered back, closing his eyes as his heart swelled with happiness.

Chapter Twenty-seven

Las Vegas, Nevada, the first week of December, the National Finals Rodeo. The place, the time, and the event that all professional cowboys dream of qualifying for.

Clay and Tamara arrived two days before the finals began to get settled and give Charger time to become acclimated to the Nevada climate, and the arena. Clay was staying at the Gold Coast hotel and casino with the other saddle bronc riders, including Billy Ettinger. Tamara was staying at the Four Queens hotel and casino with the other barrel racers. The hotels in town donated rooms to the contestants during the finals, another perk for qualifying. Jack, Terry, and Julie would arrive the day before the finals began. Julie had balked at the idea of Jack's taking such a strenuous trip, but after realizing he was going to do it one way or the other, she had checked with his doctors and gotten their approval.

"It will probably be the best therapy there is for him. Just make sure he doesn't overdo it and keep him away from the showgirls — for their sake," Dr. Miles said with a smile and a twinkle in his eye.

Clay had qualified for the finals in all three events, finishing the season ninth in barebacks, third in saddle bronc riding and thirteenth in bull riding. Tamara came into the finals sitting second overall in barrel racing.

The national finals ran for ten straight days, with one performance a day. Each of the fifteen qualifiers in each event would compete on stock that they had voted to be there. Each contestant would be competing for first- through fourth-place prize money in each performance. The money they won at the finals would be added to the money they'd won throughout the year, and the top money winner would be named world's champion in each event. The top money winner of all the contestants would be the all-around world champion. Clay was in eighth place for this title.

The excitement that surrounded Las Vegas was contagious. Both Tamara and Clay were nervous as the first day of competition began. Clay rode Whiskey River to a score of eighty-six in the first go-round of the bareback riding. It was good enough for third place.

Billy Ettinger drew Coal Black, and Clay drew Rough Cut in the saddle bronc riding. Clay was a little over four thousand dollars behind Billy coming into the finals, and he knew he'd have to ride tough to overtake him.

Billy was the first to go, on the huge black gelding. The only white that showed anywhere on the horse was the white of his eyes. Coal Black came out of the chute in one giant lunge that carried him high in the air before his front feet hit the ground. Burying his head between his front legs, he kicked straight to the sky with his hind legs, leaving Billy on a vertical incline pushing hard against the stirrups. Raking with his spurs as Coal Black's back feet touched the ground and pushed off in a high arc, Billy showed he was in control.

Billy clenched the rein hard in his left hand and pressed his thighs into the swells of the saddle. He dug in his spurs as Coal Black came back to earth, the horse's feet hitting the ground and pivoting to the left, then leaning hard to the right, attempting to throw Billy off balance. Billy used the spur on his left boot to dig into the horse's shoulder and hold himself in the saddle.

Coal Black hadn't been voted into the finals because he was easy to ride, and now he was giving Billy everything he had. After his pivot to the left, he made a hard lunge upward, then ducked to the right as soon as he hit the arena dirt.

Billy's right leg was just a touch out of position when Coal Black ducked right, and he was moved to the left, giving the horse the advantage he was looking for. One more quick jump side-ways was all it took to lose the cowboy on his back.

It was no shame to be thrown by a horse like Coal Black, but that didn't help Billy's pride any as he walked slowly back to the chutes.

Clay had his saddle set on Rough Cut, ready to ride. There were two riders before him. Billy came to stand beside him as they waited.

"I thought you had him rode," Clay said, trying to bolster his friend's feelings.

"I knew about that move of his, but he caught me off guard. I had my spur too high in his neck."

Clay only nodded. There was nothing else he could say.

Tim Laughlin rode Crazy Sal to a score of eighty-four to take the lead in the saddle bronc riding. Clay and Billy watched the ride, and when the pick-up men moved in, Clay climbed into the chute.

Rough Cut was a large bay that looked as if he might have some Belgian blood in him, but his size didn't slow him down any. His quick moves rivaled those of much smaller horses.

Nodding for the gate, Clay squeezed tightly with his legs and held tightly to the buck rein as Rough Cut ran out of the chute. Two lengths into the arena the bay planted his feet and sucked himself backward as he ducked his head, flexed his knees and rocketed into the air. Clay had his spurs in position and raked them from shoulder to cantle.

Rough Cut hit the ground, bunched himself quickly and leaped high and forward, twisting his body like a circus contortionist and making it hard for Clay to keep his balance, but he was still in control when the horse came back down. One more twisting leap followed before Rough Cut changed tactics and rocketed straight forward, trying to jerk Clay out of the saddle. Clay barely recovered from the previous move in time to react to this one, but he pulled back on the rein and locked his spurs, then raked the big horse. Three more lunges gave Clay the opportunity to show his stuff as he rode the horse with precision timing.

The eight-second whistle blew as Rough Cut ended one of his leaps, and Clay smiled to himself, knowing he'd made a qualified ride. He waited to hear his score as he walked back to the chute.

The Thomas Mack Arena was filled to capacity with spectators who now grew quiet as they waited to hear the judge's score, which came only moments after the end of the ride. The applause was loud and gratifying to Clay's ears as he heard the score, an eighty-seven, making him the new leader.

Billy smiled good-naturedly as Clay walked behind the chutes where he was standing. "I reckon if you draw all the dinks in the string, you'll end up riding part of 'em," he remarked.

"Just face it," Clay grinned back at him. "You're gettin' too old to ride these rough horses. You should have retired while you still had your youth about you."

"I may be gettin' old, but I can still pin your ears back, Junior."

"Maybe, but only if I tied one hand behind my back and stopped every once in a while to give you a shot of vitamins."

"By the end of the finals we'll probably both need vitamins. Especially you, after climbing on thirty head of stock over the next ten days."

"Shoot, that'll be about the same as spending three days working for Jack," Clay replied, chuckling.

Billy nodded. "I can believe that. It sure is good to see the old codger doin' well."

"He's almost back to his old self," Clay remarked. "You should have seen the argument he put up when Julie told him she didn't think he ought to come all the way out here."

"I'd like to have seen that fight."

"It was a humdinger. Jack threatened to fire her if she tried to keep him from coming."

"I'll bet that hushed her up," Billy said.

"Ha. You don't know Julie. She told him to just go ahead and fire her, 'cause she didn't want to work for no hardheaded fool that was bent on killin' himself anyway."

"I gather they finally got it worked out, since they're both here."

"Yeah. Julie finally agreed to talk to Jack's doctors and if they said it was all right, she'd quit fightin' about it. They not only said it was all right, they all agreed it would be good for him."

"I'd say they were right. He looks like a little boy in a candy store."

"Just wait until they honor him Sunday night."

Billy looked surprised. "What kind of honor?"

"Don't say nothin'," Clay admonished. "It's

going to be a surprise. I was talkin' to one of the PRCA officials the other day and told him Jack was going to be here. He thought it would be a good idea to recognize Jack's achievements in pro rodeo. They had a plaque made up, and they're going to present it at the opening ceremonies on Sunday."

"That's great!" Billy stated.

"Well, I got to go watch Tamara's run. She's so nervous, you'd think it was her first time to run barrels."

"I'll be here to help pull your bull rope."

Clay nodded and hurried off to find Tamara. She was sitting on Charger outside the arena, nervously chewing her fingernails as she watched the first barrel racers run.

"It sure is a small arena," she said.

"You've run in small arenas before," Clay said calmly. "It's just like any other barrel race. You go out there and turn one to the right and two to the left and come out. Don't make more out of it than it is or it'll beat you."

Tamara smiled her gratitude. "You're right! It's just another barrel race. One to the right and two to the left."

Clay stood back as the gate judge called her name. Hurrying to the alley gate, he watched her wait her turn at the entrance gate. When it was time, the gate was opened and she entered the arena at a run. Charger slowed only slightly at the first barrel before flexing his large body around the metal drum. Tamara's excitement seemed to inspire the big horse as he sped toward the second barrel in record-breaking time. Charger barely slowed his forward progress as he bent his long neck, dug into the dirt with all four feet, and turned around the barrel, Tamara's heel pressing into his side to cue him. The distance to the third barrel was covered in short order, and as with the other two, Charger slowed only a touch before turning the barrel and fairly flying back to the finish line to stop the clock at 15.01, the fastest time by almost half a second.

Tamara was breathless with excitement as she brought the big horse to a stop outside the arena. "Did you see the way he ran?" she asked Clay.

"He ran like the champion that got you here," Clay answered, patting the horse's neck.

"I'm going to cool him down, then I'll be back to watch the bull riding," Tamara said.

"I'll meet you at Charger's stall after the rodeo," Clay said, waving to her as she rode off.

All of the bulls at the finals were tough, mean, and hard to ride. Each one had earned the right to be there by bucking off a lot of top bull riders in the past twelve months. Clay had drawn number 250A, a big black crossbreed named El Diablo. Clay had drawn him only once during the year and had come out on the losing end. He hoped to even the score this time.

Billy Ettinger stood beside Clay behind the chutes and watched the first bull riders. Clay would be toward the last to ride, which would give him a chance to watch the bulls buck. He would be riding several of these bulls over the next ten days and this would help him learn some of their moves.

The first eight bulls out of the chutes won the contest, and only Lonnie Wright came close to making a qualified ride, lasting 7.3 seconds before parting company with Brawny Bonecrusher, a big Charolais bull.

The ninth rider out, Bobby Deats, rode Train Wreck to the eight-second whistle. Train Wreck turned right out of the chute and went into a tight spin for three rounds, then switched back and spun to the left, twisting his body in a series of bucks and jumps that made it hard to keep time with him. Bobby Deats kept his spurs dug into the bull's hide, never letting up until he heard the buzzer. Clay and Billy cheered with the crowd, congratulating Bobby as he came out the gate. His score was an eighty-one.

The next two riders were thrown before the whistle, and the third rider, Gary Beckett, rode Torpedo to a score of eighty-four to take the lead in the go-round.

Strapped on and ready to ride, Clay pulled his hat tighter on his head with his free hand and nodded for the gate.

El Diablo had no set bucking style. He might turn to the left, to the right, or he might buck straight ahead. Sometimes he did all three in a matter of seconds. This time, he jumped into the arena with a mighty upward lunge, came down and twisted to the left. Two spins and he switched to the right for one complete round before twisting his body back left and kicking his back feet high into the air. The combination of twisting and kicking threw Clay off balance, and he was pushed out over his hand and to the left. El Diablo sensed it immediately and did another quick move to the right, which threw Clay down to the side. Realizing he wasn't going to make the ride, Clay opened his riding hand and hoped it would come free. El Diablo helped him on that score, planting his front feet and leaping one more time to the right. The move propelled Clay forward and out, jerking his hand free of the rope and sending him through the air and into the dirt two seconds before the buzzer sounded.

"Looks like El Diablo is two for two," Billy said as Clay walked through the gate.

"He's entitled to both of them," Clay replied. "He's one tough bull to ride."

"You still got nine to go."

"I hope they're not repeats of that one. It could play havoc with my confidence," Clay remarked with a wry grin.

By the end of day five, Clay had narrowed Billy's lead in the saddle bronc riding by fifteen hundred dollars with a first, two thirds, and a second place. Billy had won one go-round and placed fourth in another.

One first and a third in bareback riding moved Clay into seventh place, but he had covered only two of his bulls and had only gotten a fourth place.

The PRCA's award to Jack for his contribution to rodeo had come as a complete surprise to him, but his good friends Will and Dottie Hightower, who had brought several bulls and broncs to the finals, were there to stand beside him. Will presented Jack with the plaque, which had a bronze emblem of a saddle bronc rider inlaid in walnut. The inscription read: "To Jack Lomas for his contribution to the sport of rodeo through his years of competition and his undying devotion to its continuance."

The only thing that had dampened Tamara and Clay's spirits was the absence of Tamara's parents. Cliff Allen was in the middle of a large land deal that couldn't be postponed. He regretted not being there and promised Tamara that if there was any way he could get free, he would fly out immediately. Of course, Tamara's mother refused to go without him.

After the ninth performance, Clay was only three hundred dollars behind Billy Ettinger in saddle bronc riding. The rigorous schedule had taken its toll on Clay's body. He'd already been on twenty-seven head of stock. He had managed to ride five of nine bulls but had taken several hard hits — nothing serious, only bruises and sore muscles. The Jacuzzi at the hotel had received heavy use by many of the cowboys, and Clay had spent much of his time letting the water jets work the soreness out of his aching muscles.

He had moved up to fourth in barebacks and a close second in saddle broncs, but remained in thirteenth place in bull riding. He had managed to pick up some nice checks and add forty-one thousand dollars to his checking account thus far.

Tamara had taken a commanding lead in the barrel racing, with five firsts, two seconds, and a fourth so far. Her winnings at the finals alone ensured her the championship title. The only two complaints she had were that her parents hadn't been there to watch and that she and Clay had spent very little time together. He promised her that before the finals were over they would take some time to sight-see.

The night before the final performance, Clay met with Jack, Julie, Terry, and Billy. He had managed to make sure Tamara was occupied elsewhere.

"Everything's set for tomorrow morning. I just want to make sure there are no questions." He looked around the room at each one of them. When no one said anything, he nodded. "All right. Tamara's parents will be here at five in the morning. Terry, you and Julie are picking them up. Right?"

"Right!" Terry answered.

"Jack, you and Billy will meet us there at ten o'clock. Right?"

"I'll be there," Jack said.

"Me, too," Billy chimed in.

"And Terry, you and Julie will get Tamara's

parents there on time. Right?"

Terry and Julie smiled. "We'll have them there, Clay. Now quit worrying. Everything's going to go just fine," Julie said.

Clay tried to smile, but his nervousness was obvious to all.

After another night in the Jacuzzi, Clay climbed into the queen-size bed and fell asleep instantly. The wake-up call came at seven the next morning, and he groaned as his aching muscles protested his rising from the soft bed. In the shower, he let the warm water run over his body for fifteen minutes before reaching for the bar of soap. Finally showered and shaved, he dressed in a pair of starched jeans and a red shirt with blue sleeves. He pulled on a pair of polished lizard-skin boots and donned his new white Stetson. He called Tamara and told her he was on his way and he'd pick her up outside her hotel in fifteen minutes. It was now a quarter to nine.

Tamara felt her excitement build as she waited on the steps outside the hotel. She and Clay had found little time to spend together since arriving in Las Vegas and now he was promising her a few hours for just the two of them. She smiled and waved as she saw Clay pull in at the entrance. When he came to a stop, a valet opened the passenger door for her. She quickly slid over next to Clay and gave him a kiss.

"Where are we going?" she asked.

"I've got a few surprises in mind," he said, glancing at his watch again.

He drove down the strip, pointing out several points of interest before turning down a side street, indicating a small building, and saying, "I want to show you something in here." He pulled into the small parking lot and turned off the engine.

"What is it?" she asked, looking at the unimpressive building.

"Something I hope you'll like, but it's a surprise. Come on!"

Tamara followed him up the steps and through the front door. What she saw when she stepped inside surprised her. "It's a wedding chapel!" she said. "Why do you want to show me a wedding chapel?"

Clay looked at the small chapel. To all appearances it was empty, though all the lights were on. He took a deep breath and turned back to Tamara. "Because, I want to ask you to marry me." Bending on one knee in front of her, he took her hand and looked into her eyes. "Tamara Allen, will you be my wife?"

Tamara stared at him in disbelief. She started to speak, then closed her mouth, trying to find the right words. "I, uh — Clay, surely you're not serious?"

"I'm totally serious," Clay answered. "I want you to be my wife and I don't see any reason to wait. Here we are, in Las Vegas, the wedding capital of the United States."

"Yeah, but I always thought we'd have a church wedding, and I want my parents to be there. I want my father to give me away."

"Are you saying you don't want to marry me?" Clay asked, a hurt expression on his face.

"No!" she quickly answered. "Of course I want to marry you."

"Then you're saying you don't want to marry me because your parents aren't here?" he asked.

Tamara nodded slowly. "Yes, and don't you want Jack to be here, too?"

"If I had your parents and Jack here, then you'd marry me?"

Again Tamara hesitated before nodding. "Yes, if my parents and Jack were here, I'd marry you."

"Then let's get married," Clay said, rising to his feet and leading her down the narrow aisle.

Tamara gasped as he took her toward the altar at the front of the chapel.

"Come on out, everybody. We're going to have a wedding!"

Tamara squealed with surprise as both her mother and father walked through a door at the side of the altar, followed closely by Jack, Julie, Terry, Billy, and Billy's wife, Diane, who had agreed to be Tamara's maid of honor.

"Mother, Dad! When did you get here?" Tamara asked in amazement.

"Five o'clock this morning!" Cliff Allen responded as he kissed his daughter's cheek.

"You knew about this?" Tamara asked accusingly, looking at her mother and father.

"Clay talked to us about it in October — after

you two had made up," her mother said.

Tamara smiled and turned to Clay. "So, you planned all this? My mother and father, the chapel, everything?"

"I had some help," he said, looking at the people standing there. "So, Miss Allen, will you marry me now?"

Tamara giggled nervously and looked at her attire. "This isn't really the outfit I imagined myself getting married in."

"That's been taken care of as well," Mrs. Allen assured her. "I brought my wedding dress along. You always said you wanted to get married in my dress."

Tears brimmed in Tamara's eyes and she tried to blink them away as she hugged her mother. "Thank you, Mama."

"Let's have a wedding," Jack said, bringing things back into perspective.

The pastor's wife took charge, showing Tamara and her mother to a changing room in the back. Jack, Terry, and Billy took Clay into another room and helped him into the tuxedo he'd rented.

After the pastor explained how the ceremony would go, Clay waited by the altar, anxiously shifting his weight from one foot to the other. Finally the door opened, and Mrs. Allen walked a few steps out, then turned to wait on her daughter. Clay sucked in his breath as Tamara walked slowly through the door. At that moment he knew he was seeing the most beautiful woman in the world. The dress she wore was full length and had been altered to fit her. "I had our dress-maker fix it up right after you left. Believe it or not, she had to alter it very little," Mrs. Allen said to Clay, her eyes sparkling.

The ceremony didn't last long. All Clay could remember saying was "I do." He never took his eyes off the woman standing in front of him, and when the pastor said, "You may now kiss the bride," Clay remained in place until Tamara spoke.

"Don't you want to kiss me?"

Clay came out of his stupor. "You're so beautiful I'm afraid I might mess something up."

Tamara laughed and said, "Thank you very much, sir. I'll cherish those words for the rest of my life." She leaned over and kissed him deeply. It took him only a second to respond and take her in his arms as everyone crowded around to congratulate them.

News of Clay and Tamara's wedding spread quickly, and by the time the rodeo started that night, the newlyweds were besieged with well wishes and admonishments for not inviting all their friends. Clay tried to explain that he couldn't have kept it a secret if he'd invited everyone, and there was no way he could have gotten them all into the small chapel, but they were all invited to the reception he'd planned after the awards banquet that night, where the world champion in each event would be honored and given a world champion buckle.

By the time the rodeo started that evening, Clay's nerves had finally started settling down. He and Tamara planned to stay in Vegas for a week, then head home at a leisurely pace. Jack laughed when Clay told him he was in no hurry to get back.

Chapter Twenty-eight

As luck would have it, Clay had drawn the rankest bareback horse in the string for the last performance. Unlucky was the big sorrel's name, and that was just what he was for Clay. Like a lightning bolt, Unlucky burst out of the chute and twisted his body into a high bucking leap that had his head turned to the right and his tail turned to the left. When he hit the ground, he lunged straight up and twisted his body in the opposite direction, making it impossible for Clay to get in time with him. Clay's right spur came up over Unlucky's neck just before the horse hit the ground, and a quick leap to the right unseated Clay as his hand was yanked from the rigging handle.

Clay landed on his feet and turned to watch Unlucky continue his run down the arena. Shaking his head and giving the horse a wave, he walked back to the chutes.

"Guess that sorry bag of bones just didn't care if you got married today," Billy kidded. "He could have given you a wedding present and kind of loped around the arena so you could stay on."

Clay grinned, but said nothing.

Clay felt his nerves begin to tense up as the rodeo continued. The closer it got to the saddle bronc riding, the more nervous he became, and Tamara noticed it.

"Hey, cowboy, you need to lighten up. It's just another rodeo, remember? All you got to do is put one leg on one side, the other leg on the other side, and keep your mind in the middle."

"I know," Clay said with a smile. "If it was someone else in the lead, it probably wouldn't bother me so bad, but it's come down to a contest between Billy and me, and for some reason it just doesn't feel right."

Tamara cut her eyes and gave him a stern look. "It's been between you two all year. You've competed against each other at every rodeo you've gone to. Billy knows what the score is and so do you. You both do the best you can, and the one that comes out on top is the world's champion."

"You're right, of course," Clay admitted. "I guess I was just wishin' I didn't have to beat the old man."

Tamara laughed and said, "That's better. Now go show Razorback what a world's champion looks like."

"Yes, Mrs. Tory," he said, kissing her.

Clay had gotten special permission for Jack to come behind the bucking chutes during the saddle bronc riding, but neither he nor Jack mentioned it to Julie, and she was now about to have a heart attack after seeing him standing there.

Clay would be the next-to-last rider out, and Billy would be the last. They had both won enough money at the finals in this event to ensure them of first and second place. It was now just a matter of which one would take home the title. The audience could feel the tension build as one rider after the next took his turn. By the time the tenth rider had gone, both Clay and Billy were exchanging nervous looks and trying to act relaxed, but neither was doing a good job of it.

Razorback was a lined-backed dun making his third trip to the finals. Clay had ridden him in Fort Worth and had won the saddle bronc riding there.

Jack helped both Clay and Billy set their saddles as their time to ride drew close.

When rider thirteen turned into the arena, Clay stepped astride Razorback and checked his equipment one more time.

"Ride the hair off him!" Billy said.

"Thanks," Clay remarked.

"It won't do you no good, 'cause I'm gonna whip you like a cur dog, but give it your best anyway."

Clay smiled, appreciating what Billy was doing. "You're too old to whip me. You're done passed your prime and just don't know it," Clay responded, grinning at his friend.

Feet in the stirrups, rein in his right hand, free hand in the air, hat pulled down, and his mind in the middle, Clay nodded for the gate.

Razorback reared, turned, and lunged in one fluid movement. Clay's feet were locked into the horse's shoulders as its front feet hit the ground. A quick push off its back hooves sent the dun into the air, and Clay's spurs sang as they raked down the horse's side.

What made Razorback such a good saddle bronc horse was the power he had, but he was also agile and could move quickly from one maneuver into the next. His first three bucks were straight down the middle of the arena, then with lightning-quick speed he went into the air, twisted his body left, and came down stiff-legged, jarring Clay's body and sending shock waves up his spine. It took the dun horse only a millisecond to bunch himself and lunge forward, kicking out hard with his back feet at the apex of his leap.

Clay was in perfect form, with the rein held tightly in his hand and his spurs raking from shoulder to cantle on each of the horse's leaps. He kept his thighs locked into the swells of the saddle and his seat firmly planted.

Razorback's next move was a real crowd pleaser as he leaped high in the air and rolled his belly upward until his feet were parallel with the arena floor. It took all the strength Clay had in his legs and upper body to keep his seat. Several gasps escaped from the crowd as Razorback descended to earth. It looked as if there was no way he could right himself and seemed that he would crash sideways into the ground, crushing Clay beneath him. The same thoughts flashed through Clay's mind, but there was nothing he could do as Razorback started back down. Just as it looked like the dun was going to land hard on his side, he twisted his body and landed on bent knees. Clay had no time to count his blessings, for the horse instantly shot forward into the air, twisting his body in a way that had his front legs going to the left and his back legs out sideways to the right. Clay fought hard to hold himself in the saddle and attempted to spur at the same time. Once more, Razorback came down stiff-legged, then sprang suddenly upward, this time in a hard lunge. His power was amazing and would have jerked Clay out of the saddle had he not been expecting it, digging in with his spurs while squeezing with his thighs and pulling hard on the buck rein. Razorback hit the ground and lunged one more time just as the eight-second whistle blew. The crowd screamed its approval.

Jack had been watching the ride from behind the chutes and smiled as Clay slid off the back of the pickup man's horse and stood safely on the ground. Billy Ettinger turned to him and said, "He's just made this a tough contest."

"If it was anybody but you left to ride, I'd say he'd just won the championship," Jack replied as the announcer called out a score of eighty-nine for Clay.

"It ought to be interesting. I know one thing's for certain. I better not ease up on this cayuse," Billy said as he straddled the chute and eased down onto Broken Cloud, a stout steel-gray horse that was in the finals for the first time.

Broken Cloud balked for a moment when the chute gate opened, then turned, leaped, and bucked for all he was worth. Billy marked him out in perfect fashion. The big gray made two quick jumps in a straight line, then turned, planted his feet, sucked back, and reared slightly, pivoting right on his back feet, then lunging forward and up. When Broken Cloud reared, he brought his head up, giving the rein some slack. Billy pulled back hard to take up the slack and squeezed the swells tightly. When the gray leaped forward, he buried his head again between his legs and jerked the buck rein forward. The suddenness of the move caught Billy by surprise, and he was pulled forward in the saddle. Only by sheer strength was he able to push himself back upright and get ready for Broken Cloud's next mighty leap into the air. Though Billy was able to avoid being thrown, he was out of time with the gray and it took him two more jumps to get set and regain his timing.

It seemed as if Broken Cloud was out to prove he deserved being in the finals by humping his back as far as possible to make it harder for the rider to spur. Three hard bucks straight up, then a hard leap forward and a fast turn to the left made up only a few of the tricks in the gray horse's bag. But Billy wasn't fooled by any of them, and after regaining his seat, he spurred with wild abandon, knowing that was what it would take to beat Clay's score.

Broken Cloud tried one more switchback and

a hard jump to the right in an attempt to rid himself of the rider on his back, but to no avail. Billy remained glued to the saddle and continued to spur until the eight-second whistle sounded.

Clay stood on the second rail of the chute to get a better view of Billy's ride. His stomach was in knots from the emotional battle he was fighting within himself. One part wanted the coveted championship so much that it ached, but the other part hated seeing his best friend lose. It was going to be a close call, and nobody envied the judges their decision.

Billy stood to one side of the arena and waited for the announcer to call out his score. Though there wasn't an empty seat in the coliseum, a calm engulfed the entire audience as they waited silently to hear the outcome of this close competition.

"Ladies and gentlemen, we're waiting for the judges to give us their score for Billy Ettinger's ride," the announcer began. "He needs a ninety or better to win this event and take home the championship. Only three hundred dollars separates these two friends and competitors in the saddle bronc competition. The winner will take home the world's champion buckle and a check for twenty thousand dollars." There was a moment's pause, then the announcer's voice came over the speakers. "Ladies and gentlemen, Billy Ettinger's score is an eighty-six, making Clay Tory our new world champion in the saddle bronc riding!"

Clay smiled widely as cowboys slapped him on the back and Jack shook his hand. The audience applauded and yelled their approval. Looking out in the arena, Clay saw Billy standing a few feet away, giving him a thumbs-up. "You earned it, Junior. That was a heck of a ride."

"Thanks," Clay grinned.

Clay broke away from the crowd to find Tamara. She was standing by the arena gate holding Charger. As Clay walked up she handed the reins to a nearby cowboy, threw her arms around Clay's neck, and hugged him tightly. "Congratulations," she said. "I always knew you were a champion."

"Thanks," Clay said, holding her tight.

Tamara stepped away and said, "I guess I better get ready for my event."

"It must be nice to know you've already got the championship wrapped up," Clay said.

"It does take the pressure off. But I've still got to make this run."

Tamara's barrel run was picture-perfect and good enough for a second-place finish.

Clay rode Big Tom to a score of eighty-three in the bull riding to get fourth place. "I'll take 'em any way I can get 'em," he remarked to Jack and Billy as they left the arena to get ready for the final banquet.

Each night after the performance there was a banquet to present buckles to the contestants who had placed first in each event for that day's performance. But the big event was the last night, when the world's champions in each event were honored. Everyone would be there, including Tamara's parents, Terry, Julie, and Jack.

Clay had booked the honeymoon suite at the Excelsior, and Tamara's parents had moved her belongings in earlier that day.

"It feels strange, both of us being in the same room," Tamara said with a small giggle. "I'm so used to you being in one room and me in another, or you in the camper."

Clay was lying on the king-size bed watching her as she moved around the room. "You better get used to it, Mrs. Tory, because I don't plan on spending another night away from you. You're stuck with me from now on."

Tamara smiled and walked to the side of the bed, looking down at him. "Stuck with you, huh? Sounds like a life sentence to me."

"Oh, it is," Clay grinned, pulling her down on the bed beside him. "And there's no time off for good behavior, either."

"Oh, really? Then what do I get for good behavior?" she asked, smiling coyly at him.

"Hmm, how about this?" he asked, kissing her deeply. When he finally pulled back, her breath was coming rapidly.

"I guess I'll have to be on my best behavior all the time, then," she said with a straight face.

"I'll see that you are." He smiled and kissed her again.

Jack checked his watch for the tenth time in

the last fifteen minutes. "Where in the tarnation are those two?" he asked no one in particular.

Julie, standing close beside him, said, "Quit your worrying, Jack. They'll be here. You keep forgetting, they just got married this morning, and they haven't had a lot of time together lately."

Jack cleared his throat and looked around to hide his embarrassment. "They better get here soon or this shindig's going to start without them."

As if that was their cue, Clay and Tamara walked through the door hand in hand. Heads turned to look at the handsome couple as they crossed the floor to join their group. Tamara wore a floor-length silver dress. It fit tightly at the waist and the side was cut to above her knee. It had a high collar that encircled her throat and a form-fitting bodice that accentuated her figure.

Clay wore a white shirt and bow tie under a tuxedo jacket, a pair of starched blue jeans, topped off with a new black Stetson.

"Jack was about ready to send out a search party for you," Julie said as they took their seat at the table.

Clay smiled and said, "I didn't realize how long it takes a woman to get ready."

"Get used to it," Terry remarked dryly.

The festivities began with a seven-course meal and continued with awards for each of the top winners. Clay and Tamara received their buckles, trophies, and the checks that went with the title "World's Champion."

Billy Ettinger was a graceful loser, congratulating Clay earnestly on his victory. "I would say you just got lucky, but that's not the case. You're the best I've ever seen. After what you've been through this year, it's a wonder you even made it to the finals, much less took the title."

"Thanks, Billy. The only thing I don't like about winning this," Clay responded, holding up the large buckle, "is having to beat you to do it. I think there's really two world's champions here tonight."

"Well, you're going to have to work hard for it next year, 'cause I've already made arrangements with Jack to start training me," Billy said with a laugh.

Jack waited until all the awards had been handed out and most of the people were milling about before he pulled Clay off to the side. "I've been waiting for the right time to talk to you," he said, looking around to make sure no one was going to interrupt them.

"About what?" Clay asked. "I'm a little too old for the birds and bees talk," he said, chuckling.

"No, it's not about the birds and bees," Jack said, grinning. "When you told me a couple of months ago that you and Tamara were going to get married, I racked my brain about what to get you two for a wedding present."

"You didn't have to get us anything!" Clay exclaimed. "You've already given me more than I deserve."

"Hush up and let me talk," Jack said impatiently. "As I was saying, I racked my brain to come up with a wedding gift for you two, and it finally came to me about a month ago." He pulled a large envelope from his coat pocket and handed it to Clay.

Clay took the envelope and pulled out the contents, giving Jack a puzzled look. "What is it?" he asked.

"It's the deed to the Lazy L," Jack said with enthusiasm.

Clay's jaw dropped, and he stared at Jack as if he'd lost his mind. "It's the *what?*" he shouted.

"Shh," Jack admonished, looking around to make sure no one was coming over. "I want you and Tamara to have it. I was going to leave it to you anyway, so I decided to go ahead and do it now."

Clay stood dumbfounded. He tried several times to say something, but nothing seemed appropriate. Finally he found his voice and said, "Jack, I don't know what to say. You've worked all your life to build up that ranch. I don't feel right accepting something that you've put your life's blood into."

Jack nodded. "You're right, I have put my life's blood into the Lazy L. I did it to build something to leave to my son. As far as I'm concerned, that's exactly what I'm doing."

Clay felt the tears welling up in his eyes as he looked at the man that had been so much like a father to him. He nodded slowly as the tears ran unchecked down his face. Wrapping his arms around the old man's neck, he whispered softly, "I love you, Jack Lomas."

Jack felt the tears come to his own eyes as well, and he held tightly to Clay. Nodding, he whispered hoarsely, "I know. I love you too."

Tamara had been searching for Clay when she spotted him talking to Jack. She was almost to them when she saw Clay give Jack a big hug. She waited a moment before walking up, realizing that something special had just happened. She reached into her evening bag, produced two tissues, and handed one to each of them without saying anything.

Clay wiped his eyes, then said to Tamara, "Jack just gave us a wedding present." He handed her the thick envelope.

"What is it?" she asked, looking first at Clay, then at Jack.

"It's the deed to the Lazy L," Clay answered.

"The deed to your ranch?" she asked incredulously.

"Yep!" Jack grinned. "All I want is a small house to live in until I die."

Tamara looked to Clay, not knowing what to say.

He put his arm around her and said to Jack, "How about we add on to the ranch house?"

"Sounds good to me," Jack said. "Then you'll

have room for all those kids you two are going to have."

Tamara gave a relieved laugh. "As long as you're not expecting them in the real near future."

Jack grinned and put his arm around her. "I don't know. I thought maybe by this time next year, I'd have a little cowboy or cowgirl to bring to the finals."

Clay and Tamara laughed and shook their heads. "You'll have to wait a little longer than that," Clay said.

Tamara kissed Jack on the cheek and hugged him tightly. "Thank you, Jack."

He blushed crimson as she stepped back and said, "I need some fresh air. I still can't believe all this."

Clay chuckled and told Jack they'd be back in a little bit.

Out on the balcony, Clay led Tamara to a secluded spot where they could talk without being overheard. "If I'm dreaming," he said, taking her in his arms, "don't wake me up."

"Well, darling, if you're dreaming, I'm dreaming too."

He kissed her tenderly and said, "I know life's not always going to be this great, and to be honest I don't know how it could get any better. We both got world championships, we have a ranch, and we've got each other. Where is there to go from here?"

"I don't know," Tamara responded. "All I

know is that I want to go there with you."

Clay smiled and looked into her eyes. "I don't have anyplace to go, if you're not with me."

They both turned to look out over the lights of Las Vegas. Even those were dull beside the flame that burned in their hearts.